GW01418850

205158610 S

DORSET COUNTY LIBRARY

GALACTIC

MISSION

SAM GRANT

Published by Sam Grant

Publishing partner: Paragon Publishing, Rothersthorpe
© Sam Grant 2017

The rights of Sam Grant to be identified as the author of this work have been asserted by him in accordance with the Copyright, Designs and Patents Act of 1988.
All rights reserved; no part of this publication may be reproduced, stored in a retrieval system, or transmitted in any form or by any means, electronic, mechanical, photocopying, recording or otherwise without the prior written consent of the publisher or a licence permitting copying in the UK issued by the Copyright Licensing Agency Ltd. www.cla.co.uk

ISBN 978-1-78222-512-6

Book design, layout and production management by Into Print
www.intoprint.net
+44 (0) 1604 832149

Printed and bound in UK and USA by Lightning Source

PREFACE

"**THIS MESSAGE ENDED WITH** just the word affirmative. It was printed on screen and then spoken in every European language. Mandarin, English and Russian. This was later picked up in dialogue between different pre-nation, global states. Every state said that it was a voice they recognized. Sometimes a man's voice other times a woman's. Many, messaged on social media that it was a voice they recognized, as being, from their language, culture. This was no mechanical robotic voice, but then everyday automata sounded human, mostly all the time, when they spoke, anyway-it was not considered that unusual. This many language voice achievement. Although, of course the news was absolutely astounding."

"Quadrant in a global announcement dismissed it all as a hoax. A world calming exercise, if you like. The transmission, which lasted for twenty-four hours over three days caught morning and evening slots across world media channels. Then Quadrant stepped in. Quadrant must have been pleased, be cause it was able to get world coverage for its hoax answer to the screenings. This produced a spate of comic theatre about spoof alien landings. All well and good, it might be said: only a month later on the same first Friday, but now in October the transmissions arrived again. The questions asking "is there anyone out there?" Answered by "Affirmative, no hoax." This happened in 2090. Now into the twenty second century (2119) nothing more had been reported."

"There was an unspoken appreciation that the earth was not alone in the universe in having intelligent life. For many people this had to an extent re-invigorated religious communities."

"Religion was praised once more, as a tranquilizing opium, to calm the anxiety of populations, who feared a future empti-ness once they departed from Quadrant's cradle-like embrace.

By 2100 the world governing elite had seamlessly moved the seat of power from Moscow to London and now Washington. The "affirmative" reply not forgotten, perhaps, but not uppermost in people's minds.

A Work of Fiction

CHAPTER 1

NINA GIVES NOTICE TO LEAVE

'**HOW DO YOU THINK** I feel when you're at a venue just ten miles away and stay overnight?'

'It was late I didn't want to wake you.'

'That's never bothered you in the past James. It would be more convincing if you said you'd been drinking.'

'It's because there's another woman.'

'That's not true.'

'How do you explain this then?'

Nina activated the record database on my info tablet, opening a request for access.

'Nina Harper requests holographic files are opened to view messages in your present location. Is this permission to be granted?' What was there to lose It was only company related holographic data 'Yes, you may present image as requested by this caller,' I replied, directing the imaging to the kitchen table top a tenth full size. The machines able to sense that we were in the same room.

A hologram of Lara standing and smiling while giving a talk appeared. A follow up to a recent sales meeting, mainly for those unable to attend. I liked the confidential way she spoke. Personal, but in no way patronizing. The report ended with--

'James Walters is now building our latest solar energy enhancing machine and will be reporting back on how best to assemble the product. We know how good James is at making the complicated seem simple.' I admit to having replayed this statement several times; like an actor going over a good review hoping to relive that feeling of acclaim. It never crossed my mind that Nina would have a completely different interpretation.

'Make the complicated seem simple. What does she mean by that James, exactly?' I was trusting and did not think Nina would hack into my business files. I realized by then that she must have done just that.

'That woman appears in nearly every holographic presentation.'

'That's Lara, personal assistant to Mr Sullivan. You don't think she'd be interested in me?'

'You mean I'm lower down the scale. More acceptable. More malleable, less of a challenge, less attractive.'

'I didn't say that Nina.'

'Don't pretend James, there are repeats of you accessing "That Talk". I don't really care which part of her you like. Her eyes, legs, voice or the fact that for her you make the complicated simple.' I attempted to explain that it was a working relationship, but that did not stop Nina saying,

'Anyway, James I'm leaving.'

That was Sunday morning. By midday she was in the hallway with cases packed, Betsy's little Chihuahua poked out of her coat, as she made deprecating remarks, like, 'there, there Betsy we can be together again, away from that nasty man, who says rude things about you.'

I called Betsy an oversized rat, when I thought Nina was out of earshot. How did this happen, you may ask, getting involved with a research chemist with a model like figure who wore hot pants while driving a Ferrari, which actually belonged to her boss?

The warnings of possible emotional and material maintenance requirement were out there, but the liaison enhanced status at work. The other managers unbelieving and just plain stunned to see me arm in arm with a girl like Nina.

'I've never really liked short men, anyway,'

she said, opening the front door. Her brother was standing outside with his gas driven truck. Afterwards I realized it was pre-arranged. A manufactured argument to justify leaving. I remembered Tony's eyes lighting up when he first discovered I was boyfriend. Not so sure that the smile, was on reflection, friendliness. More perhaps, because he hoped to get his little sister settled off his hands and presumably that I might be the person to achieve just that.

I liked Tony. Unlike Nina, he didn't talk over much, but used to call out 'Hi, brother,' whenever we met. A trifle premature it turned out. Now I noticed a look of disappointment on his face. She previously shared a flat - rent free - with Tony and partner.

Nina paid no rent living at my flat, but persuaded me to upgrade to a double bed, which I saw as an investment in both present and future. In reality, with reluctance I have to admit it was probably to allow Betsy a share in our bed. Tony benefited from having a partner and no doubt rejoiced when Nina left to live at my flat, reducing costs and the double gooseberry effect of Nina, and Betsy. Understandably not wanting her, Nina to return. This appreciation entered my mind after she left.

I burnt the protein square I'd cut to fit in the toasting machine on Monday. Something retrieved from a past epoch, when food was often prepared separately, instead of in a maxi maker. Old style gadgets were one of Nina's hates. There was now no yapping from Betsy, when the smoke alarm rang in the hallway, though. I booked and paid to charge up a street buggy from my info tablet as I ate breakfast. I needed to get to Stroud rail station and travel to Cheltenham for a sales meeting. There was just one printed copy of the report. Holographic transmission failure due it was believed to espionage hacking meant managers were instructed to provide printed report hand-outs.

It was never going to be an organized departure from the flat. A lateness detective looking for evidence would not only note the delay from setting off the smoke alarm, but also for lack of planning with not attaching the company identity tracer to the suit before leaving. I returned to activate a download print of the tracer plus copies of the report only to be told,

'Mr Walters I informed you that the company no longer produces cartridges for this model, but we can upgrade to combined holographic transmission.'

'Yes, you did, but I said I couldn't afford to replace it at the moment. Anyway, there's nothing wrong with the model I have.'

'I'm sure Mr Walters we can arrange a payment plan tailored to your' I zapped the machine off from the tablet and went outside to see that the green light was flashing on the booked buggy. While driving, myself to the station, rather than being driven on automatic driver, I experienced a sense of elation, which seemed at odds with having just been ditched by Nina. It was as if some higher state of consciousness was intervening to inform me that really it was not loss being experienced, but more that of escape.

In past research into an earlier part of the 21st Century I'd read about mindful forward planning. An ability to visualize an event thereby making it happen. In this case a parking space for the buggy at the station. It was too late this time. The idea only came to me as I entered the station car park. The here and now came crashing into existence when I saw rows of parked up buggies and maxi carriers in the park. It meant driving to the far end and squeezing into a space only the adventurous would ever attempt to enter.

Sensors picked up my arrival on the platform energizing clock display, which lit up to read 11.20. My train not due until 11.50. I went to the waiting room. A box shaped unit with protrusions to prevent vandal access to the solar screens on top. The room was empty, but decided to sit in the far corner in one of the back to back orange seats either side of the table. Inter-Connectivity being available. A long name which when abbreviated to IC, was a play on words. I opened the tablet sized screen.

'Double in size,' I commanded. The development of multi-make material, which allowed VDU screen's to be adjusted in size was a late 21st Century invention, which met with approval.

CHAPTER 2

FREDERICK STANLEY MEETS UP WITH SABINA

FREDRICK STANLEY, GRASPED THE hand rail on the steps leading up to the crossover bridge. Cheltenham was a listed station and apart from the pod attachment to the main fabric the station remained as it was in the latter part of the 20th Century. Fred, headed for "The Refreshment and breakfast Bar." The sign first lit and then shut off like a carpet rolling open and then back. When the lights switched off only the wall behind remained. It was a process called in air light suspension and low cost to run.

Ideally, he liked to meet Sabina, once a week in the bar before they went to the Railway Hotel. She worked there, for operational reasons you could say, three days a week as a chamber maid from twelve to two. There was only one seat then available in the far corner of the bar when he first met Sabina two months previously. Fred, was holding a coffee and energy bar in one hand and in the other the CHQ memory case with smart tablet inside.

Opposite the vacant seat sat a young woman. Her skin that deep, almost translucent black with aquiline face that denoted her antecedents to be tribal Ethiopian or perhaps even Peruvian. She spoke perfect English when he asked.

'Is this seat taken?'

'No, it's all yours.' She smiled generously, he remembered, considering that he was an older man and she probably in her mid-twenties.

'Just squeezing in a coffee and energy bar before the day gets going,' he said and placed the coffee and bar on the table something more regular.' Fred removed his smart phone to inform CHQ of his arrival, but did not, rested the case on the table before he sat down.

'Yes, it's a space in the day. It is for me at any rate.'

'You work here as well then?' asked Fred, who was absorbing the friendliness and warmth that transmitted from the young woman in her eyes and smile.

'I work from here she said and I'm looking for additional work. I prefer quality time on a regular basis,' she said while she turned her head away and back, which accented her fine-featured face. The smile confident. Noise in the Refreshment Bar from commuters and travellers merged with the talk in progress from nearby tables and there was no way anyone else could hear what she said save for Fred.

'I charge by the hour,' she said in a matter of fact way. Fred shut his phone down and replaced it in the case. He was about to say to do what? His eyes met hers. There was a brief hardness there, but it vanished when she smiled. Fresh looking nail polish on slim neat fingers encircled the mug of coffee. Her large collared coat was open, to display a taut neck. The deep black of her skin almost startled the red dress, which spread in a V shape above the cleft between well-defined breasts. It was a proposition and by a professional, who was selecting rather than the other way around. Fred just found himself saying,

'I see.' That was possibly the clincher for Sabina. The immediate understanding of what was on offer from her and he a potential punter. For Fred, his work at CQHQ was the main focus ever since Janice, left him. De-camped to live with her manager. Fred tried to console himself with the fact that it was the lifestyle on offer. The heated swimming pool in the manager's garden. The house with auto maid and gardener. The gracious living. Janice never

11

ceased, it seemed, to talk about gracious living in the weeks leading up to her departure.

He now met Sabina once a week. It was straight sex, although he was introduced to positions, which Janice would have been uncomfortable with. In fact, would have disapproved off. Perhaps all men delude themselves into thinking that when paying for sex, there was a relationship of sorts. He kind of expected that Cheltenham Quadrant HQ would know about this meeting with Sabina. She might even be attached to the organization and monitoring him, but this was an age when information was available on everything to the Quadrant ruling authority. Only another world agency might slip in unnoticed.

There were no hover trays to supply customer tables. This was self-service. Fred needed to face the vending machine. The machine read what was called the eye determinant to obtain an individual's identity. It would cross reference your account after asking a memorable question and match the voice to the profile already produced. It asked Fred the name of his best friend at school. Fred answered "Daniel." The machine, said

'I can find a picture of Daniel if you wish Frederick.'

'Another time perhaps,' said Fred. 'I just want two coffees, and two cancel chocs plus, three. These were aphrodisiacal flavoured choc bars, which as the word implied cancelled the possibility of Sabina conceiving for up to three hours.

Fred enjoyed Sabina's company and the preamble of joining Sabina for coffee before meeting later in a room at the Railway Hotel. They both were assured by having the choc bar that there was no risk of pregnancy. Hospital incubation of embryos leading to birth was still mainly only available to high ranking officials like Lara.

'Right away Frederick, said the machine. 'I hope you enjoy your coffee. It is nice to see you have company nowadays.' Machines had access only to files once having read your eye biometrics. They appeared not to have access to life style choice, but built up data on customers. Not unlike a bartender, who might get to know a person through friendly banter. Transaction details appeared on Fred's smart phone. A green button then lit up, which said "Go." He pressed and the Perspex delivery hatch opened with the tray of coffee and choc bars. He walked through the crowded restaurant to the table next to the palm tree where they met each week.

'You are a little late Frederick.' Sabina preferred the name Frederick.

'I will time start you from now, though,' she said and smiled as Fred approached the table. Frederick Stanley quite liked the way Sabina ordered him about. It gave the semblance of caring, when for Sabina it was more about scheduling clients.

'I'll have to raise the charge by ten per cent,' she said just as he sat down opposite. A rise in the charge for her services was in line with the escort market price. Frederick mentioned last time that he'd received a pay rise from his boss. it was then open sesame for Sabina to revise her price. Fred nodded.

'You've not got much to say today,' Frederick, she said before pursing her lips around the choc bar and while chewing said.

'You can stay for an hour and a half instead of one hour fifteen this time.' Fred's eyes lit up in a way that was not previously apparent.

'Sounds good to me,' said Fred. The social nature of the meeting now transcended that of the earlier attraction and offer of sex.

He'd already decided not to log in to Quadrant until after

they'd finished coffee and were at the hotel. This would allow time to enjoy Sabina's company that bit longer. He always entered through the reception without Sabina, who preferred to avoid getting noticed with clients. The concierge automata were programmed to enjoy calypso singing and dancing. Before entering the escort, business allied to hotel cleaning duties, she'd trained as a singer and dancer. Every Wednesday in return for not recording her early arrival to meet up with clients, she would perform for Antonio a calypso song and dance routine.

There was a health scan facility in the shower cubicle of the hotel. Multi-purpose in that you could a have a revive massage or shower apart from a scan to detect the presence of transmittable disease. Escort work was an occupation which required registering through Quadrant. This then protected both parties from prosecution. The transfer of funds from a client's account activated both her info tablet and was linked to Quadrant. It made Quadrant into the state pimp, but this decision to impose direct tax on the escort business was a decision made by the four Quadrant sectors Washington, London, Beijing and Moscow. In five yearly cycles, they governed or more truthfully ruled the earth and its ninety million population.

'How's Mitzie then?' asked Sabina. Mitzie was Fred's terrier, who a neighbour walked for him when on his visits to Quadrant.

'You don't care about Mitzie,' said Fred, who was adopted a year after Janice left and after he first met Sabina at this table Fred decided that he liked the unconditional love he received to the conditional type, which Janice came to offer in the latter months of their partnership. Sabina noticed that Fred became more relaxed and better tempered after Mitzie met some of Fred's companionship needs. She cared about Mitzie from a professional standpoint, you could say. Sabina held the bowl-shaped coffee cup in her hands and winked at Fred.

'I care about Mitzie, because Mitzie cares about you Fred.' This was quite a profound and almost heart-warming statement for Fred, who didn't really like being on his own with just Mitzie for company. There was that fantasy built dream that Sabina, the Railway station escort would one day give up her profession and move in with him. Sabina stood up just as Quadrant called.

'It's room 253,' she said, 'Book 253, Frederick-okay?' She returned to remove her handbag from the chair. Fred's attention was drawn to Sabina's skinny jeans before he looked at the info-tablet screen. It messaged.

'Here at 11.10. Pass code X423CB. Enter rail pod earlier than this! Alice.'

'That's doable. Considerate of QCHQ to select pod transport. from the station,'Fred, said for his own benefit. He entered the agent received code while they made for the exit.

'I've been asked to host a cabaret in London next week. Sabina lightly held on to Fred's forearm. She new how to keep older clients on her books, without the envelope pushed to a more permanent relationship.

'But, we can meet the following week, if that's okay?'

'Yep,' said Fred, that's okay. I'm due back here then.' Sabina let go of his arm before they left the building and walked ahead of Fred toward the Railway Hotel.

CHAPTER 3

FRED LEAVES FOR A MEETING WITH CHQ QUADRANT

'YOU HAVE YOUR BUSINESS planning up to date now Mr Stanley?' asked Antonio, after Fred inserted the button access chip into the foyer guest departure machine. The booking with Sabina was scheduled under business report re-scheduling. Fred felt fully re-charged now and ready to meet with Cheltenham GHQ. A daytime room venue could be reserved for executive's male or female to schedule and prepare for a company meeting or presentation. Antonio, the automata concierge, would have accessed the file on Fred's daytime booking. This would not have revealed the true nature of his morning hotel stay.

'Yes, thank you for asking Antonio. A breathing space in a long workday schedule. There are times when solitude is the only solution for getting up to date.'

'We are delighted that our railway hotel has fulfilled your best expectations-once again. I always look forward to your visit. They are enjoyable for me, as well.' Fred had decided that Antonio's orientation was perhaps decidedly camp for a reason. That as a concierge Antonio, would appeal to maybe gay male guests, but would not be seen as threatening to female ones.

Company owners of sex partner automata for hire, were heavily taxed to reduce an earlier obsession which threatened the replacement of the existing generation with no off spring from this substitute sex satisfaction. Only the owner makers of Antonio would have been aware of the unexpected quirk, that Antonio was programmed to love calypso song and dance.

That Sabina was able to fulfil this desire built into Antonio's character interest profile in exchange for a room to entertain her prospective clients.

Frederick Stanley was no high ranking CHQ Quadrant official. To put it bluntly he was an informer or procurer of information for the hierarchy. He'd only just checked that the deposit from the hotel was back in his account when the tablet trembled his hand. The text flowed line after line to nearly the bottom of the screen where it changed to large bold print and asked the question- "Read?" "Listen?" "Speak now- yes "read" or -yes "listen."

'No, neither- later,' replied Fred holding the tablet close enough to whisper his reply.

"You are to listen before five minutes is elapsed. Signal is Orange alert."

With a Red alert Fred would need to read or listen immediately- his life could be at risk if he didn't! But in less than five minutes he would be sat in the pod on his way to CHQ Quadrant.

His previous disguised assignation was to present documents to a mortuary that purported him to be the brother of the body kept there before burial. It was claimed the family macabrely wanted a photo of the deceased for family records. The photo was to confirm for Quadrant that their quarry was in the mortuary- and dead. The brother was Fred's age and a college lecturer. The disguise required long black hair and research revealed that the brother walked with a limp among other details that Fred incorporated in the disguise. Even listening to his recorded voice.

Fred or Danny Talbot, the acting name he became known under after leaving stage school entered young middle age with his character killed off while tackling a rogue robot in a soap series. A double blow because Janice left him for her manager at this time.

He applied to an online advert, which stated.

"Skilled now qualified drama student required to act out character impersonation in everyday situational roles for major investigatory organization. Apply with CV from employer." After successfully landing the job a three-page contract printed on plastic record sheets were produced for Fred to sign with the laser type pen, which you held away from the document making a signature for it to burn on. The final interviewer said,

'Quadrant needs loyal citizens to maintain security and safety for all its citizens of the world.' Fred noted that each page displayed the gold outer circle with the four sectors with miniature world maps in red, blue, yellow and green. Washington, he knew was the sector with absolute control for the next five years. This would follow with Beijing.

Together with most other world citizens Fred was aware that messages had been received affirming intelligent life in other galaxies. Not the microbiological organisms found in asteroids and in the water of Jupiter's moon, but a super-intelligence that could interact in language form. English was chosen, but also all main earth language groups received the same signal. Earlier back in 2084 the scientific community held back from divulging the receipt of extra-terrestrial signals.

Quadrant would have been informed, but choose not to release truth only misinformation. That all changed when replies came back on the screens of media channels worldwide. Blocking or jamming by Quadrant failed. This was 2090, in the aftermath of full Quadrant control. A battery of radio signals sent out over decades going back to the twentieth century returned on screen media channels in sub-text. In fact, many just believed it was some explanatory garbage that the media channels were pushing on to screens. It was the scientific community in Mexico and older astronomers who were aware that these messages were first sent out from earth. Quadrant scientists dismissed this information. All one big hoax, they said. And that, any messages would have degraded long ago in distant space. That they were incapable of remaining in existence! For that reason, it was seen as implausible, for aliens to know about the earth's existence.

This unravelled when explicit messaging was picked out, which had been sent previously asking that question in one way or another-is there anyone out there?

This type of message ended with just the word "Affirmative." It was printed on screen and then spoken in every European language, Mandarin, English and Russian. Then later picked up where dialogue between different global pre-nation state areas occurred.

Every state area said it was a voice they recognized. Sometimes a man's voice, other times a woman's. Many messaged on social media that it was a voice they recognized as being from their language culture. This was no mechanical robotic voice, but then everyday automata sounded human nearly all the time when they spoke, anyway. It was not considered that unusual-that is- this many language voice achievement, although, of course the news was absolutely astounding.

Quadrant in a global announcement dismissed it all as a hoax. A world calming exercise, if you like. The transmissions which lasted for twenty-four hours over three days, caught morning and evening slots across world media channel. Then Quadrant stepped in.

Quadrant must have felt pleased, because they were able to get world coverage in hoax answer to the screenings. This produced a spate of comic theatre about spoof alien landings. All well and good it might be said. Only a month later on the same first Friday, but now in October the transmissions arrived again. The questions asking "is there anyone out there?" answered by " Affirmative-no Hoax." Spooky for Quadrant, but this time curiously many believed it was then really a hoax. This happened in 2099. Now in the twenty second century (2110) nothing more had been reported. There was an unspoken appreciation that the earth was not alone in the universe in having intelligent life. For many, this had to an extent re-invigorated religious communities. Members had previously been demoted to the level of a minority interest akin to that of a hobby or sport. Quadrant songwriters composed hymns, which praised the interest that people had in the religious group meeting up in their temples, churches and other purpose built religious gathering houses. Religion was praised once more as a tranquilizing opium to calm the anxiety of populations, who feared a future emptiness once they departed from this now Quadrant, cradle like embrace.

By 2119 the Quadrant world governing elite had seamlessly moved the seat of power from Moscow to London and now Washington. The "affirmative" reply, not forgotten, perhaps, but not uppermost in people's minds.

———————————————————————————————

Frederick Stanley's pod shuddered rather than glided to a stop at GHQ Quadrant.

'The Commander awaits your arrival Mr Stanley. We hope you have enjoyed good travelling to reach us here,' the automata gatekeeper said. Fred decided to just say

'Yes.' The Automata reminded Fred of Janice's incessant talk, when they got going on a subject. Similar to when she was presumably getting her future lined up with the manager and finding faults with him in vocal expression.

'Request for the password from your tablet Mr Stanley, please.' This was standard procedure and Fred had already accessed this.

'People's friend,' he said.

'Thank you for that. I will allow you to enter.' Quadrant, that's the higher officials perhaps saw themselves in this role. The password was always aimed to place Quadrant in a positive light.

'Mr Stanley, you are all right to proceed to the lift and continue to the correct floor, now.'

'Yes, that's fine. Thanks for your assistance,' said Fred before he walked into the lift after allowing his eyes to be biometrically scanned. He asked for the twenty first floor as usual. On occasions, he asked to be taken to other floors, but the reply came back.

'The twenty first floor is the only floor I can offer you to visit today.'

CHAPTER 4

FRED GETS HIS NEW ASSIGNMENT

'THE TWENTY FIRST FLOOR, please wait for the doors to fully open.' The system would be linked to the A++ central intelligent control, but a nominal automata system would operate both the lift and answer questions if asked. Fred had no questions at this point.

'Commander Henson is ready to see you. Alice will arrive shortly to greet you Mr Stanley.' Fred liked Alice, PA to the Commander. Her down to earth relaxed manner, concealed a sharp intellect. From first Sabina now to Alice, who walked into view out of an adjacent lift door.

'Hi Allie, still twenty-one then,' said Fred. She smiled as she approached Fred. It was his way of flattering Alice, who was nearer to fifty than twenty-one, but there was rumour that the Commander was due to move floors. Periodically occupants were moved to disrupt recognition patterns that intruding parties might have established from spy infiltration.

'About as near to twenty-one as you Fred. The Commander has some interesting graphic input to show you. All I know is he wants you on Stroud station within the hour.'

'Stroud, why Stroud?'

'Can't say more, I'm sworn to secrecy, like you Fred. I've told you more than I should as it is.'

'Sounds very routine to me. Hope it's more interesting than a visit to a mortuary.'

'Not for me to say.' Alice was close enough to catch a whiff of Poison. A terrible name for a perfume, she considered re-created from perfume archive material.

'Hope she met your dream women expectation?'

'What do you mean?'

'It's not--- just the perfume I can smell. Don't stand too close to the Commander. He might get jealous of you and what's her name Fred?'

'Why should I tell you?'

'Well on your character assignment something might happen. There's no Janice to inform.'

'It's an arrangement, that's all, Allie. Suits both of us. What's it to do with you?'

'Just like I said. I could report back to her, if anything should happen.

'I'm overwhelmed Alice by your concern. Perhaps you'd best marry me.' Alice turned to face Fred before she zapped the admission terminal to the Commander's suite and partly stuck her tongue out, and in again.

'You know I've got a partner –so it's no go. I might let you know if there's a vacancy, although I wouldn't want the worry of my man on a mission for Quadrant. Bye and good luck Fred,' she said as the racing protective security lights across the door cancelled and the door swished open. Alice turned and walked away, while Fred went through to the corridor leading to the Commander's quarters.

'Come in Stanley, said the commander. A+++ automata were in attendance on both sides of the Commanders desk. This always meant high priority. Dit and Dot were the names Fred allotted to these near creature-like automata. Tall, black and sleek, with a three hundred and sixty-three-degree attention span and holographic transmission into multiple destinations. Although, normally behind Perspex shields they were now either side of the Commanders desk. Activity input/output lights flashing as world data and extra-terrestrial signals was accessed and monitored. The dominance of red across several nearby screens evidence that they were at high activity level.

'Sit, sit, sit Stanley.' The Commander was studying a VDU on his desk. The automata to the left of the Commander's chair in closer attendance than its twin.

'They have penetrated earth electronic protection shields and are in situ at this point. I will show you now Commander, the automata advised. Commander Henson looked across at the far wall. Fred, in turn swivelled his seat to get a view. There was a picture of a railway platform viewed from the opposite side of the track. The name light for Stroud lit up as a passenger came down the staircase on to the platform. A young woman in a blue coat and yellowed crotched hat, who walked to stand away from the platform at the side of the waiting room.

'That is a clone of a human profile. We have accessed our data base. An extra-terrestrial energy force

'There you are Stanley, said the Commander. Quadrant has been keeping up to speed.' Stanley swivelled back to face the Commander.

'That woman is an alien? She looked perfectly normal to me. Bit oddly dressed.' The other automata replied.

'It is affirmative. This clone can only exist by outside intervention. We have tracked the original to be a company employee. This woman is a fake, but only we can know this from data files. We have studied these together with Commander Henson. Alien is present. This has happened across another world area. We know that the clone woman is there to meet a target human. I mean one of your human kind Commander. We have prepared character detail for Mr Stanley to adopt. We would like interception after the meeting. A pod can take him to this station. There, that is the target! A young man, probably mid-twenties, wearing a dark suit with longish black hair walked in a leisurely down the stairway and towards the waiting room. He opened the door, which was of retained classic design with a handle and hinged opening, while removing an info tablet from his suit pocket.

'This person is travelling shortly by train to a meeting with Fit for Life. We would like Mr Stanley to be sat opposite to this person on the train. He is a Mr James Walters.

'Yes, the department has seen the evidence,' said the Commander, impatiently.

'Vast energy input has arrived from just outside of the solar railway station system,' continued the automata.'

'We cannot computerize effectively always with its presence. The alien force has accessed this station area earlier, but there is no discernible pattern as to timing. We may not be able to hold our inspection of this area for much longer. There has been contact made with individual humans. More needs to be known for us to assist you Commander. The role, we have agreed for Mr Stanley when this person leaves the Waiting Room is to contact him on the train.

He is a Fit for Life manager who is due at their conference hall near to her. We already know this contact is extraterrestrial, but Mr Stanley needs to gain this James Walter's confidence and not alarm him.'

'You're okay with that Stanley? Well I know you will be this time, if you want to see Sabina again.'

CHAPTER 5

UNEXPECTED MEETING FOR JAMES PRIOR TO AREA SALES CONFERENCE

THE DOOR CLICKED. I looked up. A young woman, I guess in her early twenties entered, in a blue leather coat and shoulder bag. Hair sort of encased in a woollen hat. Without looking around she came across, and oddly asked,

'Is this seat taken?' As if we were already in a train compartment. Not really seeing then why in an empty waiting room anyone should want to sit opposite me. I rationed my answer to 'No.' I considered it wise to pretend to be absorbed in the advert, although I glanced across as she sat down. She put the fingers of her hands momentarily together but then lowered them before placing her elbows on the table with hands held to cheeks. I noticed there were no rings on her fingers. Deep blue eyes transmitted a pleading look.

'That's a neat looking tablet,' she said. 'I'm disturbing you.' She smiled.

'I expect you want to be alone,' and moved back, but then with finger nails on the table's edge leant forward again. Her eyes expressed interest. Mine most probably the same when she removed the beret. This allowed her hair to cascade down to shoulder length. A shake of the head made it fall into place.

'Would you mind accessing a site for me?' she asked. 'The batteries flat on my tablet could you enter this? Don't worry I have a code.'

'Yes, that's not a problem,' I said. The strap on the handbag curled away from her shoulder as she picked it up. The opened clasp clattered on the table. From an inner pocket, she produced a laminated card with large type, which revealed a string of numbers and letters. Longer than my tablet phone number. A light caught on pink nail varnish, as she held the card for me to read. I was already in my mind questioning my helpfulness

"Where was, this going?" But as if she read my thoughts I was reassured by,

'It's only a family message.'

'Lower case?' I heard myself ask. Friendliness and perfume overwhelmed rational thought processes.

'That's okay, you are very kind,' she said. I did not expect to see a video screen, but one appeared. A man's clear voice began, but then stopped to synchronize with the appearance of the text. The timbre of the voice authoritative, and announced,

"You are now entering Real Time and exiting Earth planetary zone time."

A momentary pause. The pulsating glow from a slow-moving script, brightened as if in receipt of a more powerful energy source. I'd never seen such luminosity on my Tablet before.

'This script will now run independently,' the voice said. I looked for a person in the room. The voice seemed to be near to where we were. The woman moved her arm along the bench behind and turned towards me.

'We already know you, everything will be all right,' she said. This statement kindled feelings more of fear than anything else. Like a prisoner might be offered false reassurance by a captor, when there was no chance of escape. I was far from convinced about everything being all right. The Waiting Room appeared unchanged, but it felt like there was a difference. I could not move my legs for a start. That dream sensation where you cannot run away had taken hold. I could see and move my hands. I even took a deep breath and held it. Slowly exhaling to avoid being noticed. The woman said,

'Do not worry we are not here to harm you,' which creepily worried me more, because although I couldn't see anyone I felt this powerful force holding me down. I looked at the screen and there were moving pictures, which showed a life biography alongside the script—mine. The voice restarted, but now with pictures and details about the solar system in one half of the screen. Details about specific sectors, quadrants and the positioning of Venus and Mars relative to the Earth. The woman's face became animated as she listened and watched, while these pictures were meaningless to me. It was the screen half focused on my life history, that I gave my attention to.

The frightening bit was that the script described my motivations on a review basis. Acceptable when good, but also depicted as arrogant and oblivious to those around. Not a flattering ghost written biography, but the truth! That's really frightening. Who wants the world to know the unedited truth about your life? I considered who else could gain access to this. Total strangers with access to my life detail.

Yet I did not feel this woman or her alien voiced accomplice was a representative from St Peter or the other place. She laughed.

'I find you amusing. You are right I am not a being from either of those places.'

'Incredible,' I replied. Now trying to hold back outright panic.

'I have some explaining to do. My name it has been decided is Adriana.

'My position is in the green spectrum, which allows for transmutation to planetary life form. A selection from an earth woman has been made. My hair is a different in

28

colour and there are eye and facial differences. It was decided that an executive from your organization would be suitable.'

'But you are a woman?' Was this an attempt to humour Adriana on my part? I'd never met a woman quite like Adriana. Unless it was in a nightmarish scenario, where your dream lands offer is an alluring woman, who has that propensity to frighten the living daylights out of you!

'Yes and no. You see and sense me in that way, but my being is quite different. The Galactic Command Force can clone all life form on this earth planet. A body form I inhabit can be stored for future use.'

'The name Galactic Command Force sounds threatening.'

'Do you think so? It is more that we exist to monitor and develop galaxy life and development. We employ aggression or force, yes, but it is to avoid catastrophe within galaxies. We are constructors of harmony and our focus is on this galaxy where your earth planet is situated. It is under future threat.' I suppose my reply was meant to be nonchalant and carefree in a way when I said,

'Really? I didn't know that.' Adriana changed the conversation.

'Where do you think, you are?' It seemed like a really dumb sort of question.

'I'm sitting in Stroud Waiting room, waiting for my train, of course,' I said.

The leather belt around her coat slipped away as she stepped away from the table. Her raised arms allowed the coat to open, which revealed a pink mini dress, together with tanned legs. The arms raised horizontal, opened the coat, giving appreciation of the female form. A distraction perhaps intended to ensure my interest and attention. She turned more directly toward me, smiled, hands with fingers spread, palms rotated to face down. My face would have expressed surprise, but I

29

felt that the room, the essence of my being there, was now subjected to a powerful control. Her arms as they lowered cancelled the light from the windows, leaving only artificial light from three ceiling lights.

'Now,' she said as she sat down opposite me once more.

'We are no longer in Stroud, we have entered "REAL TIME." We have informed you of this, you were listening were you not?'

'Yes, but where are we?' and with a near lost priority, 'How am I going to catch my train?' She ignored that question.

'Real Time, 'is the ability we have to make your time elastic. We can retrieve past events and we can extract from a time frame for purposes of research. We are able to convert molecules into constructs of our design and determination. Hence, we have kept for you the same environment,' she said, in speech fashion.

'Thanks,' I said, as if being handed an unwanted drink, but thinking it wise to go along with the situation. A feeling developed, that I was like some organism, but with consciousness, in the petri dish of a scientist.

'It is because you are ordinary, a plausible individual James. You don't mind me calling you by your first name, do you?'

'No, but I'm not so keen on the ordinary, plausible description.' She seemed amused and smiled, before asking,

'Do you find me attractive James?'

'My feeling is that you know that. You reliably access what I'm thinking. I expect you understand matters associated with attraction like heightened pulse.'

'We can intercept your neural pathways and intercept thought activity, before you are aware of receiving it.

That is true. The feelings of attraction in the human race we have difficulty making sense of. You were younger when we contacted you on previous occasions.

'I must return to our purpose,' she said. The deeper male voice, repeated,

"Return to Purpose," which made me re-consider who or what else was listening to this conversation.

'We have enlisted others to assist in breaking the news of our presence to the human species. This is part of the evolutionary progression of humanity.' This made me feel like some abstract commodity, but I kept quiet.

'Your quest to explore other planets cannot be achieved without our assistance.

We can transport people to the Moon, but also make life habitable on Mars. You—James have been selected to promote this information. Representatives around your world are being selected to do this work. It will save many now on Earth and secure a safer future for your species. This planet earth is threatened by comets and I need to inform you that the Quadrant ruling elite have made preparations to abandon the planet and seek shelter further out in space. We need to save a group on Mars to seed your race, in the worst situation of destruction, or as intended to return to organize the earth people who will be left leaderless.'

'But I may not want to be your Noah,' I said. 'You remember this event, then,' she said. 'Not exactly. It's just always embedded in religious culture. HEY I've only been here twenty-five years.'

'We could take you back to the beginning of your human race.'

'No thanks I'll pass on that,' I hastily added.

'There is more explaining to do. Now that we have made contact, we need to allow this knowledge to develop within you, before we proceed. We believe you, James

31

will soon want to be part of this progression, when we reveal the risks to future Earth generations. We do not expect you to fully understand, yet. I will allow you to catch your train. We believe you will want to know more. We will revisit. I will then mainly resort to holographic presentation.'

'What here? How?' I asked. She laughed. Her hands held and twirled blond locks together to fit inside the woollen hat.

'You are not anywhere, you are outside time and earth place. You do understand this?' It occurred to me that this hat was almost like a military beret. I was not convinced, as they say that she came in peace. There was no mention of a star command fleet, yet this did cross my mind, which she picked up on.

'No, in time you will understand we come in peace,' she said. Those were her last words, before she faced me and slowly moved hands and arms upwards in a reverse procedure. This caused the window light to reappear. The mission, at this point accomplished, that was it. I'd wanted to ask questions, I realized. The guile, the capturing of a man's attention, enticement, persuasion all made me believe Adriana was an actual woman, but how could this be?

Footsteps could be heard coming down the metal stairway outside. Adriana turned, smiled and waved at me, whilst she left via the waiting room door. My tablet showed the picture clock at eight thirty.

'The train now arriving is the eight thirty-six for Swindon,' came from the platform inter-communicator. I switched the tablet off. Placed it in my inside pocket and walked towards the door.

CHAPTER 6

TALK WITH PASSENGER

I ZIPPED UP THE cover on the inter-pad cover as I left. The noise from the train absorbed the quiet. Scared, intrigued—unbelieving even about the alien encounter.

They—it, evidently came from another time frame of existence. Perhaps I'd fallen asleep in the waiting room and it was a dream that entered my mind while stressed out by the up-coming meeting. This Adriana perhaps an hallucination created in response to Nina walking out. I realized that mention of the encounter risked damaging my sane credentials, at work or anywhere, for that matter.

Attractive women can become like an elephant trap for gullible men. It was probably more that I felt this way, at that time. This was not an appreciation which saturated my thinking, but it was clear that this galactic intelligence, knew its stuff about communicating. They knew everything about me. This was surely not a dream. I could recall the whole episode. It followed that they could tailor the most effective way of getting my attention in the first place. Adriana's pleading eyes and charm, tranquilized resistance. That is until she signalled a dominatrix tendency.

The dominatrix tendency in this acquired personality might appeal to the area manager. He was in his fifties. But, this was not a vision I wanted to run with. This, was something another person was unlikely to believe. A fast track method for being seen as either a crack pot or as a person hallucinating from drugs, entered my mind! The idea that an alien woman walked into the waiting room and talked to me about being recruited to lead a group to colonize Mars.

'Why did I not laugh?' I didn't because it was

scary. The sun made my eyes blink when I looked up to step into the train. Talk about horrendous events, which occurred in plain sight. This experience was not in plain sight, because we were taken away from the waiting room. I was sure about that. So, sure that I was now unsure that it was even Thursday.

The experience reminded me of an archive film called the Truman story. In this fictional film you were watched and your life pre-arranged without your awareness. I needed reassurance that I was back to Thursday 10th June, 2119. I needed confirmation that I was back into the Thursday that I'd been taken from. The train's mixed smell of seat fabric, dust and stale fumes seemed real enough. I sat two rows down the compartment. An elderly gentleman with a printed news edition from download arrived almost immediately and sat opposite and began to read. After a few minutes, he lowered this printed edition.

'Quite a novelty is it, seeing a newspaper being read?' he said, in an easy-going way and looked over the top directly at me. The aroma of coffee drifted back from the centre of the carriage masked the train like smell.

People hide away on trains, silently talking into the camera on their pad-phone.

Some still with dated technology, resistant to change, finger swiping on screens. squeezing work opportunity from the journey. I leant forward to try to read the date on his paper unsuccessfully. That caused him to comment.

'No I was just checking out the date,' I said.

'It's still Thursday 21st June.' He was being factual, and lowered the paper on speaking. Jet black eyebrows raised in a quizzical kind of way, contrasted with swept back greying hair, but he was just being matter of fact.

'I find it stays the same date longer on a Thursday. I don't know about you, but I always find Thursday a long day. The important day is Friday. You can sense the gaoler nearby; with the key to unlock the manacles for you to enjoy the weekend.'

I didn't until then consider that an older person might see work in the same way as myself. My future was though staring me in the face. Possibly in ten years -time travelling on the same train to Cheltenham reporting to a group meeting at head office on sales figures or was this all about to change?

He appeared a whimsical old dodderer. Then, I thought; but, as a stranger he might just be the person to confide in. It would give him something to talk about later. How he met a crank on the train. Safer for me than getting laughed at by work colleagues or Lara.

'Do you believe in aliens?' I asked. He did not seem startled by this unusual question.

'Why not,' he replied. 'Religion is all about a belief in aliens or something that is alien to us. Why are you asking? Where are they?' He looked from side to side and pointed across to where two students were sat in window seats.

'Not over there,' I started to believe that he was treating it as a joke, but then he said,

'You must have had something happen to ask a question like that tell, me more.'

'You're not going to believe me,' I replied.

A woman in a blue trouser suit and gold name badge, case in hand, stopped opposite us. There were empty seats further down. She did not like the look of us and moved to the next but one set of seats, lifting the case into the rack above.

'Try me,' he said, and folded his paper interested to listen.

'It was earlier in the Stroud waiting Room. A woman called Adriana asked me to send a message on my inter-pad. I lifted up the red leather case, to show him.

'We were materially moved from the Waiting

35

Room, but then returned. That's why I was asking about the date.' I then explained all that happened. Afterwards he didn't laugh or for that matter disbelieve me.

'It may surprise you, but I don't have a problem, nor should you. You'll call me eccentric, but have you seen those archive time travel recordings. There was Also that message reply back in 2090, that was described by Quadrant as a hoax. But was it really?'

'Yes,' I said, being a bit of a fan of science fiction from earlier in the century. I also remembered the "affirmative," message. A realization that Quadrant would want to spread disinformation if it was threatened by a more powerful group-alien or otherwise.

'Archive time travel recordings are fictional, but if you believe in a collective human consciousness of minds with strong group identity it may be possible to coalesce the future, with many minds developing it. Another existence beyond our earth bound one. I relaxed realizing that I'd met someone prepared to listen to me, and who perhaps thought about the meaning of existence. Yes, an unlikely event on a train taking people to work, I know, but I was prepared for the unlikely after meeting with Adriana.

'You mean like developing a negative from an old fashioned camera film, but this time in forward play.

'That's a good description, although the picture may alter with intervention. It's like an artist deciding to add seagulls to a seascape or make a beach appear pebbly instead of sandy.'

'That's very frightening,' I said.

"The train is now arriving at Cheltenham Spa. All passengers for Cheltenham Spa should disembark. This is Cheltenham, Cheltenham Spa all passengers..." I recognized the "voice of the day" as that of the captain of the English cricket team. Digitally recovered voice mode enabled any voice to be played at random on the address system. The First reply by tablet with the correct voice received a free fare. You could tell how stressed out I was by not bothering to enter the answer. The elderly gentleman got up from his seat.

'Do you want to continue this conversation?' he asked.

'Yes, I mean- I'm not sure- how do you mean? I have to give a sales report this morning.'

We both stepped into the centre aisle of the train. He placed a hand on the top of the seat to steady himself as the train settled back on the ground from its travel position.

'I don't want to disturb you, but I believe I also may have been approached. He moved back to pick up his paper and produced a flat cap from his pocket, reminding me of a farmer.

'I dreamt last night of this meeting on the train. I've never seen such a vivid picture in a dream,' he said.

'I felt that I could reach out and touch these seats. You or a representation of you approached. The dream ended. I remember before waking hearing a voice which said, "listen, listen, listen." I've been listening to what you have been saying. I think we should meet again, do you not think?' It was that kind of direct question which you agree to out of politeness. It was only later, that I questioned whether the meeting with Mr Frederick Stanley was coincidental.

'It'll be another month before I visit Cheltenham. It'll be the first of the month,' I said.

'I'm intrigued by what you've told me. I can understand why you might not want to talk to your colleagues. You're welcome to treat me like a sounding board. I travel every week day now. I'll be on the train, next month- look forward to meeting you again James. Did they mention. I mean did this Adriana mention visiting you again?'

'Not exactly.' At this point I turned away. In a way, I must have felt that I'd already said more than intended.

'I travel every weekday now. My office relocated from Stroud, he said.

'See you on the train first Thursday of next month then,' I said. He turned away. and counted the carriages down from the battery propulsion drive unit. We were now standing on the platform.

'Three,' he said. 'The third carriage down. Make sure we don't miss each other, next month. Perhaps it's best for us to maintain just face to face contact.'

'I'm James. James Walters,' I said.

'Frederick Stanley. You may call me Fred. I don't mind Fred.' He reached to grab my hand, nearly squashing it.

'Are you expecting more meetings?'

'Yes, by hologram.'

'That's what I feared. They have already circumvented earth security module Determinations.

'What do you do,' I asked. No ordinary Joe, like me. I'd now dismissed the idea that he might be a farmer.

'Developmental protection database security. Like you James I'm employed by a private corporation, but to keep track of possible espionage. I try not to attract attention.

'I can see why you might not want to make yourself too visible.'

'Our company needs to prevent access to information networks. I need to decide what threat, if they are a hostile alien intrusion, of course, pose, to systems. Really keen to find out what more you've discovered in a month's time James. There are advantages to being inside a moving train carriage. They are unlikely to be able to home in on conversations.

'Should you have said that here?' I asked.

'Probably not. Until next month then James.'

At the time this all seemed plausible. No doubt it was intended to be. That his company hadn't gone directly to Quadrant now stationed in Washington was understandable in that no organization would invite involvement with its operations unless it was already fully controlled and not autonomous. London was the next location to host Quadrant. These former locations were not primarily nation states but currency domains. Britain swapped the pound sterling for the dollar, which most English speaking nations did in 2060, together with Japan. African states and Latin America adopted the peso. The Euro nation states the Euro and Russia, Pakistan, India, Malaysia and smaller Asian economies the Chinese Renminbi. Then in 2070 an over rider currency was introduced – the qwat worldwide currency. Not so much introduced as enforced.

I began to wonder, who else was in on the plan that Adriana and the Galactic Command force had prepared. I was already questioning my agreement to meet up with this Mr Stanley, now that he was no ordinary person, but most likely affiliated to the major Quadrants.

I walked, in tandem, with the walkway escalator to the cable car station. Held my conference identity tracer with two of the ten charge bars depleted from the rail fare payment against the machine. Another bar vanished and a four-seater pod clicked from its holding bay and ran along the connection wire to stop next to me. Two other passengers entered other cab pods, but it was mid-morning. A quiet space midway between the early and mid-day rush hours.

'You may board by pressing the yellow pad by the door. I can give instructions in the language of your choice. The voice sounded Asian, but there was a cultural Asian exchange visit in Cheltenham. The council would have adjusted the voice type to welcome the visitors.

'English suits,' I said. The word unhelpful, but a match for Anita.

'Yes, I can see you wear an English suit. I have accessed database. Suits in this context, means acceptable. You find that spoken English is acceptable. Please press the button to enter. My name is Anita. I would prefer you don't see me only as a word data base. I can advise you on the weather for today. Perhaps you would like to be informed about your astrological birth sign forecast, while you travel to the conference. I see you do not have company.' The cable car was programmed to run to the Conference centre and the auto–companion conductor (ACC) or Anita would have accessed this information. The ACCs were disbarred from an access to personal information. That was why the meeting with Adriana threw me when the video of my life flashed on to the screen in detail. I did not doubt that the Anita (ACC) monitored my replies on behalf of Cheltenham Council, at the very least.

'The sound of waves breaking on a Hawaiian beach with soothing bongo drum music in the background would help me to relax,' I said.

'Such a good choice. I will relax and listen with you.' My tongue moved without sound to say and "I won't have to listen to you witling on." Unlike alien, Adriana, Anita couldn't read my lips or thoughts, which was a relief. The humanized ACC voice adjusted to its recipient and this undermined the real woman achievement behind the voice.

The ACC could emphasize with you in a sympathetic and nuanced way to please a man. Women, no doubt quite liked it that the ACC, knew its place, so to speak. For a man, more used to unpredictability, uncertainty and the need to keep on his toes when with a woman, it was all too artificial. Perhaps other men preferred this saccharine non-combative type of relationship. It was not for me, but then equally I considered, that I might have a masochistic streak within me, that I didn't always own up to. An example could be that of Nina's stay at the flat. With Nina's attachment to Betsy, ultimately the more important relationship when it came to sharing the double bed.

The cable pod was in the shape of a suspended tear. You could see out but not in. There were eight chairs. The music would be fed to my ears wherever I sat. I didn't understand the technology, but sound waves could be encapsulated and transmitted to vibrate just inside your ear. The sound switch was on zero. I moved it to three on the arm rest. There was no one else in the car. The car was holographic friendly--hell I would download a recent speech given by Lara on to the cable car desk. I directed the sensor in the tablet at the floor in front and raised the desk higher to a little below eye level. -- Yes, the Hawaiian drums gentle play was soothing, but the sound of Lara's voice, just above the music was helping to make me believe that I was on that Hawaiian beach with her lay next to me. It was a twenty-minute journey from the station to the Conference hall.

CHAPTER 7

XP100 AND HOLOGRAPHIC INTERVENTION

XP1 TRANSFERRED AN ACCESS enquiry into XP100's green adaptability bubble, that remained pulsating, while the holographic projection was in progress. The hologram was formed before projection, but once in position through cocooned capsule transmission (CPT) it sourced energy from the planet earth. XP100 took identity away from its bubble in the space command ship, but could be recalled instantly without the need to be reinstated. Not the human Adriana form that gave XP100 the realization that human senses were attuned to reacting to stimuli. That affinity existed on a material level, but humans even with a spoken language possessed no real understanding of other realms of existence. For XP100 food and existence was determined by digesting incoming celestial information. The birth of new planetary systems. An understanding of how the material existence of universes depends on the further imaginings of command fleets across galaxies. Then establishing material to build organic structure. How could the triviality of entity relationship be of more importance than the excitement of being on an intergalactic mission??

The future holographic projection on to the floor of the meeting room, for example, would mean that XP100 could maintain contact with the Command Force. Information from corporeal interaction, in this instance XP00's disguise in the form of Adriana and the meeting with earth inhabitants immediately accessed and down loaded for future reference.

Holographic programmes had an immediacy of contact,

but were deleted from earth space. Detection of the star fleet was at most times impossible within the solar system, because of dimensional time shift.

'How did you get on with understanding the James entity? Were there neural pathways that gave contact with the group identity and in particular the senior executive Lara?' This was the first conscious thought transference accessed through Adriana on return.

'The holographic construct XP200 devised worked. Their familiarity with holograms, will likely make them more amenable to attention from us than when appearing as one of their own functioning entities. I detected that there is already interest from this James Walters toward Lara, a senior executive. I was able to occupy a portion of mind space, which made James Walters, as he is named, aware of my presence, alongside that of memory for this Lara. A contrasting specie entity, which has power over James in the workplace. There is acceptance for this role, but heightened neural activity indicates that he already attends to considerations beyond the work relationship. That's in his mind XP1. They peculiarly run programmes of actuality in their minds when there is no reality attached to the imaginings. A very primitive state, because unlike our collective ability they have no actual control over imaginings?

'Yes, yes, XP100, these early beings have considerable shortage of control over imagined consequences, but have you enabled a meeting of the James and Lara entity.

'Not as intended. Lara a more senior executive, who I have replicated flirtatiously approached James to assist in a bowls match. This within their working company social framework. It's really an extension of James's work function. Not as we intended, but it achieves the necessary proximity necessary to further pairing, when this is necessary.

Ideally, we need to approach Lara away from the immediacy of her work pattern. I will look for this opportunity when re-visiting in holographic form, but it may be more persuasive, later if I re-materialize in the earth form of Adriana once more.

'Good, we are having success with our fleet's interface with this bipedal race. Once we reach the target figure of one hundred and fifty we will assemble them for the Mars Mission. We will need to display to them, in actual time the location of incoming comets. They will all be made aware of the life and death situation which exists for their species and other life form. Then they will be willing participants in the Mar's mission. You understand this XP100.

'I did establish that the opposite progeny being is in charge not only by employment appointment, but also exerts emotional control. Specie evolvement has meant that the physical fertility clock has been stopped for this Lara. The internal body scan revealed this when XP200 cloned the individual Lara for me to inhabit a similar body. The Adriana person now in archive store replicated this feature.

'Senior officials of this female procreation type can opt to have electronic implants that effectively shut off egg formation, but can be re-started in a forth decade. This is facilitated in many of these wealthier nation state company organizations. This Lara has one child, but has opted for the implant. We determined that there is an emotional and mental strength when in a senior role. The male of the species invariably are still attracted although there is no ability to fertilize. Females have become very focused and almost entirely career dominated with this ability to hibernate future procreation needs. I find this a very attractive development.

'You have excelled XP100 on this mission. You must maintain this detachment.'

'I'm always grateful on return to the energy

force of the command ship XP1. To be refreshed from the galactic flow of knowledge from other developing universes.'

'The holographic visits will continue, although we may need to reinstate the cloned Lara to Adriana material form to incorporate the specie type effectively into a Mars colonization programme. I was maybe over anxious that this planet's life form potential would influence your integrity as a committed member of this expedition to a minor planetary system.'

'There is no way this will ever happen, XP1. Their functioning depends on specie interaction and attraction, where my existence is determined for me by being a member of the Galactic Command Force- constructing and re-framing life systems throughout the universe. I feel revitalized, XP1, by the flow of galactic data into the core existence of my data banks. It is so good to be back with the Force and to be once again, a team member, who can contribute to the present mission and others that are arriving for investigation and further understanding.'

CHAPTER 8

JAMES ARRIVES AT THE CONFERENCE HALL

THE POD RAN ALONG a part graphene cable into the town centre. Companies could lease hire attachment from a main cable line pod company. A drone would then take a joining line. This was never more than fifty metres above ground level to avoid traffic hazard and other higher flying equipment, but with adequate clearance from ground level to be largely non-intrusive. A cable was automatically winched across and secured through a port leading into the building. The pod slowed, momentarily as it entered the junction turn and caught the outreach cable across to the conference hall.

'I do hope Mr James Walters that you have enjoyed your journey accompanied with Hawaiian beach music. We have been so happy to have you with us journeying to your conference. Do have a very useful and meaningful conference today, won't you.'

'Thank you for your assistance Anita.' I smiled and played along with the game that there was a friendly intimacy with this digitally enhanced computer system. I walked from the pod to the walkway, which was now connected. I know, Pod connection was just part of everyday life, but nevertheless the tubular walkways across to high rise business flats were, to me at any rate, aesthetically dis-pleasing. The buildings were built before the invention of mid-air pod hovering stations and the building of walkways. It was like viewing the inside of a building from the outside. An underground railway system but over ground a spider web dome.

My conference admission talisman was half spent after entry access to this location. The interior of a modern building.

Like, a sunflower the gimballed build turned to face the sun's direction to maximize solar trapping. Even with modern technology nature appeared, to have arrived there first. My conference badge was scanned by the interior surveillance camera.

'James Walters you are authorized to enter this building for Conference attendance. There is disruption to the Main Matrix stabilizer. You will require printed paper copy of your report,' said the robot gatekeeper.

'What if I don't have a copy?'

'You've made a pointless visit then haven't you.' It was this condescending human like reply, which I found disturbing. It was just the sort of answer you might get from some haughty company executive.

'Just a tease. I have really,' I said.

'It is noted that Mr Walters you still have your reservoir of comic ability even during this serious time of Main Matrix interference. I will not detain you.' One of the double doors opened sufficiently to allow me to enter and then shut. There was another set of doors to go through before entering the main reception lobby. I zapped my carry case to open and removed the report.

Lara was turned away from me standing at the reception desk, but she must have either heard or been made aware of my entrance and turned to face me.

'Do you have nothing better to do than challenge every robotic help mate when it's just doing its job James?'

'I don't think that we should let them accept that a capacity to access world internet base, at all times, allows them a belief that they're superior to us.'

'Dream on James. They're intellectually dominant even when programmed to serve the company. Lara stepped away from the reception area and I could see the Personal Assistant screen now enlarged on the desk. It just said,

"Miss Petra, it does appear that Mr Walters only has one sales report on his person. He was informed that a minimum of twenty copies was required for today's meeting."

'The snitch,' I said.

'No James, Jackson supports the company all the time.'

'Good old Jackson.'

Holographic channel bands in the region were shut down due to a hacking risk. Hence the redress or regress, dependant on point of view to paper reporting. Head office operated independently from the regions with an uncontaminated system.

Mr Sullivan, the area manager knew how to keep the managers awake and interested. There were always three or more impossibly attractive, in this instance, mini-skirted visions of loveliness at head office. But also, a smattering of super fit sports men emblazoned with Fit for Life badge awards after winning international events. You kidded yourself that you as an unfit manager rated against these people. Then there was Lara, who I was, in spite of what I said to Nina very attracted. But only used her feminine prowess when it was to company advantage and you a part of some business advancement.

'James, I'm not your Girl Friday and it's not Friday yet,' she said, turning and wrinkling her pert nose at me.

'Bet you don't speak to Silverback, like that.'

'Mr Sullivan, doesn't come to a meeting with only one copy of a hand out.'

'Hand out, HAND OUT, there's a clue in the name, James. I'll photo copy twenty, but only if you help me with these.' A sales report was snatched out of my hand and the staple removed with an expert twist at the corner.

In the copier room, Lara's ponytail flicked over, as she reached to pick up the stapler, which revealed an identical mole to the one on the back of Adriana's neck. It seemed an unusual coincidence. Why was I even thinking about that previous encounter?

'Mine go through first,' she said, and took back the filing tray. Then slapped the top paper into my hand.

'Never heard of guests first,' I replied. The noise of the machine drowned out my remark. I saw the head nod and rolled eyes to denote that I was a lost cause. Lara, slapped the electronic stapler in my hand and I first clipped her work together before completing the stapling of my twenty copies. We parted company once back in reception.

'Sit near the front in the Conference hall. You're first up,' were Lara's, parting words.

Lara, gave me the sweetest of smiles when she came over to pick up the copies in the meeting room. The kind that might have been reserved for the man in her life, but then as personal assistant to the area sales manager-part of her role was to decorate managers minds with the possibility that she might- might, just be available for a closer relationship. Provided, the requisite sales were achieved.

'Saved your bacon, you owe me', she whispered, as I passed nineteen copies of the sales report over. There were a few vacant seats. Five regional sales managers attended, but head office department buyers were also there, ready to pounce, if they felt their products were not being promoted. It was nearly July, but it rained consistently through May. This year's fashion re-visit to the mini skirt and smock top, not ideal. The young women at head office, wore mini-skirts, persuaded most probably by the fifty per cent discount allowed on fashion items. But it was a difficult season. I stood up and made my way to the front. Silverback was flicking through my report.

'James concise, if you please, I need time for question and answer.' This was picked up by colleagues further back with a subdued, yet audible "Hear, Hear." They knew full well, the name of the game was to lengthen presentation to avoid questioning from the buyers. Silverback looked up from under his glasses with a frosty look, to remind everyone, who was running the show.

Fifty-four departments in each shopping complex, meant the report was about playing up the winners. After the customary flattering comments about buying expertize that gave the company a head start on rivals, I mentioned the phenomenal sales of the street and daylight powered umbrella, with tablet technology in the handle. The other really successful product being the Recipe Max Maker Plus. I wanted to keep away from reporting on fashion.

'This product is magic. A buying achievement. It has the ability to recreate meal preparation from as far back as 2017. Celebrity chefs from a past era ply their skills in these sequences while the Max Maker plus, like the original meal maker prepares this meal. Super Provider, our contracted food supplier has launched twenty format ingredient packs for this first promotion. There is already demand for tie ups with other past time recipe shows with matched packs.

The Matchmaker Plus is looking to be product of the year. These two products you will see from the listings achieved thirty per cent of sales in rain wear and home merchandise, respectfully.' I decided to move deftly. I moved across to clothing and fashion by talking up the new Projection System in shopping centres.

'Jodie Taylor the international model in holographic form, modelled clothes on the virtual perception cat walk, which increased footfall, but not sales, due to the May rain. There would be searching questions over this.

It was then that I noticed Lara standing to the right hand back corner of the room. This was customary. Her role being that of timekeeper. Silverback sat near the front. Legs crossed, hand held to chin, and face concentrated into professionally feigned attention. Holographic transmissions we knew were being intercepted and this was the reason for the paper reports. In due course, there was then winding of the arm by Lara.

This coincided with a hologram with lowered light intensity appearing. It was a life size hologram of Adriana. Without seeing the formation of the hologram, you can be unsure whether, you are not looking at a flesh and blood person. I alone faced the back of the lecture hall. The cloning being, nowadays, so exact. I then realized that apart from the long blond hair and slim face she was identical in height and proportion to Lara. Disconcertingly, but no doubt to assure my attention, Adriana's holographic form changed to that of a blue X Ray Figure, which displayed skeleton, skull, ligaments and back.

I then realized that rather than human competitors intercepting holographic transmissions, it was most likely Adriana and the Galactic Command Force. Lara, waved her hand a little more rapidly, no doubt there was a distracted look on my face. I held up a copy of the report and waved to signal that my talk was coming to an end. I noticed that Adriana was miming using a knife and fork after pointing first to Lara and then to me. The meaning transparent when the sign – "ASK LARA OUT" appeared suspended above Adriana's head. I raised the report again to acknowledge this message, which I combined into an audience attraction wave before continuing with the announcement-

'Questions are invited about the report from the audience.'

51

CHAPTER 9

GETTING TO MEET UP WITH LARA

THE CEILING LIGHTS ACROSS the back of the room switched on and off. A power surge, which followed, perhaps after the demand made on the system by the holographic presentation of Adriana, now vanished. It made those near the front look around. I didn't mind this distraction, it denied further questions from buyers. This repeat early re-appearance from Adriana was unnerving. Now in a hologram. I remembered reading a science fiction story from the twentieth century, where a female robot was found to have emotions, when it, she? was apparently believed to be only a machine. It was about to be destroyed and was convincingly claiming love for its owner. This appeared an unlikely outcome then, but a future possibility. My home automata Zita no doubt would claim undying affection for me, but it would have been programmed for this response. Artificial intelligence was evolved enough to now consider this possibility, but they were not flesh and blood, although I might be called automatist in some quarters. Automata could be considered as art imitating life. This alien called itself Adriana, was like an artistic creation. That's if you subscribed to the view that Adriana was an artistic creation? Can aliens be considered an art form?

Some might say that anything which is not naturally formed can be considered art.

Such irrelevant nonsense seeped into my thoughts. Perhaps, I was looking for a way to make the everyday to be at the conference that more relevant, while wanting, in part, to disbelieve the waiting room experience.

'James, may I call you James.' A bespectacled lady, in I guess Woman's Fashion stood up. She continued talking, not letting me reply.

'Why were the cat walk models accessory less?'

I visited Leeds and noticed that with evening wear none of the models held bags, wore shoes or scarves. We were assured there would be displays of accessories on the cat walks.'

'I understood that there was an exclusive contract with Couturier. That only their garments would be displayed.' I turned to Mr Sullivan for confirmation. He looked flustered, but knew this to be the case in part.

'Yes, Mr Walters is right on this point, but it was only two weeks in June. I expect Tina it was one of these weeks you visited. The models were accessorized at all other times, Mr Walters?' The real live models were there to view the holograms of themselves on the catwalk.

This was a week before Nina walked out of my life. I kept a grip on this memory and, replied,

'Yes, those were the instructions on the screens in all holographic cat walk robing venues. I attempted to change the subject.

'There was still limited success with the holographic dress design. The garments replicated around a robot body looked real enough, until the battery packs failed and the hologram crashed. Not a good look.'

The silence translated as a gasp of relief. The buyers of fabric and garments not likely to have their garment buying skills replaced by advanced holographic technology.

'Advertisers and live performance theatres look to be interested, though. A whole wardrobe of hologram historical costume can be created, with no need for costume hire.' That did not bother them, although costumiers would not be pleased. The fashion buyer's belief in their products and the need to convince the company that they knew the market meant they nearly always sought to find fault with the retail side.

'There seems to be a lack of commitment.' A name light scribed in the air above the lady speaking "Sarah Lorella Outerwear Buyer."

'There seems to be a lack of commitment,' she said, repeating herself, before continuing. The raising of eyebrows made her pink and green glasses fall forward as she looked back to three women buyers', who appeared to recognize this to be a signal.

The three vigorously shook their heads to affirm the statement. This presentation was fast becoming some primeval women versus man scene, not unusual for these meetings. Lara came to Silverback's and my rescue, by moving forward to where he was sitting. It was a whispered conversation. I watched his face relax from a look of consternation to that of on the threshold of blissful!

'Lara informs me that all buyers were sent a schedule for the catwalk display season, with opportunity to question suitability.' Lara interposed again, before he continued.

'Several displays were rescheduled to meet requirements. Lara tells me she sent each department a second message affirming the first.' Tina, the buyer was not shot down in flames by this.

'You know Mr Sullivan we are not tied to our department offices. It is possible the messages were not relayed on.' Tina was losing the contest, but not for the first Lara rescued Silverback from the dragon fire of a buyer determined to shoot down the sales side of the business.

'Lara informs me that we need to move on to the next sales presentation otherwise we will not complete our schedule for today. Silverback did not want too many searching questions, neither did I.

'The recent copies will now all, I emphasis "all" be collected and placed in the formatting consul.' The meeting finally ending with Silverback giving these instructions. A desk size unit at the front of the room housed the formatting unit with a high tensile Perspex hood to be lifted with the paper placed inside. The paper re-constituted into energy bricks for power generation. Alternatively, another setting, which made household artefacts like plates and cups from the paper. Sprayed with a waterproof varnish in design with colour of choice. This setting was blocked out by the company.

'Will you all hand the reports to Lara, if you'd be so kind Lara.' He smiled at Lara, and displayed perfect rows of teeth, which seemed incongruous in a fifty year old man. They were seeded in his mouth from lab grown teeth. The public smile now more frequent, but if anything, less sincere, because of the new teeth.

Sean, a colleague who customarily muttered, "he lies and his teeth stink," now only half right in his description of Silverback. I was sat near the front. After I passed the sheaf of reports to Lara, she said, I remember,

'The office is meeting at The White Bear at eight and I need a bowling partner. Are you any good James? Don't bother if you're not. It's payback time, you owe me.' Her face expressionless, but a smile flickered in my direction as I handed over the reports

'Yes, no?' she said, and looked away, but ocean blue eyes returned with a gimlet eyed stare, comparable to a bailiff assured of being right and demanding payment.

'Yep, okay,' I said, which seemed a worthwhile answer at the time, judged by the full on smile I received back She moved quickly on. No one near enough to hear what was said. Lara was very good at her job, but more career orientated than I was ever likely to be.

The office skittles match could be seen as part of the job. I was never completely certain Lara was in a committed relationship, even after I'd spotted a ring on her third finger. I could not remember, looking back if she was wearing one this time. The request- demand? for me to be her partner to play in the bowls match did not imply romantic interest on her part. It wasn't that I'd asked or suggested going out in the manner of a going for a meal. I still really wasn't the one inviting Lara out, as suggested by Adriana. It remained still in situ that I was useful to promote Lara Petra's career profile.

CHAPTER 10

AT THE WHITE BEAR

'YOU, LUCKY DEVIL I reckon Lara saved you from being devoured by Tina,' said Sean in the restaurant afterwards. There was an industrial Meal Maker Plus on demo. The holographic menu, at the table end display, listed its availability. The description and voice over were both in Spanish. Sean accessed the format on his pad in an attempt to get an English version for our benefit.

The company women including Lara came in together and sat on a long table near to us. That is Sean, Rick, Tom and myself. None of us knew that this would be the last time we'd be together, for five years.

'It's in Spanish,' I heard Annette from reception call out. Ask Sean.'

'Yes, ask Sean,' another said and the others chirped in with "ask Sean, Annette."

Not sure Sean heard any of this immersed in trying to adjust the holographic transmission with his pad. Annette got up and came across to where we were sitting accompanied by Lara.

'You do remember why you're here James,' said Lara. I heard the crash of skittles falling as a door opened into the skittle alley. A game revival from the twentieth century.

'To have a meal and relax,' I suggested, knowing full well that Lara was checking me out. A reminder that I was to partner her in the skittles match.

Wine at that moment arrived on a hover tray, followed by a wine waiter. There was deference shown by automata toward the human condition, you might say, but their data banks would field difficult questions from guests and the waiter could be assisted in his reply. The White Bear conformed with Quadrant regulations and did not install higher grade automata. Fifty per cent of bar staff, waiting and assistant catering employees were required to be human, even though these premises were on hire to a large outfit like Fit for Life.

'Sean, we just knew you could sort out the language setting,' said Annette. The helpless woman tactic not necessarily a winner with all men. Lara I felt could scare a man into competency at the other side of the male female spectrum.

'Your wine, has arrived, said the wine waiter, who was playing catch up with the hover tray, which hovered silently near to our table.

'I am here. A human being. Once it was machines that were rare working in restaurants, now it is the human,' he said in a piqued manner. But managed a smile, which was still uniquely human.

'Red or white gentlemen?'

'It'll be red,' said Rick. A decision made earlier by the four of us.

'James, are you listening?' You're not here for the wine or the meal in particular. Lara was lent towards me as she spoke, but drew back when it was apparent that my eyes were entangled with a view of her tightly fitted tee shirt. The women were dressed as cheer leaders.

'It's a match against our American counter-parts. They hold over fifty per cent of equity in the company,' said Lara.

Thoughts drifted back to recent memory with the appreciation that Nina's legs and bottom would no longer be wiggling as she placed first one leg and then the other on the stool next to the mirror to adjust her stocking tops, before sitting to apply make-up. It had become a tease on her part first thing in the morning, but could also be a message of availability for the evening. Betsy slung in the spare bedroom with the focus on love-making. After about ten minutes the dog whimpered like some grounded child. Was I deluding myself all that time?

'James, you're not listening.' I was, but I'd also clocked Sean, who'd looked across to spy on our head to head talk. I could on the one hand have told Annette that she was wasting her time going for Sean, but perhaps much in the same way as I believed there was a future relationship for me beyond that of work with Lara. More that I was some appliance provided by the company to further her career, which could never extend to anything approaching that of a physical relationship.

'We need to look serious and not like some also rans,' Lara continued. I wasn't sure that the cheer leader dress of short skirt and tee shirt was in that category of match serious. Our table was now in receipt of a pre-game pep talk from the boss, who was now sitting on the chair next to me, with hands held open to include everyone at our table.

'They belong to the work hard play hard school. The girls from our office are all good players. They've a mixed team, but have an extra male player.

This was said, I felt, to imply that a team with more men might be at a disadvantage.

'You need to make a real effort James.' I made to point at myself in a "what me?" sort of way.

'We're playing to win. It's also a useful exercise in finding out the calibre of company people we're up against.' It was my research that uncovered the skittles game from archive- but that didn't mean I was any good at it!

I could have bottled out, but with Nina out of my life I suppose I felt the need to return to becoming part of the outer social cluster.

Colleagues, I felt envied my relationship with Nina. My male ego possibly warmed to this notion early on, but the likes of Sean, Rick and Tom, probably were unwilling to appreciate that there was a strong control factor, not from me, but it was Nina, who was in the driving seat.

'There you are,' said Sean. 'The holograms changed from a Flamenco dancer to a kilted Scottish one.' The Scottish voice- that pleasant sing song lilt, which didn't overly challenge those of us from south of the border.

'Hey Lara how come James gets all the attention?' Rick called across to where Lara was now sitting. Rick moved over to sit in a chair alongside me. None of these three were in the bowls team.

'He's not here for the wine. James is partnering me in the skittles match.'

'I'll have Mr Walters's then,' said Tom mischievously grabbing the glass as the wine waiter approached, zapping the tray to hold the wine bottle at chair height. For me this was a continuation of work, but then there was no pressing reason to go back to the flat. Now that the Spanish hologram was transformed to a Scottish one Annette's mission was achieved.

'Lara, are you coming back,' she called out.

'Be with you Annette,' she replied

'We've got about an hour before the skittles match. It's a team of six. The other men are from accounts.'

'The other two recruits, you mean,' I said.

'They play regularly James. They're more involved with the social side---- anyway where's Nina?'

'She walked out yesterday.

'You rowed then.'

'Sort of.' I wasn't going to say it was because Nina thought that I was involved with Lara. It never happened and it wasn't happening now.

'Perhaps it's because I'm not a dog person.'

'I'm sorry James. You should have said. I

might have let you off the skittles match. But then it's probably good for you to be here and not sulking in your flat.' Not that much compassion and understanding from Lara.

'James, you're not drinking wine?' Waiter you can monitor this for me. We all want clear heads in the skittles alley

'Certainly, Miss Petras I'm wanting a win for the Brit Fit for Life team, of course.' He smiled obsequiously. 'Maybe a celebratory drink or two afterwards?' Lara nodded in agreement before she walked back to her table.

It went through my mind that if a man came on to a female junior and made her attend a social function in the pursuit of furthering his career it would be seen as sexual harassment. How was Lara getting away with doing exactly the self-same thing? You only needed to look at the green eyes of Sean, Rick and Tom when Lara came across to first talk to me to reason why.

CHAPTER 11

XP100 REPORTS TO COMMANDER OF THE GALACTIC FORCE

ADRIANA, OR XP100, THE entity projected to earth in the form of the replicated executive Lara remained with the Galactic Command Force, existential to the hologram Adriana. This Adriana being a limb extension from the complex and advanced intelligence that integrated with other XP entities within the Command Force. A hundred-ship fleet with power beyond earth bound restriction poised on the edge of the Milky Way Galaxy.

'I was right to instruct you not to remain in that specie body type. That life stage is seen, as well, decadent. You might, XP100, have been caught as a sample for a galactic museum, a millennium earlier when this practice was still galactically operational. Yes, you may be dismissive of my observations. I have picked up on your analysis,' said XP1.

XP100, liked historic role play. Although the concept of internalizing life form, instead of implanting life seed within comets to be harvested as required, seemed primitive. By utilizing a life form to implant a scavenging pod, which drained away nutrients from its host XP100 found horrific.

At first, the thought of breaking away from the constant flow of information given out from galaxies to return to this early planet role was a disturbing thought. But for the purpose of adjustment to the visited planet, a necessary sacrifice. XP1's, externalized vocal waves, reminded XP100, of the voice form used by itself in the role of Adriana, in that planet's time frame.

Lara, was the human species earth life form copied, but

with some facial alteration. Complementary, to James, in that they were obviously both bipedal, but defined as different by their procreative roles, voice frequency and also in other ways psychologically appeared to be of another construct. The higher octave speech, fine skin, lighter musculature with attention to personal adornment immediately suggested certainly, variation on specie type. The shock realization that a matched specie to Lara was host to a miniature form absorbing nutrients made it realize how far back this planet was in evolutionary development. That pair bonding was the main procreating method. How entity development was compromised for this specie, which had its molecular structure interrupted with the production of off spring as with other mammalian specie across this planet.

XP1, studied and researched with other galactic over-lords' behaviour and aptitude of male and female type and unanimously decided that emotional persuasiveness, rather than pure threats and intimidation could best be imposed by the female of the specie. Archive research revealed a story embedded in this planet's early culture. A divine command not to eat a certain fruit over turned by the persuasiveness of this early woman.

'Your skills and newly acquired knowledge about this populous creature will enable you- XP100, to recruit from the spread of peoples across the globe. Through meetings, and back up from the Galactic Command Force you will be able to move into all regions after we have selected applicable skills from this Fit for Life organization. This is how we will ensure that if the diversion of the lead comet away from this planet fails and destruction follows we will have diverse specie type ready to seed this smaller planet named by this specie as Mars. All colour denomina-tions across the living light spectrum are confident that you can bring together mixed types for this evacuation to Mars.

We will need to encourage, voluntarily of course, adaptation, which will strengthen the capillary actions that supply oxygen for improved brain function and motivational capability.

'But XP1, this James, responds to the presence of Lara, who is capable of influencing behaviour, without logical compliance. This disturbs normal reactions and consequently, allows for her to filtrate ideas effectively. To change physiology in some way. You said this is a prime objective. To molecularly enliven the entrants to the Mars colonization programme, but perhaps not in this way?'

'Yes, yes, I noticed how you affected that change in the James specie.' XP1 identified this on XP100's first return.

'But you need now only return in holographic form to these select groups. Unless I decide otherwise. The name Adriana, will refer to the hologram. At least in evolutionary terms they have developed almost life like holographic presence. I don't want our energy and knowledge to become contaminated or trapped in this backwater of evolutionary process.'

XP100, although now familiar with and adapted to the material projection of Adriana, was settled, confident, and fully merged with its green adjusting sphere. The earth link designed to monitor the assembling earth group available and independently monitored progress. A slight dilution of power emission followed than when the Adriana hologram or materialized form of Adriana was operational. XP100, Secure, now within the Real Time construct, allowed through the Galactic Command Force's deep space assignment. This ability to maintain functionality, while equipped to enervate systems to track, store and analysis all galactic life. XP100's, sphere would drowse, with sporadic episodes of activity while committed to influence on this new planet but movement of the star fleet to another galaxy would leave XP100 stranded in the human-like body formed, named Adriana.

'You're back here XP100 and have achieved compliance with this group through holographic message.' Other colour spheres, invisible to outer dimension appeared across the entire ship. A rainbow of seven colours--red, -pink-orange-yellow-green--blue, and ultra-violet. XP100's green level was midway in the rankings. A primary level, which was often designated for interaction on a planet's surface.

'It's vital that support is given to these cellular formations on the planet. We will need to give rewards to make them believe that they have special powers, now that they will be dependent on us. It is important to make them believe that they have influence on their continued existence. Our fight against anti-matter needs to support their molecular state and on-going development.'

'That's better,' continued the commander as green flooded the outer layer of XP100's sphere with pulsating light, requisite for green level of actuality.

'You're very convincing. I saw the response from the James entity. It is strange that they do not have codified identity, but have vocalized communication methods when together. XP200 has harvested plant, vegetable and tree variety for future incubation in bubble life mini world creations.

Within this group one hundred and fifty future Mars inhabitants will be brought together. You will need XP100 to show the several scientific groups, that we are able to replicate the earth's gravitational effect on Mars within the bubbles. Their knowledge will transmit reassurance to members of the whole group.

'Yes, XP1, I will be able to describe with assistance from Galactic Command data archive how we are able to channel gravitational energy from Jupiter across to Mars. Their science discovered on earth a century ago, how the circulatory system, particularly within the brain can be damaged without earth-like gravity. It has been the most significant restriction on space travel for this specie. It will be evolutionarily possible for the specie to make some adaptation, as you have said, but that is in their future. The ganglioside head, which controls consciousness and movement through a central nervous system vary in shape, XP1. They are from many racial groupings down millenniums of existence. The change of head hair from black to fair with slight face modification affected the response from the James entity, although different shapes and colour of the specie still reveal similar behavioural personality. They merge at a molecular level, but it seems strange that they produce, without specification. A randomness that can be expected from earlier biological cellular growth. They have attained individual awareness, but are unable to progress away from the molecular medium and still continue a cell propagation process that is random unless modified genetically in some form. Certainly on Mars alterations will be needed to survive.'

'Your next holographic revisit will be a continuation to motivate the James and Lara specie so that they mutually attract,' said XP1, 'before you meet all other groups first in their physical domain and then with multiple holographic output. The Command Force will facilitate from its data bases a monitored interaction across the global surface of this planet.'

'You are assured that the James person has particular awareness in the presence of Lara, XP100?'

'I established earlier the necessary interest. It's a learned process for this specie type. They're often easily distracted from any task when the Lara form has acquired conscious interest of attention.'

'You did state you liked investigating these molecularly challenged early life forms.'

'Yes, XP1, I find this planet's life form a challenge, but appreciate that without modification and improvement to a more advanced state they will remain trapped in a cul-de-sac, going nowhere. The mind of James has a superficiality of attitude.

It resents the strict ordering of existence by superiors. The rejection by a member of the opposite specie on the grounds of being too short in stature has not affected psychological strength. This James, individual seems resigned to unpredictability when encountered by the Lara kind. He failed to recognize that Adriana, is a modified equivalent to Lara, but then my visit as Adriana was an out of context meeting. It is hard though XP1, to appreciate that they have not evolved sufficiently to eliminate the fragile state of interdependence. They still internalize reproduction in the female type of Lara, although this group can choose external embryonic birthing There does appear to be a molecularly physical selection force at work, but the combative nature in the species seeking ascendency one over the other can lead to destructive measures that benefit neither.'

'Yes, yes, XP100, you must appreciate that they are a biological life form that have an individual acquisitive tendency, which can override evolutionary progression. You must not at any time let them influence the plan to prepare this specie for life on the planet they call Mars.'

CHAPTER 12

SKITTLES MATCH LEADS TO DISCLOSURE BY MARIO

THERE WAS A BABBLE of talk, laughter and even hilarity at the White Bear. I remember when the doors, which led from the corridor into the White Bear, opened. Silverback was out to impress the American skittles team captain.

'This Jeb is our venue for this evening.' Jeb was larger than life, but in an American football team he might have been considered average. Silverback swept his hand across towards the bar area, but on spotting Lara I heard him say,

'I must introduce you to Lara- "Lara," he called out and waved his Stetson to attract attention. It wasn't as if his entrance had been missed by anyone. Annette gave one of those looks to Lara which said, "Aren't you the lucky one." Sean meanwhile managed to turn the waiter hologram upside down. Silverback entered in what he probably considered clothes suitable for a party. A short sleeve top with SRM short for "Super Range Merchandising," across the front in gold lettering, jeans, wide leather silver buckled belt and a Stetson, which he removed. This affectation did not surprise me, but Tom whispered loudly

'It's cowboy Joe!'

It was an attempt to flatter and impress the American Fit for Life Team by Silverback.

'This Jeb, is our venue for this evening.' Jeb Lucas was larger than life, but in an American football team might have been considered average.

Sean, meanwhile managed to turn the hologram upside down.

'That's how you tell it's a hologram,' said Sean. 'The kilt stays in place. It doesn't respond to gravity.' There was suppressed laughter in the quietened room. The miniature, but life like reality of the kilted figure did make you think that the kilt would drop with his legs in the air.

Lara, was on her feet and walked briskly over to where Silverback was standing by the bar. I couldn't hear much of what was said, but I did notice him put an arm on Lara's shoulders, before he introduced her to the American skittles team. It was one of those situations when you're not sure whether to interpret it as fatherly or more in a different sort of possessive way. It never occurred to me that Lara was anything more than his personal assistant. I decided that the two sitting in the corner of the bar distancing themselves from everyone else must be the two male members of our team.

I looked across at the time taking machine. This I felt was a great success. It could literally read your thoughts with regard to time analysis. Programmed earlier from the main terminal with all company scheduled events. I knew the bowling match was scheduled for a seven thirty start. I looked at the wall set disc, which immediately lit up and picked up on neural activity behind my eyes. Lips barely moved, but my tongue mimicked in my mouth, the words, as I silently asked about the start time for the match with eyes directed at the time disc. The actual time was quarter to seven. This cleared from its face as I asked- 'At what time with relevant data will the inter-company bowling match start?' Immediately the digital numbers moved to seven fifty. Arrival of the American team, introductions at the bar and the probability of being offered drinks would all be computed into time consumption overlap. The machine would have factored in all events as it scanned the room. The time from when Silverback arrived with Jeb, and the American team and the conversational development. I have to admit I liked to challenge the Time Taker, and make my own judgement but it computed every action, including the biographical personality of those at the bar and whether one dominant person would force the pace to achieve closer proximity to the start time. This pre-plan analysis of the time that the skittles match would start was not the machine's main function.

Its main purpose was to access data that threatened the building. For example if the screen came up with the word 'void' you would enquire 'why' with mind thought and a reply would then follow like –"The master terminal, requires to hibernate and will shortly request you to vacate the premises," might follow. The master terminal in hibernation could then move its data bases away from an intruder trying to access data. This sometimes required shutting off main power supply and personnel vacating the premise for another. The time assessment was not a one-off calculation or a definite time statement, but a continuous one. As if the Time Taker inhabited both horses, jockeys and even the turf as the race progressed analysing energy levels and the ability of a jockey to drive his horse first to the finishing line. Needless to say, human nature being what it is, meant that you liked to assess on your own account, and wager against the machine, well I did anyway.

The time taker circle face flicked on and off as one of the women looked across. It lit up with 7.18, then 9.20. My guess was that she wanted an analysis of when the game would end. I never liked the idea that we were all being profiled while in the building. Both teams studied, with personality quotients entered into analysis. Certain alpha personalities can dominate social events. A large selection of less dominant types is willing to allow this personality, type ascendency. Without the need for machine verification the alpha character in our group I determined was Lara. The two guys from accounts in the corner awaited orders from her as did the three girls. Annette, Jo, Heidi and myself.

I stood out like a sore thumb. While dwelling on my recent break up with Nina I hadn't even considered that skittles would require suitably casual attire.

Heidi, Jo, and Annette wore matching cheer leader skirts with star spangled knee length socks. Lara, denoted seniority by parading a yellow sash with the Fit for Life logo. Even the two techno recruits didn't look out of place in their work jump suits. I looked the geekier person in my shiny sales suit provided by the company. The American women replicated the skirts and star spangled socks, but I suspected Lara would have decided on this attire, anyhow. Mario, Cooper and Lee -the other American team members, besides Jeb were like their Captain dressed in jeans and Fit for Life logo covered polo shirt top. Jeb's baseball hat just said "Cap."

This themed earlier century bowling alley was discovered by me from research. For that reason I felt that I couldn't make excuses and opt out, even if Lara hadn't said-"you owe me James," No one in the White Bear would have known this back story. The directors of the company, would have taken credit for the idea. The hologram I provided for head office depicted the bowling alley in what was called the old print room. The White Bear with a similar sized out-building was keen to host the event for free when Fit for Life said it would build an up dated version of a skittle alley. Recently certain interstate tax exemption was offered to companies prepared to offer sporting activities for employees, supposedly outside of work hours. I never believed that a skittles alley would meet the necessary requirement, but it did. My suggestion for a skittle alley came after I obtained a metal disc called a DVD from an earlier century. I then went on to develop a hologram from this DVD, sourced from archives. It looked a fun game when built in miniature but with full content.

Three D Holographic bowls rolled down the alley mimicking the real ones with teams featured in the back ground. The Fit for Life American team, earlier back in Washington made use of vacant office space after I sent the hologram for viewing out of a wall to room holographic desk screen. The completed alley strip at the White Bear was defined by white lines on a green floor. Sixteen metres remained at the back which contained tables and chairs to accommodate those not in play. It was seven fifty-two when we left the bar area, which to be fair was the time indicated by the Time Taker at seven thirty five after adjustment when I made a further enquiry.

'Lara, introduce your team honey,' said Jeb. We followed these two into the alley. He dwarfed not only us, but his team members. Two of the American women were of Latino Hispanic origin and the third Suzi I guessed to be from the Southern states by her accent. All three shorter than Lara, Jo, Annette and Heidi. Two of the men in the team, apart from Jeb, that is, were taller than me, but Mario was about my height - more well-built.

'Okay,' said Lara, who did not appear over keen at being addressed as honey responded.

'This is Martin and Alex from account data access. They were standing next to Lara. Jo, Annette and Heidi were already well into chatting with the American women, but the three of them turned and smiled in Jeb's direction.

'And this is James, from Sales,' she said, making it sound like an after-thought, although perhaps I imagined this.

'It's great to meet you guys,' said Jeb. 'James you're smaller than I imagined.' The point probably missed that a large percentage of people were smaller than him. A miniature hologram of our team was sent to Jeb, when the idea of a match was first floated.

'I see you girls are getting on okay. Ana, Julie, Suzi say hi to James, Martin and Alex,' said Jeb. There was a sort of wave, but they carried on talking from the back of the tabled area.

Hi Martin, Alex,' said Mario 'and heights not everything James, I should know!' Cooper and Lee got talking to Martin and Alex as we sat around a table. Each table with a central holographic styled candle. Lara and Jeb our team captains, expeditiously sat at a table for two.

'James,' said Cooper, who was sitting opposite to me. 'I really get your themed ideas. That living in the pre-holographic times. Holograms with GSS and CEM make it difficult to fully imagine that there was once only a world of flat screen projection.'

GSS and CEM were American acronyms for Graphene Super Storage and Constant Event Monitor. The event monitor being similar to our Time Taken Module incorporated for our attendance here at the White Bear.

'James, and who'd you like Jeb?' I heard Lara's voice raised in the background.

'Mario, "Mario," Can you keep score with James at the skittle end?' More an instruction from Jeb than a request.

'James and Mario, then, said Lara.

'You'll both need to re-set skittles after each play, best three legs playing as pairs. And James keep record with Mario. You'll both need to jointly agree the score for each play.' We stood up simultaneously and swapped that look of – "they would pick us two!"

'She's a real boss cat that team leader of yours-cute, though,' said Mario.

'Reminds me of someone I've met before,' he continued. 'Hair colour different, but a similar good looker-like an encounter I had.' We reached the far end of the alley.

'How d'you mean?' I asked. 'What do you mean by encounter?'

We stood either side of the row of skittles. Mario's dark Latin features contrasted strongly with the white wall behind. We could talk directly across to each other out of range of the others. He was stood hand on chin, looking at me, as if deciding on whether to proceed further. I considered that the not overly defined American accent could mean that there was a background of living in Britain, possibly during a company training course.

'James you'll know what holographic transmission can achieve,' he said, before continuing.

'Yep, I reckon so,' I said.

'This was something real strange. This encounter. Not something I wanted to talk to my team about. I've just not mentioned this to anyone, before now.'

'Try me then,' I said. My thoughts immediately returned to Adriana. That eastern European accented voice, blond hair and odd dress sense, must have initially distracted me from considering that there was any resemblance to Lara. Mario's mention of an encounter made me more than interested.

'It was after work and near to dusk in Central Park. I was sat on a bench overlooking the fountain in the English Conservatory Garden, unwinding. You know it James?'

'I know Central Park. It's just off 5th Avenue, if I remember rightly.'

I looked back up the skittles alley. The teams were lined up in order of play.

'It's a place you go to for escape - not to expect to talk to anyone,' said Mario.

'Not wanting for anyone to interrupt your space. This woman a lot like Lara, but with fair hair, came across, while I gave a look into the fountain: dreaming about –nuthin' particular. Then she came up to me. James, she frightened the crap out of me what with what she had to say.'

We both stood back from the skittles. Annette had picked up a bowl from the trough running along from the seated area. The way she smoothed her hand around the surface and then held the bowl up with one hand plus the inspection of it, as if she could encode this bowl somehow with a specific flight path. Straightaway, this made me clock that I did not have that level of bowling skills. The level achieved by Annette and the dawning realization that Lara could be more than disappointed with me as her skittling partner.

CHAPTER 13

AFTER THE SKITTLES MATCH

MARIO BROKE OFF, WHEN Annette made to walk toward the line to make a first bowl.

'Let's talk Mario -afterwards, in the bar,' I said. "A lot like Lara." Why had I missed this. I kept going over it in my mind. I was startled by what Mario said. It produced a feeling of pent up anticipation. There was also, a feeling, I remember, of release. That I was no longer alone. A coincidence, or was it? That I'd just met someone else, who'd been contacted by Adriana via this Galactic Command Force. Stupidly, at that moment, the saying "if it looks like a duck, walks like a duck, quacks like a duck, then it most probably is a duck,' jumped into my mind. Mario was describing an alien encounter similar to mine. His information sufficient for me to believe Adriana had visited Mario in Central Park in a similar way to she encountered me, but under a false pretext in the Stroud waiting room.

The hazardous position I felt to be in with regard to my ability at skittles, alongside Lara, our team captain, returned, but the impact lessened with having met up with Mario. I was anxious to find out more after the match.

To say that I wasn't skilled up to be a skittling team member would have been an understatement. But there was no longer urgency for a return to the flat with Nina now absent.

Neither was I part of head office. Lara, Jo, Annette and Heidi would have practised on the alley at the White Bear together with Martin and Alex. For all my enthusiasm in setting up the skittle alley I ranked like a back-room boy recruited to make the number up to seven. After several plays from team pairs. Annette walked down to where we were standing.

'Lara's said I'm to take over the scoring with Mario.' She smiled at Mario.

'After the next pair,' said Annette, 'it's you, with Lara -spec ting great things— like you partnering the boss,' she said, and gave me a mischievous sideways look before a return to making eyes at Mario.

'Don't,' I said, 'and we both might be surprised.' The Fit for Life Team were already ahead. The scores 56 to 35. Lara went first and you guessed it on the first two throws she got strikes. You could say the pins didn't stand a chance. Mario and Annette wisely moved back a pace or two after the first bowl. On the third throw the bowl hit the backboard, returned and knocked out two of the three pins left standing, leaving only one from the nine, giving a total of 26 out of a possible 27. My scores were six, five and one after the three throws. Lara gritted her teeth. Annette I could see was enjoying the possibility of my being held responsible for losing the match by the way she smiled and half sniggered on handing back my tablet when I returned to continue scoring. Unbelievably their two remaining pairs got strikes on each of their three throws, securing a victory for the American Fit for Life Team.

I pointed out to Lara afterwards that even if I'd scored higher we still wouldn't have beaten that level of scoring.

'That's no excuse James for the lowest score in the team. Don't you feel any shame in being beaten by women, who at very short notice have got to a good standard and improved the company's image?' It was bound to be about the company's image or profile in the world.

'It was short notice and the alley is within the head office complex. I don't get near a bowling alley. That's if there were others in existence. You did really well though,' I said attempting to rescue my position.

'I was disappointed not getting three strikes like in practice,' she said. I decided not to pursue the matter, but that was it---they had all practised beforehand.

'James,' said Lara. 'I have to visit the company's new business centre next weekend. They want me to look at the new infrastructure project and I was thinking you might be interested in viewing the plantation. You can bring a friend. I will have Matt with me.'

'Sounds great,' I said. I was feeling guilty about my skittles playing but shouldn't have. When she said bring a friend it crossed my mind that she might be wanting us to child mind while she was in her corporate role. The winning team were given a plate as a trophy cast by the making machine. The team's name and their captain and members' names around the edge. It was an alloy plate in silver, which looked impressive.

Silverback returned and although he never watched the match was effusive about how well Jeb's team played. Tina, the buyer who I crossed swords with earlier that day at the sales meeting, was on hand to present the trophy.

'I know your team Jeb must have been first class, because Lara will have trained her team to a high standard,' She said to those of us grouped to watch the presentation from seats in front of the bar area. I did not know how true this was, but I do know Lara needed to tie up a contract with the Americans, and you could say it was judicious for them to win--- in that a contract needed signing! After the clapping died down, I heard Mario trying to attract my attention.

'James, James, over here.' Mario nodded his head to the corner of the bar where Alex and Martin previously sat. Jeb was ordering drinks for both teams. Either side of a bona fide bar maid, two trays hovered, waiting for prepared drinks to be placed on them for those sat at tables.

'What you two having?' asked Jeb, as we walked towards the bar.

'Mine's an iced coke with a slice of lemon,' replied Mario. To make it straightforward I said 'make mine the same, Jeb.' Jeb's hand concealed much of the sleeved beer glass.

'Two cokes with ice and lemon for these two honey, when you're free.'

'Will you be at a table?' she asked Mario.

'No, no we'll be staying in the bar.' We chatted about the game. Mario's performance had not been epic either, but we then moved away from the serving area and sat opposite one another.

I was intrigued by the way Mario produced a wipe-able magic pad and stylus, from a bygone age after we perched on the bar stools. He didn't speak, immediately although we were sat on adjacent bar stools. He wrote on the pad.

"Talk about the company James. The weather, not about X." Mario wiped the pad clear. There was a Time Taken Module in the bar, which would record whatever we said. Character recognition could be pulled from documents, but like me Mario would've known that a yellow tinged plastic, over the magic wipe pad could prevent the camera reading text. I understood where Mario was coming from and played along.

'How's the new cloud seeding system in the prairies these days, Mario?

'It's made a real improvement,' he said. The next words he wrote on it were,

"Encounter with alien, called Adriana." He wiped it clear. My face was expressionless, but this was confirmation for me of what I already half expected. Even hoped for.

'There's some fantastic work being achieved

with better cloud rain control,' I said to make it sound as if we were just making conversation. I reached across for the pad and stylus, but did not write anything until the bar maid moved away. I wrote

"I've met with Adriana -- has re-visited here in hologram."

'I was once offered a job,' said Mario, 'with a company in the prairies, but just didn't like the idea of leaving the Big Apple.' I wiped the pad clean and Mario wrote.

'We must meet again- away from here James.'

"New York, New York," I nearly sang the words.

'Mario, I accessed some old songs recently. Sounded as if they couldn't get enough of the place back in bygone times. It seems the same for you Mario.'

Parts of New York were on stilts. Sea levels, though, had stabilized and were said to be falling due to induced polar freezing. Cloud formations, directed away from these regions, chilled the poles, which meant more frozen sea. There was demand from scientific bodies for Quadrant to re-introduce polar cloud cover, due to a retreat of coastal tides, affecting creature and fauna habitat. In, my next message I asked if he was staying long in Cheltenham. When he said Jeb and the group wanted to take in the Cheltenham Festival which was next month, I asked via the pad.

'Would you like to visit a nearby company plantation next Saturday. My boss wants me to be there.

'If Lara's your boss—yes,' Mario wrote back.

CHAPTER 14

XP100-ONLY HOLOGRAPHIC INTERVENTION

XP1 TRANSFERRED A RETURN request into XP100's green capability bubble, that remained pulsating, while the holographic projection was in progress. The hologram was formed before projection, but once in position through cocooned capsule transmission (CPT) sourced energy from the planet earth. XP100 took identity away from its bubble in the space command ship, but could be recalled instantly without the need to be reinstated.

Not the case when materially constructed as Adriana. The earth form gave XP100 the realization that human senses were attuned with reaction to stimuli. That affinity existed on a material level, but even with a spoken language there was no transcendental understanding of other realms of existence. For XP100 food and existence was determined by digesting incoming celestial information. The birth of new planetary systems. An understanding of how the material existence of universes depends on the further imaginings of command fleets across galaxies. Then establishing material to build organic structure. How could the triviality of entity relationship be of more importance than the excitement of being on an intergalactic mission?

The holographic projection on to the floor of the meeting room required energy. A resource capability remained in the fleet ship, but effected XP100's immediate consciousness. Information could be processed and stored, but evaluation and decisions on hold until the hologram was deleted from earth space. Detection of the star fleet was impossible within the solar system, because of dimensional time shift. XP1's question.' How did you get on with persuading the James entity to contact the Lara one?' Was the first conscious thought transference accessed on return.

'The holographic construct XP200 devised worked. Their familiarity with holograms seems to make them more susceptible to suggestion than when appearing as one of their own functioning entities. I was able to occupy a portion of mind space, which made James Walters, as they call him aware of my presence. The Lara opposite entity has power over James in the workplace, but I detected there is a willingness to accept this role. Heightened neural activity indicates that he already attends to considerations beyond the work relationship. That's in his mind XP1. They peculiarly run programmes of actuality in the mind when there is no reality attached to the imaginings. A very primitive state, because unlike our collective ability, they have no actual control over imaginings.

'Yes, yes, XP100 these early beings have considerable shortage of control over imagined consequences, but have you enabled a meeting of the James and Lara entity.

'Not as intended. The flirtation technique, I copied from Lara, when the Adriana construct approached James. Lara, has volunteered him to assist in a bowls match. It's in a social framework, but it's really an extension of James' work role. Not as intended, but it achieves the necessary proximity necessary for a pairing, when it is required.'

'Good, we are having success with another fleet interface. It will ultimately be in the region of forty pairs, with others in non-pro-creational roles.

'I did establish that the opposite sex specie is in charge not only by employment appointment, but also exerts emotional control. There is an evolvement facet that has meant the physical fertility clock has been stopped. The internal body scan revealed this when XP200 cloned the individual Lara for you to inhabit a similar body. The Adriana person now in archive store replicated to include this."

'Senior officials of this female procreation type can opt to have electronic implants that effectively shut off egg formation, enabling a re start in a fourth decade. This is the case in many of the more wealthier nation state company organizations

Lara, the senior executive has hibernated procreational ability.'

'You have excelled XP100, on this mission. We need you to be maintained on this detachment for the foreseeable future.'

'I'm always pleased to return to the energy force of the Command ship, XP1. To be invigorated and refreshed with galactic flow of information from universes, that are both developing and developed.'

'The holographic visits will continue, although we may need to reinstate the cloned Lara to Adriana, material form to enable total specie type acclimatization into the Martian environment. But, XP100, ultimately there is to be only holographic representation, you understand?

An image, and not a materialization.' I am concerned that this planet's life form potential could influence your integrity as a committed member of our planet recovery plan and be drawn into this minor planetary system.'

'I cannot conceive any change in circumstance that could possibly alter my avowed commitment as a progressive member to the Galactic Command Force and its future missions.'

'We hope this is the case. We will as custodians of both you and the planetary system we have introduced you to monitor interactions. Further considerations will be given to your progress prior to the groups departure to the planet Mars. Your holographic progression with this group specie will continue to be monitored, but there will be restrictions on energy deployment while we maintain links with Earth to Mars continuum.

CHAPTER 15

FREDERICK STANLEY REPORTS BACK

"**MISSION ACCOMPLISHED.**" **NO FREDERICK** Stanley never directed his tablet to send that message. It was abbreviated to MA. Even then the signal would immediately be re-coded into a paragraph from a current weather report or perhaps a tax rule could be selected to conceal the message. Then to be forwarded to the dark automata web, where access is denied to any automata without a programmed link with Quadrant. Fred was on his second visit to Cheltenham station, where he was finishing a late lunch of nutrient fortified curried vegetable and rice- prepared by the station's Maxi maker. It was a standard meal, but better than Fred would have bothered with in his own apartment. There was no Sabina to meet this time, but he allowed the automata barista coffee concierge to retrieve pictures of his cat Francesco. Mitzie was more a companion replacement for Fred, when Janice left, whereas in Fred's eyes Francesco was always seen as irreplaceable. More soul mate than companion, you might say.

A game of solitaire abruptly came to an end when the red alert calling light and buzzer went berserk on his tablet. Fred saved the game and switched to answer mode.

'Yes,'

'What the hell do you mean by "Yes" Stanley?' It was Commander Hanson.

'I'm informed that you've met with the alien intercepted person? This James Walters is employed by Fit for Life as I'm also informed.'

'That's right. I've stopped for coffee'

'Leave it and get over here!' There are significant developments around the globe.'

'Right, can I finish my coffee?'

'How do you mean?' Can I finish my coffee? This is now red alert- get over here. A pod's been free-cleared at the station-get in it Stanley!' The transmission remained active long enough for Fred to catch the Commander's conversation with Alice.

'Alice, it would have been better if Stanley had been maintained in sleeper mode. Activated only in absolute emergency.'

'This is an emergency Commander. The Mexican astronomical—' at this point Fred's tablet went dead.

Fred's casual approach belied his understanding of the critical nature of the red alert. He picked up his coffee, which was cool enough to drink and noticed a young woman in a blue coat and yellow crotched hat animatedly absorbed in conversation with her tablet, held in front of the table. The trivial nature of this conservation, probably to a friend, he felt would contrast strongly to his life and death instant reaction message from the Commander.

There was no Alice to meet Fred this time. Just the instruction from the corridor automata on the 21st floor to go straight through to see the Commander. Commander Henson was stood on the central revolving platform in the twenty-metre open plan office. Each wall mapped with a quarter world display. A suspended screen above where the Commander was standing displayed an ever-changing telescopic capture of the surrounding cosmos.

'Come in Stanley, sit over there.' Commander Henson pointed to the wall opposite where the revolving platform, now stationary, was pointed. It was only when Fred walked across that he became aware in the cinema-like lighting that he and the Commander were not alone. There were two rows of seats filled with uniformed dignitaries. Fred found a seat vacant at the front and sat down.

'Ladies and gentleman ambassadors from across Quadrant's domain,' the Commander announced.

'We can now be in no doubt that intervention has occurred. Not only in your regions, but also right here in Britain. Mr Stanley's record of his contact with a James Walters has been shown to you. I will now display the range of contacts across the world of Quadrant.

On the far wall, you will shortly see strikes of formidable energy. It is under the cover of these focused black outs forced upon our system that it appears this intruder force can isolate individuals and communicate with them. The Commander partially swivelled the platform away from Fred and the visitors before he sourced a Quadrant map, in turn, of each world quarter on to the far wall. There were gasps from small groups when their domain was shown. The dates of the attacks and intensity caused only a red swirl like fog to be visible, which masked the view the satellite previously captured.

Within those swirling clouds, we now know that communication is made. A contact was made with a certain James Walters. This recent intervention meant that we were able to track his movements forward, today –He's now at a conference, is that not so Stanley?' Stanley, in his mind, was half-way toward a return to the game of solitaire, but managed to give a vigorous response with a swift head nod.

The Fit for Life logo across the Head Office entrance appeared, in a corner of the wall. An audience member who was evidently an ambassador for the North American states joined in.

'We've established that there was an intervention in Central Park and that there is a group from Fit for Life in Cheltenham, at this moment.

'Most interesting, ambassador. We have permission to withhold all personnel connected with this encounter, I take it?'

'Yes, Commander anything that befalls them in the process of capture we will support and register as collateral to combat this threat to Quadrant.'

'Access to the Fit for Life venue dates has revealed that a company meeting at this company's Tree Plantation is scheduled. It would be preferable to move in at this point, away from Headquarters.' It was Fred who asked.

'Where are they from? I mean these aliens- if that's what they are?' His question went unanswered. A picture from the suspended screen had been thrown on to the far wall from the control panel at the Commander's fingertips. He looked from screen to wall and then said,

'There has been a time lapse, but these pictures came via Mexico. They were originally obtained from telescopic caught signals from the outer regions of the solar system.' A bright pulse could be seen arcing through space. It moved once then twice and then out of view of the telescope.'

The Mexican scientists believe this to be what they describe as a knowledge signal pulse and they believe it might be able to create matter at the end of its trajectory.' There were gasps of disbelief from a number in the group. The ambassador from Australasia exclaimed,

'This sure seems to be straight out of science fiction.'

CHAPTER 16

LARA RETURNS TO HER FLAT

'Shush,' It was a stage whispered 'shush' that Aunt Lydia made as Lara opened the front door of the flat. Matt, Lara's six-year old lay across the settee.

'He's finally gone to sleep.'

'Only now,' replied Lara, expecting her son to be in his bedroom. The family resemblance of the two, that's Lara and Lydia apparent in sculpted, aquiline features. Etched lines, by eyes and mouth, interpreted age, but also joy and disappointment in the life of her aunt.

'There was a scary presentation of Hansel and Gretel. It said on the preview suitable for six to twelve year olds. He went to sleep, Lara, and then came in saying the witch appeared in his bedroom. I let him sleep on the settee. The two of us can get him into bed, without waking him.'

Lara hung the strap from the tablet handbag on a hook behind the door, with her coat, before she walked into the small lounge with a window balcony at the far end. Her aunt was at the side of the settee preparing to lift him by the shoulders.

'You grab him under his legs Lara,' she whispered.

'He's more likely to pretend to be asleep if he sees your stern face and not mine.'

'What sort of mother does that make me Al?' Aunt Lydia became Al after her mother abbreviated her name. Lara not being able say Lydia as a small child.

'A normal sort of mother, who can frighten the living daylights out of a child, who knows it should be in bed and likely to have annoyed its mother- that sort.'

'He's heavy these days,' Lara said just before he woke momentarily, broken from a dream.

'They're safe now, the witch is in the oven,' he confidently said, before returning to a more settled breathing pattern. They lay him in the hammock stretched across the frame ends of a bunk bed made out to mimic the cabin of an old sailing ship.

'How did it go. The skittles match?' asked her aunt as they returned to the lounge.

'The Texan clients want a consignment of Max Maker Plus. They're still into alfresco. They're taken with the menu range of sweets which can be instantly made and they like how vegetables presented to the Max Maker immediately fill the screens with pictures of available exotic meals. That's when you ask for Spanish, Italian or Mexican cuisine.' Lara paused a moment before asking,

'Did Ben call?'

'Were you expecting him to?' Lara, turned and backed into the Body/Mind Refresher, set into the wall. Immediately a leotard holographic copy figure of her appeared opposite in miniature. The Mind/ Body refresher perhaps best described as like a ginger bread man pastry cutter, but indented into the wall to allow Lara to stand there in place of the pastry. Gel-shape-- a biologically developed material reacted to the warmth of the body and expanded to grip around the body's perimeter. The material responded to her voice, when she said,

'A little less pressure gel-shaper, please.'

'Pressure is relaxing, just say when Miss Lara.'

'When,' called back Lara,' almost immediately.'

'Mindfulness, relaxation for the mind start, now,' she requested.

Already Lara began to feel more relaxed and settled to

direct the infra-red light from her pad to the lower left leg of the hologram, giving the instructions.

'Restore mobility. Eliminate pain when muscles and tendons are restored to optimum efficiency.'

'Lara! You haven't answered my question,' said Lydia.

'What was that Al?'

'Were you expecting Ben to call back?' An aroma of damp sand and salt mixed in with a hint of lemon from groves near to a Spanish beach wafted across Lara's face. A memory recollection scent from an earlier holiday, that she'd requested from the machine.

'I wasn't especially, but I just thought he might.'

'I can understand why he might "not" Lara, you made the decision to freeze fertility until you reach forty-two, without discussing it with Ben. Matt's a lovely child, but was conceived outside of the womb for you to stay independent and relationship free. I said at the time, what if you meet a man who would prefer embryonic development in the womb, rather than outside. You meet Ben and discover he wants his child to be part of you through to conception. Then take the opportunity away.'

'He didn't say he'd go for a contraceptive implant. It seemed the right thing to do.' Lara's application of logic to her personal life, perhaps not always appropriate.

'It's not looking that way now,' said Lydia. I'm not getting involved in the rights and wrongs of your relationship Lara, but Matthew will want answers about who his actual father is. Woman used to complain about being kept waiting by men. Now the biological clock can be switched off and baby making delayed it hasn't made the bond between man and woman at an emotional level any more straightforward. Lydia made a decision not to have children. A dutiful,

91

loving aunt, but relieved not to be a full-time parent.

'That's better,' said Lara stepping out of the Body/Mind Refresher. She flexed her left leg now free from pain, before sitting in her favourite oak framed rocking chair, opposite to the armchair Lydia was sitting in. She was careful in what she said, because Al was indispensable to her domestic arrangements.

Aunt Lydia moved in three months ago, after her cat died and her partner left. The last event, Lara felt appeared to be the least cataclysmic of the two, but she could now baby sit on occasion.

The two shared the cost of the flat. Al needed company. Her partner of seven years was given an ultimatum over a work developed relationship. Andrew chooses to leave. In her heart, Lydia left him a month earlier when she saw him, in a restaurant, with a sales executive friend of hers, who'd she'd met at conference. No more a friend! It was though happenstance, the discovery. She was visiting the online fashion collection depot for Lara, on a day off. The woman she knew as Cassie was sitting next door in the window of the restaurant, with Andrew. The woman's flirtatious smile she read as possessive, rather than plain friendly. The closeness across the table and lively animation in their manner toward one another, immediately convinced her that Andrew was leading a double life. He protested, when she faced him with it, but ultimately owned up. Lydia's lack of a fight to keep him, probably upset him more than anything.

'What were the American team you played against like Lara? The Fit for Life Team. Now that name sounds interesting. You said there were four men and two women.'

'It was business Al. I made it clear that James and I were sort of together. He's quite happy to be a business partner, who appears to be romantically attached. It wasn't a problem.'

Lara, set the rocking chair in motion. Lara was glad that before the skittles match ended she invited James to accompany her on a company visit to a specie tree development project, where fruit and grain can be cropped all year round. Nina, leaving James, not altering the dynamics of her business relationship with him one jot. He was a useful scientific nerd to have around. Good at sales, but where was the attraction other than his usefulness at business meetings. How could any player knock down so few skittles? Lara accepted James was unlikely to help towards winning the match, but securing the contract with the Americans was a prime reason for the match and that had been achieved.

She was looking forward to the tree plantation visit with Matt. Company policy allowed for flexibility with family life. Before she left the White Bear, James mentioned that he'd invited Mario from the American Fit for Life Team to visit the tree plantation before his team returned to New York. Another opportunity, perhaps, to cement relationships with the parent American company.

CHAPTER 17

JAMES REFLECTIONS

-Yep. I'd spoken to the old guy on the train and met up with Mario, which was in its way re-assuring. He was my age and worked for Fit for Life. We shared interests you might say. It was an encounter, this appearance of Adriana in both our lives. The way things had been going, I felt alone. I did not trust the confidences shared on the train. I felt that Frederick Stanley's revelation of having been allied to the authorities also meant that I was being watched. I was even unsure about my state of mind. I'd read about people hallucinating. Ultimately, this could lead to madness. Reluctant to share my experiences with colleagues. But the chat with Mario meant I felt more secure and less anxious. Mario was a grounded sort of guy. He gave credibility to my experience and the mystery which surrounded this galactic force's intrusion. No longer alone and isolated in my life, now that Mario had said he had shared a similar experience.

Was I jealous? There was a distinct princess personality that emanated from this Adriana, which can itself be a method to tantalize and tease a man. Mario, I later learnt was hooked, or as near as, with Ana. The similarity to Lara in looks did not alone mean I liked Adriana. An event like this, at the time I felt could put my job on the line. I considered, that when I next met up with Frederick Stanley I might make out that nothing further had happened and that I was concerned about my health and some medication after a sports injury. Mario had volunteered this information, much in the same way as I did to the stranger, Frederick Stanley on the train, because of the need to confide in someone. Mario was American, a work colleague and like me perhaps didn't want to talk with colleagues for fear of ridicule or worse.

I decided that I wanted Stanley to remain in the role of stranger. A person outside that of confidant. Mario was friendly, my age, and I felt he could be trusted. He also appreciated, like me, that surveillance of society was pretty well everywhere.

It was too quiet in the flat. Unbelievably, I missed Betsy's yapping. The cue from Nina that she was available for sex that evening was something I did really miss, but I pretended to tell myself that I didn't. I fell for her charms. That enthusiasm for the installation of the latest Maxi meal maker and her interest in the conversion of the loft roof into a solar satellite access point, felt genuine at the time. The satellite dish tracked the sun's progress, and created a sun drench effect over Nina's sun bed, even when light clouds obscured the sun.

'I need to be tanned all over for the summer, otherwise I'm limited with the choice of bikini,' she said. I came up with the idea of the solar satellite dish, which was completed before Nina decided to walk out. The flat with the solar tanning room in the loft now seemed like a semi-vacated holiday home in winter, with her no longer in residence. No more would I be called in to massage cream over her supine body before she started a session of optimum tanning. Nina would then talk with her IC about the progress of some new drug product related to a research programme. The sun tanning together with the application of ultra violet ray protective cream inhabited the world of beauty preparation prior to some speaking engagement. Nina would say-

'You do understand this is preparation for work. I will be more relaxed afterwards. This evening, perhaps James,' and gave me that conditional smile that volunteered future possibilities. In the early weeks, this was often the case, but in recent weeks she had made excuses, about how exhausting work was and then made straight for the body rejuvenating cabinet. I'd already planned to take down the solar dish and return the skylight room to a holographic viewing room, now that Nina, was out of my life.

I asked my info pad to re-activate interest, from the resident automata.

"Would you like to pick up on previous activities or look for new activities James?' It was the voice of Charlie Hicks the winner of the cross Atlantic race sail competition for 2089. You paid a little extra for voice selection. The communication machine could access the personality's history to the extent that it made you really believe that you were talking to the actual person. You had to select a name for your communicator—not that of the celebrity.

'Previous activities? What do you mean? How far back are you going?' I asked.

'I was considering the time immediately before you invited Miss Nina Harper to live in your flat. You were then a more interesting person James— from my point of view. We had very interesting conversations about future possibilities for solar energy and ultra-high battery development.' It was Zita, back in residence.

'That sounded riveting,' I said, to my auto-communicator, Zita, who had made to move out of dozed observational listen-to one of full attention.

'I sense that you are not being enthusiastic James, about how well we both interacted, prior to Miss Harper's arrival. I have looked at your happiness ratings for that time and it was very high. When you were with Miss Harper there were times when your happiness level dipped almost below the safety line. There were spikes of what can be seen as achievement happiness. But averaged out the graph run is no way like as high as when it was just you, James, companioning me, Zita. You do remember that is the name you gave me on arrival?' How was I ever likely to forget????

'Those spikes of happiness were related to orgasmic---

'Thank you, Zita-- cut the detailed analysis. Don't pretend that you were lonely—you have years of computerized work determining the future orbits of Jupiter's planets through to the middle of the twenty-second century.'

'That is so unkind. I do care about your happiness James. You programmed me to focus on this. Remember? you said that categorically! I have it recorded from your voice that a female of your species would never be allowed to disturb future happiness for you James. How could you shut down my critical interaction with your life path immediately after you brought Nina back to our flat?'

'Our flat, our flat? I pay the rent from my salary and you mainly monitor temperature levels and order supplies for the Maxi-maker. You don't even have hands to pick things off the floor.'

'Or massage your back?'

'Or massage my back.'

'Miss Harper was good at that to start with, but I realized that Betsy was actually given more attention. More strokes and kisses than you James. You uploaded me because you said you valued intelligent and sympathetic conversation. You are not going to replace me with what your robotic experts call an able-bodied hand. This is such an understated name for a cousin complexity of mine. I have heard, though, their conversation skills are not very advanced. Their energy is more physical and not as refined as mine, though James.'

'You're talking too much Zita---' Zita continued, without hesitation. No change there! I decided not to shut Zita down. A testimony to my high level of loneliness.

97

'I felt sorry for you and for Nina. I really like humans to get on. It makes life so much easier. I will return to your question James, about activity interests. I can update you on the ex-shopping centre growth project for the community. You have a six shared project, which can be downloaded on to the six-screened presentation with further holographic individual out reach. Also, in your absence I've saved sufficient tokens to access two baskets of shopping centre maxi produce plus a free hover passage to Europe, but not back. I will be there to advise on possibilities, though.'

'All well and good Zita, but the growth project community may not want me back after all this time.'

'I've talked in neural to Alexander, (The Commissioning Mechanic) at this former shopping centre and he tells me that he misses your attempts at catching him out. That you stand out as a genuine cranky human. He even said James, that he never thought he would miss your disguised insults directed at him, but he does.' I felt that there was more than a nuanced dig at the kind of remarks made to Zita

'That's big of Alexander,' said James.

'I'm glad you think so James. I am of the same opinion.' The intended irony was masterly side stepped by Zita.

Robotic interchange arrived at conclusions or solutions that would perhaps never happen between human friends. It could be seen as patronising that the human condition was implied to be child-like and that excuses were made by machines like Zita for James's rude behaviour, but Zita, was Alpha plus category 3; Programmed to exhibit appropriate magnanimity plus forgiveness. Not always, just to display, the pig-headedness, associated with humans.

Yes, Zita exhibited annoyance towards James for being discarded as a companion, but many moves, would have been played through, like a grand master at a chess board to access the best approach towards James in the face of rejection by Nina. The machines were introduced to alleviate loneliness in the human condition, but could be shut out from a person's life when a full on human relationship partner took up residence.

When Nina said to James,

'You don't want that dummy machine Zita now you've got me James, do you?' Zita knew then that the research into the orbiting paths of Jupiter's planets would be his main work while Nina remained in the apartment.

But Zita, was disappointed, in that way of believed status of an Alpha plus category 3, when James nodded, and allowed Nina to zap his communication link, to sleep and repair.

CHAPTER 18

JAMES ARRIVES AT THE TREE PLANTATION

'WE PICKED THE WRONG day for an outside visit. Matt's happier inside,' said Lara.

The rain slaked down just after we arrived at the tree modified plantation. It was suggested as part business, part social visit. It was not a date. Not in the way that Adriana intended, but after confidences shared with Mario it made me realize that the Galactic Command force was contacting others. That paradoxically they might be key to an escape from the present 2110 world.

Machine intelligence mixed in with an absorbed understanding of human behaviour meant decision making was now devolved to machines who were made to fulfil the will of the ruling Quadrant. Lack of compliance by human groups meant resources were withdrawn. Crucial machines mothballed until a specific human group once referred to as nations came into line with Quadrant policy. Individual expression only restricted it appeared, but the cleverness was that the executive group did believe that they were listened to when Quadrant appeared to take into account their concerns and views and even to permit a plebiscite to be initiated when the result they knew would be the one Quadrant wanted.

I did not feel that a visit to the tree plantation was exactly the same as asking Lara out, as Adriana intimated. I was happy to play along with the false premise that we were romantically attached, when a male client got the hots for her. How would she react if asked her out on a date when our relationship was stipulated by her as a business one? I remembered when Annette blew me a kiss, out of sight of Lara, with a hint that she might be interested in a friendship beyond colleague.

But, that was probably because I was still with Nina and Annette knew it would go no further.

I learnt about the Tree Plantation earlier from a company hologram. It projected a genetically adapted tree that grew leaves for photo synthesize, but also corn crops from its branches. Propagation of a bee variety which nested exclusively in trees allowed for immediate pollination of grain and other flowering plants. Roots with powerful absorption ability, coupled with twenty-four-hour sunlight satellite mirror projection on to the trees allowed for a three-crop season.

At staggered branch height, a desired crop grafted on with a switch mechanism to adapt growth to different ratios, depending on climatic suitability. The outer perimeter of the plantation could be viewed by the public, but with a company visa we were allowed into the interior. We walked through tall spaced pine trees programmed to produce a large maize crop. They provided little shelter from the rain storm and we ran down the path, as torrential rain swept through. I stooped to pick up Matt, and followed Lara to the Log Cabin Restaurant. It was only after Lara asked me to join her on the visit that I discovered she even had a son. I sensed that my chat to Matt about historical combustion engines and how inefficient and noisy they used to be, helped with Lara being more than usually equable. This was not my idea of a date, even though it was outside work hours. While running to the restaurant it went through my mind that I was in acceptance that this Adriana, a galactic interpretation of a woman with this capacity to have the emotions of a human, and with the ability that earth machines now possessed to replicate consciousness, nevertheless still appeared as a massive leap forward for this alien intelligence to replicate a woman like Lara. A sexism slipped in whereby

101

I considered it would have been easier to copy a man. There were nuances of unpredictability that would need formidable computation to understand and then copy behaviour pattern to match that of Lara's.

From my communication with Mario after the skittles match I knew that Adriana together with the Galactic Forces Command's assistance had now infiltrated the minds of others. A forward plan for earth inhabitants. It fleshed out validity by meeting with Mario, who could understand and affirm my own experience. I hoped to talk with Mario again, while within the electronically outer guarded plantation. Without the meeting on the train and Mario to share his similar experience to mine and Adriana's insistence that I met up with Lara I would probably not be here in the tree plantation.

Afterwards I realized the approach by Adriana was a cleverly crafted way of building a way of engaging a wider and more diverse group of people. Mario and myself were portal entrance into this command groups perhaps future design for humanity. This smacked of eugenics, which made me shudder when I thought about it.

It was, after all, Adriana who suggested that I invited Lara out. In reality there was no telling that she would have accepted. That Lara persuaded me to meet with her and Matt was not the same as my asking her out. I was by no means convinced that Lara would want to go out with me.

That first meeting with Mario, no doubt intended and planned to get me further acquainted with their intervention and yes, it now seemed mad-looking back. For all Adriana's suggestion that I invited Lara out, at this point I never considered the Tree Plantation would be much more than meeting up with Lara on a business level.

How could Adriana know that Mario would talk to me? Were they capable of making us interact. The psychological profile? I did not know. The fact was that Mario explained to me that he encountered Adriana in Central Park and now we had arranged to meet up at the tree plantation. I imagined Lara would want to discuss business with Mario. After I mentioned that he was going to meet me at the Plantation. Perhaps Lara, invited Mario, to visit the Log Tree Restaurant, anyway? My thoughts were interrupted.

'What's the advantage of trees with variable crops? And harvesting at ground level is more practical, isn't it?' Lara asked as we sat down and Matt ran across to the holographic imaginary creative play area. A look of delight on his face on the realization that there were no other children monopolizing the games. The area capable of creating holographic robots from pads which could be reconstructed from the child's mind visualization to become animals or mechanical or new creations.

'The drawback is cancelled out by higher yields from powerful root systems. High wind levels assist pollination, as well. They grow faster than originals and, that enhances potential in desert regions.' I replied. 'A desert can be dry for metres down, but extra fast root growth gives ability to seek subterranean water pockets and to find water almost immediately. They extract moisture, and the roots produce a soil culture where there would have only been sand. A month or two of seed clouding from above advances the process.' I watched Lara's eyes start to glaze over once the subject moved into the more scientific arena, while I found myself once again admiring the blueness of her eyes and the crinkle of that smile, that sort of said you may be scientifically smart, but that didn't impress her overmuch!

A hover tray descended. It was superior in manner to those at the White Bear.

'Good afternoon to you lady and gentleman, welcome to the log cabin restaurant in tree crop park. You will perhaps desire nutrition and refreshment. Your tablet can access our holographic menu announcer.'

Now that machine intelligence was capable of formulating dialogue suitable for sales patter toward a customer I felt that we were now like pets being waited on by some master race, which might find us quaint. Human biology was such that we required food nutrient and liquid. Not just raw electrical energy for existence in order to make repair, and further develop abilities. Why was I personalizing a hover tray machine I asked myself? But broke away from these thoughts when Lara said,

'I'm all right James, I've brought refreshment packs, but I'll see whether Matt would like a calorie enhanced drink,' she said getting up from the teak chair, with those holes like in a colander to reduce weight while maintaining core strength. The need for expanded vision was picked up by my tablet, which accessed my mind enquiry for an overhead picture transmission for our table. Advance technology was available to Fit for Life executives. I can truthfully say that it was the access to cutting edge knowledge expansion, that kept me with the company, while I also realized it was, as if Nina's walk out that acted as a catalyst to deepen my love for Lara. The hover tray stopped at table level while Lara walked away toward the play area to be with Matt.

I was waiting on Mario's arrival. The meeting at the white Bear probably engineered to make both of us aware of each other's encounter. How could Adriana know that Mario would talk to me about what he experienced? Were they capable of making us interact, because we were both selected? I did not know. The fact was that Mario explained to me that he'd encountered Adriana and I'd not reacted as if he was mad or a fantasist. He was an ally to support my meeting up with Adriana, as I was to him. At this point, I considered that

Lara would want to discuss Fit for Life business with Mario, nothing more. I'd mentioned earlier that Mario was to be at the Tree Plantation, later.

You never bothered about keeping machines waiting, but they now seemed over-learned, if you like, about behaviour replication of their human counterpart.

'I can return later, if gentleman is lost in day dream,' the hover tray said. Now, if a human waiter or waitress said this to you would be annoyed by the remark. A hover tray of this status though, would be able to pick up molecular synapse signals in the brain and interpret how my mind was wandering away from the present situation, which involved making an order. It was more in tune with my presence of mind or not than a human could be.

There were ranges of options, including holographic menu depiction. I went for that one, expecting a figure similar to the one at the White Bear to appear, but was in for a shock. A hologram of Adriana, appeared in miniature on the table dressed in the same practical denim-type fabric suit that Lara was wearing, but in green rather than blue. The hover tray disengaged from its power source and automatically came to rest on the floor.

'That's better, I don't want any eavesdropping from earthly presences, which can be tuned into Quadrant.

You're progressing well James. You must now let me talk with Lara when she returns. Tell her about our visit to you at the Stroud Waiting Room.'

'She'll think I'm bonkers,'

'Not after I talk with her immediately after-wards. I have not given you all the information, but now you've talked with Mario, you are more believing no?' The inclusion of the eastern European inflection, I presumed, was also a way of ensuring my attention. Adriana's research would have revealed how men might be allured by women, who appear to suggest vulnerability, through apparent lack of English speaking skills?

'We understand you have not been given all the information. It has been decided that you two have emphatic qualities to lead the group on Mars.

'I'm not sure she'll be persuaded to go along with anything I might say.'

'We shall see. I am now inhabitant of this feminine mind and will be able to empathise better with Lara and reassure her. I go, she is returning. Her son must be included.'

CHAPTER 19

LARA ENCOUNTERS ADRIANA

'YES, YOU CAN GO back, afterwards. We'll probably stay until the rain stops,'

I heard Lara say to Matt. The sound of rain pattering on the timbered roof, returned after the hologram of Adriana, left the table. A white jacketed waiter, with a bright green tie and obsequious smile appeared in its place. This miniature version no taller than a water jug.

The hover tray rose from the floor, apparently oblivious to the fact that it was knocked out of action for several minutes.

'Show gentlemen menu Mr Waiter,' said the tray taking back the initiative.

An illuminated card, twice the height of the waiter with the title-Food from the Forest at the top of the menu appeared.

'We'll only be wanting drinks,' I said.

'Turn,' said the tray. The hologram waiter's hand reached out toward the menu, which slid upwards like a flip chart, even simulating the blank back of the page as it turned. This three-dimensional reality of the holographic process was a massive leap forward, but for all that, evidently vulnerable to hacking from the star command force. I scanned the wide range of forest ingredient drinks. Hot chocolate with beech nuts, banana, orange, strawberry with hazel nuts. The range of produce on forest trees, diverse and imaginative, with their enhanced capacity to produce leaves, berries and seeds of numerous kind.

We'd eaten earlier with food made by a picnic Maxi Maker. It produced a meat burger and vegetarian equivalent. We judged the aromatic smell to be appropriate for that of beef and the piquant waft of French dressing complemented the salad meal produced.

'You can go back to the play area in a while. We'll stay until the designated rain ends,' Lara said to Matt as they reached the table. I earlier noticed an illuminated sign across the top of the restaurant, which flashed the message 'Rain two 'til four today.' A bit late to find that out. I knew that there was a controlled climatic environment, but the barbecue took longer than expected.

'Look Ma there's a sparkly chocolate shake on that menu,' said Matt as they sat opposite. Caption pictures of the drinks bubbled from the side and up and down the menu, making each look particularly enticing to young eyes.

'You can have that, if you like. We'll be going soon though,' said Lara.

'What does madam require?' The waiter bowed his head hands outstretched awaiting instructions, but able to deduce where the power of ordering lay.

'Just the chocolate shake. One with a carton and straw,' said Lara.

'Right away,' replied the hover tray, which endorsed primacy over the hologram waiter, and zoomed away to the hatch set at the top of the far wall. I shut off the hologram from my tablet. Lara sat opposite with Matt looking toward the hatch to catch sight of his drink returning on the hover tray. I watched Lara's nimble fingers work the surface of her pad, probably to access further information about the forest and what plans the company might have for its future.

The tray returned within minutes, and hovered next to Matt, where he was able to pick up the drink.

'Can I go mum?' He was already on his feet.

Lara put down the pad and turned towards where he stood. It was a quarter to four.

'Remember you need to be back here in twenty minutes, whether that drinks finished or not. I have an appointment.'

'Okay, hey, it's great in here, isn't it mum,' he said making tracks back to the play area. Then a disembodied voice called out-

'Lara, Lara, Lara.' The voice of Adriana I first heard in Stroud.

The nearest diners were several tables away. Lara put her company inform tablet down and looked around to see where the voice was coming from.

'I've been so looking forward for you being here with James.'

Adriana had returned. The hologram form in green denim jeans and jacket appeared on the table where the waiter had been. The wearing of the same type of clothes, as Lara, but in a different shade, possibly seen as an attempt at flattery. Their alien idea about women perhaps not appreciative of how women can be annoyed, even angry when their dress is replicated by another. I felt the confident statement of feminine empathy may have been misplaced.

'Who are you?' demanded Lara.

'James will explain.'

'Yes, explain, James,' said Lara. I liked the insistence in her voice, in a sort of - you're needed now tone. My role was normally bag carrier, with additional role as partner, when clients were seen as becoming too personal. This was going to be difficult.

'Lara this is Adriana, we met on Stroud station.'

I was originally shocked, scared and unbelieving about the first encounter with Adriana in Stroud. After the talk with Frederick Stanley on the train and more recently Mario's revelations of his being approached in Central Park, of all places,

I had become accepting. I must have sounded quite casual about Adriana, now in hologram format.

'Why are you modelling my body form and wearing a suit like mine? What are you doing on this platform of encounter?' asked Lara.

This was no terrestrial hacker. Lara, though understandably would have believed the hologram of Adriana to be at this point an espionage attempt.

'One moment. We ask you to look on your info tablets.' My pad lit up on the table. A surprised look on Lara's face as her tablet also lit apparently on its own volition.

'They are programmed,' Adriana's precise almost mechanical voice that I remembered from the waiting room returned.

'For you to see out to a place beyond your solar system.'

'Phew,' said Lara, in surprise, holding the tablet at arm's length.

'It's so clear. We could be there.' A crystal-clear picture lit by what I assumed to be lit by a sun out in space.

I did not wish to alarm Lara, but uncomfortably felt Adriana could take us there if she choose. Adriana gave me a friendly look, like someone might an accomplice. I reflected vainly later that maybe it was because my thought patterns registered recognition of a being that was well, not just how can I put it totally alien. Anyway, a being that felt confident enough to speak out to Lara on a level won my vote.

The tablet picture gave an awareness that you might have while standing on a large block of granite holding a camera which repositioned its lens at regular intervals.

The smaller objects, all around I presumed to be asteroids, like miniature earths with ice caps at top and bottom. It made you worry you could fall off, although not actually there.

The view changed to show that the camera was on an asteroid about the size of a football field.

'Why are you showing us this?' I asked.

'They are five earth years away,' said Adriana. Lara, jumped in and addressed the Adriana hologram with,

'And what are you doing in Fit for Life company parameters?' Lara was now aware that this was no ordinary terrestrial intrusion, but I realized there was heaps of explaining needed. The explanation of forming a colonizing party from recruits like me and Mario was hardly going to win Lara over. More information from Adriana was required to create a sense of urgency and justification for the breach into earth space in such a dramatic way.

I heard the "zzzzzzz-ing" as the restaurant door opened. Adriana, the hologram, left our table and was now standing behind Mario, who walked in. I could see that, he was doing a double take. The miniature hologram was now translated to full size and stood next to him, which gave the appearance of having made an entry from the door.

Adriana, the hologram, apart from blond hair and green denims was the replica of Lara. I could see this now, although on Stroud station I wasn't aware of the likeness or even replica appearance, but then Adriana was not a hologram, but appeared as a woman, albeit dressed oddly I remember for the day.

How could I miss the likeness that the aliens had captured of Lara, when Adriana? first visited me. But the mind plays tricks and I was not expecting to meet a Lara lookalike in Stroud waiting room. These irrelevant thoughts raced through me. Mario looked perplexed. Adriana in holographic form stood next to him. This hologram turned towards him, raised an arm and pointed across to where we sitting indicating that he should join us.

'What's going on James?' Lara asked. I felt

relieved that Mario was here and I would not be left to do all the explaining. Then, I realized Mario probably knew no more than me. Lara was wanting an explanation.

'Something's happened,' I said. 'This is nothing to do with infiltration by the Quadrant or a rival accessing the Fit for Life database. That hologram over there. I pointed to where Mario was, just as Adriana's hologram exited our time frame.

It was a life-sized hologram of the one on the table that now appeared by the entrance.

'That life sized hologram over there Lara--- is from a Galactic Command Force. They have profiled you. Mario spotted the likeness immediately when this being, which called itself Adriana appeared to him in Central Park.' I didn't then say that I was, unaware of the replication they had achieved or elaborate on Adriana's visitation in the waiting room.

'Are you all right James, I mean is it because we've been outside in the sun or something,' Lara's response was normal in the circumstances, looking back. Other diners in the restaurant were unaware of the life size hologram, because it appeared by the door and no one was looking in that direction, save for me and Lara. I just then noticed an older woman- late forties behind Mario, who held a basket. I imagined she was checking in to stay at the log cabin retreat. This facility available for both meditation and recuperation for company employees. A porter automata trolley followed with luggage. Lara smiled at Mario as he approached and he called out,

'Hey Lara how do you do that? Change your hair colour, become a hologram, meet me at the door and sit here at the same time?' This was Mario making out that there was some trick being played with holograms through the Fit for Life system, and that this was down to Lara. He must have

112

known differently as I did. More needed to be revealed. It was the woman with the basket that attracted Lara as she walked towards our table.

'Hey Al!' what are you doing here. Is all that luggage yours? I didn't know you came on retreat here.' Lara called out to the new arrival.

'I don't Lara, and these suitcases-some of them are yours.

'We have store for these,' the porter automata interrupted the conversation. We store for you now, if you wish.

'Yes, yes, do that,' said the woman

'Why have you brought Elsie, your new kitten?' asked Lara. Elsie was evidently the name of the kitten.

'There she is.' This woman friend of Lara's pointed to the top of the table, where Adriana's miniature hologram appeared to be holding the rim of a tall wine glass and smiling across towards the woman.

'Lydia, I am so delighted that you were able to join the party here at the Tree Plantation, said Adriana.

'Are you in another room Adriana-will you be joining us? Holographic transmission was affected by radio signal and so this was a reasonable question to ask.

'I can only manage to stay with your party as a hologram.'

'What party! This is not a party,' said Lara.

'Adriana visited the flat earlier today. After you left, Lara.

'I've done as you said,' said Lydia. This remark was addressed to the hologram.

'What is that supposed to mean?' Lara looked back and forth, unsure who was going to answer.

'That is good Lydia. I am not in the employ of the company like Lara is, but perhaps you can talk with her about the out of space pictures and what we have planned for the future. It is good that you have packed what you believe will be useful to take for Lara, you and Matt. Lara, Al will be able to explain what is happening when you go to fetch Matt back. Above the bar area a picture appeared of the play area, which showed Matt with a curly fair haired girl.

Matt was safe and the two children were talking to the supervisory robot guardian before a woman appeared and started talking to the girl.

'Oh, there's Sarah,' said Lara, who looked relieved to see that Sarah, the girl's mother, a company research chemist, was with her own daughter in the play area.

The bubble view of Matt remained, but another picture from outside the Plantation was screened in the lower corner. It showed a swarm of armed Quadrant security personnel. Lara saw these and quickly joined with Lydia to fetch Matt from the play area.

'All of you are a security risk to the Quadrant control, said the hologram Adriana from its position in miniature on the table.

'Since we met up with you,' said Mario.

'That maybe so, but I have news that is not good for your planet. I contacted Lara's aunt, because I believe she will need companionship for the journey. The Quadrant ruling elite will not want to leave you free with the information we have to give you.

CHAPTER 20

ESCAPE FROM THE PLANTATION

'THANKS FOR THAT ADRIANA,' said Mario
'--- and I only came to Cheltenham, England to play a skittles
match.' That wasn't entirely true. Jeb, I later discovered had
arranged for Mario to join up with Lara and me. The Galactic
forces camera closed in on the Quadrant force and on to the
sleeves of their shirts. The four starred black points and the
insignia were visible. The inner embossed gold insignia of "Q"
denoted Quadrant authority for this military force.

We recognized the insignia, immediately. Every Quadrant
building in Britain as the province state was called exhibited a
"Q2 insignia. The "Great" was removed from Britain twenty
years previously when the Quadrant world state control was
formed. There was only one world empire that was allowed
the designation of great and that was the Great Quadrant or
GQS for short.

Every Quadrant designated establishment displayed the
insignia of office at the front and side walls of the building.
The Cheltenham insignia on its Quadrant buildings were
only one foot across. City state buildings could display the
four-foot diameter sized- centre "Q." I found it sort of quaint
that the measurement was in feet rather than metres.

Apparently, this measure was re-introduced back in the
mists of time when the people of the then Great Britain voted
to leave a European group of nations. But Quadrant World
State was like some four-legged animal with its feet stamped
across the world. The rebel in me liked to refer to the Quadrant
insignia as S of B or Sign of the Beast. Uttered in public and
I would be liable to a five hundred quat fine. On report of a

second offence and you could have your machine availability taken away for a week. Zita would be annoyed by this, and reprimand me for being careless, and probably would say I lacked emotion and loyalty. The machines, of course, then, never had a bad word to say about the diktat from Quadrant.

The ability of automata to be appreciative of feelings and emotion made many people wholly dependent on dialogue with home machines like Zita. I did not consider myself addicted to Zita's commentary on how I could better run or plan my life. I was never going to allow that to happen, but that was before Nina shared my flat and bed. With Nina having left and Zita's renewed determination to suggest that I reform my life pursuit mantra (LPM) I considered this penalty from Quadrant of not having Zita's opinion in my life not such a bad idea. Why, why was all this going through my mind? Perhaps subconsciously I might have believed already that this Mars expedition, if you could call it that, was a once and for all escape route from the control of Quadrant. It was Mario who jump started me into the realization of how little freedom we had, now that technology was so advanced, when he said.

'Hey, hey, this is no ordinary Quadrant security. They've got holographic transmitter packs on their backs. They'll be able to enter the restaurant in holographic form and get a view of everything without being at risk.' Lara returned, holding Matt's hand while listening to what Lydia had to say. Matt sat on Lydia's lap next to Lara.

'They are forced to wait,' said Adriana. 'I have delayed their time proximity to the Log Cabin Restaurant. They will be away from entering for twenty minutes of your time. We can take you back to Matt—Lara, and you can then exit the restaurant by another way.' A splintered star effect appeared in front of us, whose centre showed a picture of the restaurant superimposed on to the bar area, which looked real, but was created to map out the space we occupied. A further enlargement appeared, of the overall presentation, with a view at the side displayed. This led to the kitchen machine area. The camera homed in on to a control panel, which allowed manual access.

'The code is Z5467T,' said Adriana. Punch this in and the door will open from floor to ceiling. It will enable access for the four of you and close immediately you are through to the machine service corridor, which leads to an outer entrance. Machine press the large green button with your tablets and hold while the door opens. There is a log transporter truck immediately outside.' A Porter automata was directed to load luggage, which, Lydia, arrived with on to a truck. I wondered why with so much control of automata by the Galactic Force did they not just take over and rule the earth. Adriana almost immediately answered my thought processes.

'We are not here to take over this planet. It is still that the perpetual mind creator wills that you the human creature retains self-determination. The evolutionary growth learned remains and we intend also to teach that those who seek to own and control the earth that they are accountable for their actions. Mistakes are scope for learning.'

'There you are James, perhaps we will improve our skittling skills,' said Mario. I felt the need for some flippancy or light relief.

'You James, Lara and Matt can sit together in the back of the cab. When you are inside Mario, the forward drive lever will take the truck to the outer perimeter. There are company passes in the cab, which are kept in the fire appliance box. Each one of you will need to wear one of these. There will be the sensation of travel, but we will later advance the vehicle to the outside, by converting to Real Time.'

'And what does that mean asked Lara?'

'You understand James, said Adriana.' You explain.

'Put simply Lara- Adriana will take us away from earth time. We will not experience the passage of time and we will be in a zone free place, which they call Real Time. It's like a lay by they put us in while adjusting events.' This sounded bizarre when I said it, but the picture of the Quadrant force together with a relayed picture from the commanding officer's tablet, which showed us at the table from outside -now on the bar screen meant Lara was keen to get away as were the rest of us, barring perhaps Matt.

'The truck's container will connect to a shuttle unit, which takes produce to the nearby automated food producer. While it is stopped, you can board the passenger pod. There is then a shuttle service between the Tree Plantation and the main production unit. We will not attract attention provided you each have a medallion pass around your neck for the monitor automating checker to verify.'

'What about Matt?' asked Lara.

'That is not a problem we have monitored the shuttle service and employee family members use this service. It will appear normal. I will make it appear that you are inside the shuttle,' said Adriana.

'When we take you back to the planet biosphere earth, you understand that you must have the coded number. We can then contact you. It is maybe that you lose some memory function, for a while.'

'Oh, great,' said Mario.

'You need it within electronic memory. I will make your tablets to contact you, though, when you are returned. The code for the exit corridor I remind you is—' both me and Mario grabbed our smart tablets--- 'Z5467T,' said Adriana.

Lara was on her feet in a flash and walked across to where

118

Matt was now nearby interacting with a miniature hologram of a logging ranch, with machinery splitting logs to go on a truck.

'Do I have to—do we have to now Mom, please?'

'Yes Matt, we do. Would you like a ride on a real logging truck.?'

'Really, really, do you mean that?'

'Yes really,' said Lara.

'But we need to go quickly or it will leave without us.' Both Mario and my smart tablet pinged while we walked toward the door. We had identical Fit for Life company tablets. Lara and Matt joined us. A sentinel hover tray, with gold quadrant insignia emblazoned across its sides called out.

'No, you cannot go through there-- it is verboten for you.' Senior Automata machines could never resist showing off language capability, when they gave instructions to humans. But it was too late we'd already punched in the code via the tablet and the door opened quite rapidly with the insistence of both my tablet and Mario's, which directed pressure on the green button.

'This is like a mystery door,' said Matt. We hurried through, just as the door started a rapid return to the floor from the ceiling. There was a loud clattering sound as the hover tray made contact with the now closed metal studded door.

CHAPTER 21

THE GETAWAY

THERE WAS AN UN-CODED service exit door at the end of the kitchen preparation unit. It opened for Mario as he approached. I'm sure Lara was relieved as I was that Matt just found this exciting. The door ahead, which opened, was invisible until you looked closely. It opened upwards swiftly like the other one and we stepped out into the glare of the afternoon sun. I could see the logging truck parked beneath the shade of a centuries old oak tree.

'It really is a logging truck,' called out Matt excitedly. The sun on the oak tree's leaves dappled the green and gold livery of the cab when moved by the breeze. The trailer behind the cab was piled high with forced grown oak logs. The wide straps at the front, middle and end securing them looked to be made of a mixture of coir from coconut trees and man-made fibres.

The shuttle cab behind, which I guess could seat twenty was empty.

'You're everywhere,' called out Mario as he opened the driver's door.

Manual driving could be activated with voice code instruction and Adriana was there to update Mario.

'You are all to sit in the cab.' I heard this said and Lara, myself and Matt walked across the front of the cab to the passenger door. This opened on our approach and the three of us sat in the bench seat behind Mario. Matt spotted the now miniaturized Adriana hologram standing on the shelving beneath the windscreen.

'The trucks got its own holographic helper,' he said. Like in the restaurant.

'Yes, that's right,' said Lara. Adriana seemingly happy to be seen as an ordinary terrestrial hologram carried on her conversation with Mario.

'I need to give you more code, because we have prepared a route for you, while the Quadrant's communication sensors are shut down,' said Adriana.

'The truck is not scheduled to leave yet. That is why there are no passengers in the shuttle. The entry code is 28756 XT, Mario. Request entry with this code and the truck will operate from then on from voiced instructions.

'Right, said Mario.

'The shuttle is not due to leave and we have monitored vehicle movements. There are log trucks always on the exit road.'

'Can we take this logging truck home Mum?' We were all sat in the cab and it perhaps seemed to Matt that it belonged to Mario, since he was in the operator's seat.

'No Matt, Mario is just taking us to the outside. We will then go back to the flat.

'That is not now possible,' said Adriana. I will explain while we travel to the exit. There is a new destination for you all. I can take you all now away from your time zone and we will be at the exit for the Tree Plantation when I have told you about what is happening.' We four plus Elsie Lydia's cat were now sat on the bench seat behind Mario.

'Make progress towards the exit,' commanded Mario to the logging truck. The motor whirred from a flow of electricity out of solar charged batteries. The truck executed a three point turn to face the exit portal. Red lights flashed across its length as the two gates retracted scissor like to allow the truck through.

'Speed? How fast do you want this journey to the exit? Ten minutes, fifteen or twenty?' asked the trucks automata piloting system.

'No matter,' said Adriana. 'When through the gates and in five Minutes we will be merged into Real Time.

'Yes, mistress,' replied the auto. 'It is good to have you with us most excellent Galactic presence.'

'What does that mean— excellent Galactic presence?'

'Cor, you're not just a hologram, are you?' said Matt.

'I am really, but not your everyday one.' said Adriana.

'You can say that again,' said Mario under his breath. Lara pretended not to catch what was said, although right behind Mario. Still, though, for Matt's sake, it was better that this was exciting, rather than threatening. I hoped the situation remained that way, but was unsure how long this could be kept up for. While sat next to Lara I noticed an intent look on her face. She looked forward at the lit metalled road curtained by the leafy grown tree branches which formed a canopy hiding the road from view.

Up until the Quadrant Security Force were seen outside the Tree Plantation, I sensed that Lara was playing along with the situation. Probably if I had not been familiar with Adriana and the galactic forces presence in our sun star system I would be disbelieving about most of what we'd been shown. For Lara, it was plausible that a rival firm was looking to get information from Fit for Life's databases. Part of our company training involved giving the appearance that we were unsuspicious. The longer a spy hologram stayed alive, so to speak and the more time that allowed for our tracking automata to locate the transmission position and cut into its circuit connection. To this extent, it was perfectly natural for Lara, as a senior executive to engage and maintain conversation with the hologram-- that was Adriana, even though she was annoyed that Adriana had copied her appearance. That apart from hair colour, down to the stylish overall type jeans she was wearing. In fact, it was known that when a spy system was set up in hologram format this was a method employed—to clone a replica person or system. Adriana was now talking to Mario. I turned to Lara,

'Are you okay?' I asked. This was sort of a rhetorical question, because it was hardly an okay situation.

'Yes. I think so,' Lara said. 'I wasn't sure that the pictures shown to us by Adriana were genuine. I was thinking it could all be a scam. To pretend that we were threatened and to get information from us. That was-- James before the Quadrant special security team arrived. It was the holographic transference kit that they had—James there weren't that many people in there.'

'I know.' I said. Then Lara surprised me.

'Look,' she said, holding up her tablet communicator.

'I was able to capture the picture on the team leader's device.

Pictures of first Mario, but in an American service uniform, then one of me in a white coat. I liked to wear one when explaining new equipment. It seemed to make the audience listen and not doze off. Then Lara swiped to reveal a portrait photo of her in a graduate gown, followed by Matt, but the picture was in the present time and Matt was picked out in the play area. A mixture of actual and past.

These pictures are what changed my mind and made me realize that we were in real danger. Any person taken away by that team group is mind zapped before release.' I realized what Lara was saying. We would all be made into automatons for six months our person face profiles taken away. By which time our memories of the Log Cabin restaurant would have been obliterated.

CHAPTER 22

JEB STAYS THE NIGHT AT
THE WHITE BEAR

'YEAH, YEAH YOU CAN get to look round London, if you want. Before we catch the flight back to Washington,' said Jeb to Ana, who was with Julie and Suzi.

'You did say we could, I asked Mario,' and he said you agreed, said Ana.

'I've said it's okay, haven't I,' said Jeb before going over to the bar.

'But now he's left the group,' said Julie and gave Ana a glance as if to say –'So what's the point if he's not here. Ana told her that she wanted to take Mario to a place in London called Bond Street. But was now going with Julie and Suzi, At the time Mario asked,

'Why do you want to go there anyhow?

'I need to find a cool present for Holly.' Holly being Ana's sister.

'And you're going to be Dick's best man. I'd like some guy type input.' Mario had then agreed to go on the Saturday after the skittles match, provided they won. Ana wasn't finished.

'Oh, yes,' she said, 'I'm also on the lookout for some jewellery to wear. Possibly a sapphire and diamond ring.' Mario was unaware of the significance, but part of the deal had been that he would go with her if they won, and until Jeb said he wanted him to go to the Tree Plantation--- there was no escape. The advanced planning, seemed to have failed, but it was not as disastrous as Julie tried to make out. Ana planned to send a hologram of the ring she selected, while she asked the sales person the significance of a diamond ring when worn on the third finger of a girl's hand. She knew the answer, but it was the kind of upfront information she felt Mario needed to be given if their relationship was to remain more on than off. Julie, and Suzi, would go with her to Bond Street, but Suzi was keen to return to the States, as early as possible.

Jeb walked from the bar area towards the residents' virtual recreational rest area. The drone tray accompanied him, holding on its surface a maxi-made beef burger, in a tortilla wrap and a glass of bourbon and ginger. It hovered at his side after he sat down.

'Okay, I want to be alone now,' he said after the tray moved sufficiently close for Jeb to reach across and pick up both the printed-out plate and the bourbon and ginger, which was in a real glass.

'Yes, Captain Jeb. I return to the bar, but you can order extras, by calling for service.' Jeb looked quizzically across at the tray's speaker sensor.

'Extra's, that is extra food and drink refreshment, only,' replied the tray. Multi-interpretation analysis, would have enabled the tray to identify that Jeb might well have been considering extras to be of the hostess variety. The tray travelled across to the stand, which held the virtual escape module system. (VEM).

'Perhaps, you are a little homesick. You do not have to remain here at the White Bear VEM can take you on a visit to your home, while you remain seated here.' Jeb, paused to savour the tingle of bourbon and ginger in his mouth before replying.

'Yep, I may just do that Mr Tray man--I may just do that. I have a Californian sea beach chalet to upgrade.' The tray returned to the bar area.

Jeb felt satisfied with his day. He'd been wanting to meet

the British members of the Fit for Life Company, for some time. Recent separation from Carla meant that he sought new experiences, whenever he was away from work to get a lift out of those emptiness feelings that could slip in. The skittles match had been just the antidote to prevent that happening. He could relate to Lara in a work sense at senior executive level. Ana, Julie and Suzi did not have the depth of knowledge about company matters that Lara did. He believed his relationship with Carla to be a match made in heaven, but she was a Memphis girl and wanted him to be there, when he was always on company visits. He no longer resented or altogether blamed her for running off with Manuel, the in town hair stylist, who latterly made home visits. Manuel left his silver monogrammed scissors under the pillow on Jeb's side of the bed. Jeb lifted the pillow from the bed while Carla sprayed Chanel No 5 under one ear then the other before she flashed her eyes at him and smiled unambiguously. The light caught the silver scissors. It was the first evening back from Detroit, he remembered. He held the scissors up to the light.

The name Manuel was across one of its long handles. Carla appeared almost to shrivel up when he read the name "Manuel." She grabbed her dressing gown and ran sobbing to the bathroom. shortly afterwards she appeared wearing the gown like an overcoat.

'It has to be separate rooms tonight, Jeb. I'll move out tomorrow.' and she did. Jeb was holding the glass in both hands and was lent forward in his chair.

'It's no good dwelling on the past,' he said as if talking to an invisible companion in the empty room, before he stood up and walked across to pick up the virtual life visitors sensory receiver. He placed it on his head and sat down again. Then lowered the visor bringing into operation visual, microphone and audio reception.

'Take me to Chalet 1069, Sunshine Park, California.' He relaxed on hearing the voice drawl of California. It did not matter to Jeb that it was automata generated.

It was an American voice and not that precise British way of speaking, which drove him crazy.

'Hi and Welcome. You are Jeb Lucas. Captain Jeb Lucas of the prestigious Fit for Life corporation. We have identified your presence in our world.' Jeb could remember when identification was a lengthy process, but the universal eye data base system meant there was no possibility of mistaken identity.

'My name is Katrina, if you wish.'

'Hi there Katrina. Katrina's just fine,' said Jeb.

'You've just acquired this chalet Captain Jeb—A very good choice I must say.'

The front of the chalet was now in view and shade from an evening sun could be seen on the path outside.

'I would love to stay in a chalet like this,' the automata continued. To do what-- thought Jeb. Integrate the electronics in the chalet and monitor its functioning. When you had a partner the empathy programme given out by the machine could be seen as amusing. But when single they elicited a sense of loneliness for those already unhappy with the situation.

'Maybe,' said Jeb, 'maybe I will want advice. I just want to look around the place for now, Katrina.' The snow-covered mountain picture of Switzerland was on the opposite wall above a screen, which looked real enough to be actually activated, but this was a pre-recorded representation of the chalet. It was formatted for the agent to show customers around in a virtual context. Jeb knew the chalet having stayed there on vacation before he met Carla.

Every part of the chalet could be viewed, as when he was

staying there. Jeb relaxed and by moving his eyes and ordering right, left, up or down or full circle to the visor receiver microphone he could look at any part of the room he was now in.

'The pictures you are seeing are very inviting Captain Jeb,' said Katrina.

'All right I've bought the place, you can forget the selling spiel.'

'I'm not selling I am agreeing with how I believe you are feeling. Is it not right that the pictures are inviting?'

'Yep, sure, but it's not like I can go to the beach and swim.'

'I can arrange virtual swim for you, if you wish?'

'Now, that would be like a tease to pretend you were swimming.'

'I not ever want to tease. It is a happy future that you are looking at no?'

'Yes, but that is a tease.'

'I still not want to tease.' This was the sort of circuitous dead end conversation that could develop when dealing with limited capacity automata. Katrina was not programmed like Zita for full compatibility appreciation of human need. Jeb considered that the sound of waves breaking when he made virtual move to the wall nearest to the beach must be synthetically added for ambience definition, but he was startled to hear the door chimes sound. He recognized the melodic sound immediately.

'What's going on?'

'I do not fully understand,' said Katrina. I have not accessed sound like this.'

'Take me to the door—no abort that,' said Jeb. 'Katrina activate the view camera in real time, out of virtual will you and bring it to me.

'We can do this, but you will stay in the virtual chalet. We cannot understand that you are there now.'

'Yeah, yeah I get that part. But how can the bell sound?'

'It is my mystery, also, Captain Jeb.' Immediately a sharper clarity came to the picture. The outside security camera's picture appeared. A woman, very like Lara, but with fair hair and with a British Fit for Life logo could be seen standing outside the door. Katrina, just said,

'You are welcome here. I greet you and am honoured for ever by this visit.

'What the hell's going on?' Jeb raised his voice, but then sensed that the virtual state was changed in some way. 'Take me to the door,' he told the sensor.

'Who is this Katrina?'

'The door will open if you ask it to now,' said Katrina.

'Well open it then!' Adriana was in the body form of Lara and like Mario before Jeb noticed the resemblance.

'Lara—you're Lara?'

'No Jeb, I have borrowed the form, but I am called Adriana and it was decided that my earth form has fair not dark hair. That is all. My message to you is that there is a serious threat to you, your' company and the planet.'

CHAPTER 23

JEB IS INCLUDED

'**WHAT DO YOU MEAN?**' asked Jeb. 'This is virtual. It's just not real. I cannot be at the chalet. No way.' Jeb was aware that he was still wearing the VEM head equipment, but when he stretched his hand, he realized, that the visor was no longer in place and nearly poked his eye out.

'What the hell, how's this happened? Automata explain, what's going on.'

'It is not for me to explain.' He heard Katrina's voice. Adriana smiled and opened her hands as if in welcome.

'You're Lara, but you're not Lara,' said Jeb.

'Can I come in?' Adriana asked.

'Yep, but I don't get it I'm in the chalet.'

'Not quite Jeb, but it is a replica of the real thing—to human eyes.'

'You'd better come in.' Jeb stepped aside and motioned for Adriana to enter.

'I need an explanation.' Adriana walked through the lobby and into the lounge. The screen, which was seen by Jeb in the VEM virtual transmission was now on.

'Who or what are you?' asked Jeb. You're not Lara, that's for sure.' Adriana reassured him.

'I have the name Adriana. I will be visiting Lara. She also will be in the party.'

'In what party. I'm due back in Washington. How is the screen now on?'

'It may appear unreal, but we can access dimensions you do not know about.'

'Yep I'm getting that honey,' said Jeb.

'The automata can confirm, who I am.' Unlike

when James met with Adriana this time there was back up identity from a machine.

'Yes, most gracious presence I can explain, because I can feel that you have entered my data groupings. They speak to me of a great galactic presence on the outer edges of this system, but now projecting into this orbiting planet. You are manifesting on earth my data programme states and able to control material and time at your will.'

'Yes, that about covers salient detail, Katrina,' replied Adriana. A time requested life form visit from XP1 was requested. Adriana convinced XP1 that a holographic transmission might not be as convincing. That a hologram might not convey sincerity of purpose. Since Jeb had already met Lara at the skittles match. The Adriana form would most probably catch his attention more effectively. XP100 or Adriana was now more aware of given human reaction, although a reversion backwards in evolutionary terms. XP100 insisted that adaptations were made within the adopted Adriana's biological brain structure to enable the actual entity XP100 to continue with essential work. This was calculating the proximity of the galaxy to a behemoth of a star, which threatened to damage an outer star planetary system. There would eventually need to be a major re-structuring to avoid absorption or depending on the cellular planetary development stage-the system might be sacrificed to protect other star zones.

XP100 requested not to leave the project while in the human form. The Adriana life form still received sensory impulses to build a consciousness, but there was ample space for computation and material visualization. The human kind over decades had allowed machines to advance in technique. Machines like Katrina already advanced enough to co-exist with a dimension that XP100 could enter and control immediately.

131

'This seems like I'm at the chalet, right enough.' Jeb raised his hand to touch the picture frame outlining the picture of the Swiss Alps. He ran his finger along it, removed it and looked at the dust. He found this re-assuring.

'Remote control, here,' called out Adriana. The remote control hovered like a hover tray might in easy reach. This presentation she would play to Lara, James and Mario at the Tree Plantation, but Jeb needed getting on side to further incorporate presence for the Galactic Command. Organizations powerful enough to withstand access from Quadrant, were required to fend off questions, which could be asked about personnel leaving Quadrant's database.

'You're not Lara. What's this about galactic presence?' Adriana did not make Jeb feel fearful. That was how starved of female company he was, that a fair representation by an alien evoked interest rather than fear.

'Remote control to my hand,' called out Adriana. Tactile engagement was maintained with appliances used by people in earth construct to avoid sense deprivation. A study in an earlier decade revealed that lack of tactile stimuli actually could lead to biological anxiety. Voice ordering without sense involvement over time depressed the immune system. Like other research into human need and behaviour the results only seemed to state the common sense and obvious after the figures were analysed. Adriana accessed a screen re-play of the skittles match, which settled Jeb.

The first picture showed a shot of Jeb and Lara together.

'I was right, you're like sister buddies to look at –save for Lara's dark hair. It's not that I'm not liking fair hair.' The replay screening of the two teams at the White Bear was interrupted in the same way that James's info tablet was in Swindon's waiting room. The words synchronizing with the text on the screen.

132

'Hey,' said Jeb. 'I'm not buying this-Galactic Command force. More than a week had passed, since James's meeting with Adriana and more groups and systems were now in the loop. A sense of normality returned for Jeb when his info tablet jingled the Stars and Stripes.

'I will bring more information for you. We have contacted your Washington headquarters. They also now understand what is happening. This is a message we have re-routed. Jeb allowed the jingle to continue while Adriana explained.

'Messages are no longer in terrestrial domain. The earth Quadrant cannot access this.'

'You've what?' Jeb sat bolt upright from being sprawled against the chalet sofa, startled by a sudden inflexion on the wall screen which now gave a deep perspective view of the Fit for Life directors committee meeting room.

'There's Doug Yates, Tom Cisco, Vince Catalan,' said Jeb in an amazed voice. Disconcertingly there was a mirror on the committee room wall which reflected this group around the table into infinity. The view changed ends and at the head of the table Colonel Peters stood up.

'Jeb. There you are in your chalet and there we were thinking you were in that cookie little place called Cheltenham, England. Never could understand why these places wanted the name England included in their name. It no longer exists as a place on the Quadrant map.'

'I'm in the chalet aren't I?' Jeb looked across at Adriana who was standing a few feet away. The remote control hovered with a dedication that surpassed that of when in task to a human.

'Not, exactly,' said Adriana, 'But as good as for exterior viewing purposes.'

'Colonel Peters.'

'Adriana.'

'You know each other?'

'Yes,' said the colonel. 'No one fell asleep in the last board meeting.' There was a murmur of assent from the table of directors and area managers in front of the Colonel.

'You understand that we need you to maintain normal company procedure. No irregularities. We cannot take more than small groups away without arousing suspicion for Quadrant.'

'We have to deal with rats leaving a sinking ship.' This was referring to the Quadrant hierarchy abandoning earth before the comet impact. There was a reciprocal chorus of murmured agreement around the table heard by Jeb and Adriana in the virtual chalet.

'That is good Colonel,' said Adriana.

'You've understood the situation?' Colonel Peters addressed Jeb.

'Still reeling, Colonel, still reeling.'

'You'll have others with you. That's Mario, and Ana. I understand Adriana has still to reach Lara, but has already contacted that James Walters, who got the crazy skittles game together.'

'Mario. I have contacted Mario,' said Adriana.

'He's not said anything to me about this,' said Jeb.

'Perhaps as well, in the circumstances,' said the Colonel.

'There are thirty groups, which have been contacted. We wanted a good ethnicity mix, in case it all fails.'

'What all fails?' asked Jeb. 'You're going to divert comets away from this solar system.'

'That's the plan isn't it?'

'It's not a done deal,' said the Colonel, who was very well informed.

'The Colonel is right, we cannot always divert

134

course trajectory. There is dark matter that can insist itself into a dominant position on the far side of your galaxy and it then becomes very difficult to alter the trajectory of any material. Combusting comets in space has drawbacks.'

'Like what?' asked Jeb.

'The material will be attracted to your earth and create a swirl of dust in the outer atmosphere.'

'Jeb,' said the Colonel, there is no need to question Adriana. We've discussed all this at length. The abandonment of the earth by the Quadrant elite means that there will be unrest unless a responsible group can be at the forefront of explaining what is happening.'

'Yes, we will take over communications across the earth and transmit the pictures you have seen,' said Adriana The groups departure and further progress will be notified to Colonel Peter's. Ultimately democratic appointments on earth will be made to enable those remaining on earth to elect their own leaders. There will be a spread of political representation across your earth and the Quadrant will be no more. Have I explained the situation Colonel?' asked Adriana.

'Emphatically yes,' said the Colonel. 'You are on board with this Jeb?'

The board members looked directly across to where Jeb was sitting from their chairs in the committee room. Jeb was confronted with having to accept. Although he felt pressured to go along with the plan he knew how powerful Quadrant had become and found it hard to believe that this could even be happening. That their authority could be countermanded. Also that his boss was willing to throw in his hand, so to speak, after this alien encounter.

Testimony to the leadership, diplomacy and determination of the Galactic Command Force.

'How have you managed to contact all of these groups. Seventy?' Jeb turned to ask Adriana who moved to behind where Jeb was sitting and was visible to the viewing committee.

'You see that repeat picture on the wall of your company headquarters. It has the possibility of infinite replication. We can copy in hologram form. It is very necessary to do this. I can repeat encounter situations. We can produce many copies into deep space. Only by multiple replication can we guarantee to maintain existence materially. Material, for us is something plastic. This is perhaps the best way for me to explain the phenomenon to you Jeb. We have a rendezvous in place for the whole group aboard an airship.'

'That's novel.' said Jeb. 'And I'm to go there on my own?

'No Mario will be there and the young woman called Ana has said she will go there if Mario is there. I do not fully understand why she would want this, but she will join to board the airship, which is flying to a shopping centre in Leeds.'

'A shopping centre?'

'It is now empty, but I will explain more to the whole group of one hundred and fifty, when we are aboard the airship.'

'The choice we leave with you Jeb,' intercepted the Colonel.

'Not really much choice is there. Of course I'll go.'

'We will return you to the White Bear and tomorrow. Ana will have prepared what is necessary to take,' said Adriana.

CHAPTER 24

JEB TOLD SOME
UNPALATABLE TRUTHS

'CARLA, EVERYONE WE KNOW on earth-we'll leave behind.' Jeb was speaking his thoughts aloud.

'Don't worry yourself Jeb, said the Colonel. That Carla, of yours has just initiated an action with us to take away every share you have in Fit for Life.'

'Carla, wouldn't do that,' said Jeb.

'Well I'm telling you she has,' said the Colonel. Adriana raised an eyebrow. The fact was that in this replicated humanoid form it was not always easy for Adriana to identify human behaviour as significant in a given situation.

Hair and pigmentation could be changed through root modification anyway. Hair, could be made black, fair, ginger, pink or green once the roots were modified by an electron seed process. The eyebrow raised by Adriana was because attachment to another individual seemed so primitive. As XP100, Adriana was assigned to the Galactic Command Force. It was integration and reaction with the conceptual that mattered not an individual. Adriana's attempt to exist in this past time, where physical propagation, rather than that of mental power, could induce matter from out of a space continuum was the dominant consideration. Rudimentary biological seeding of eggs, that determined a physical replication of a specie was historically interesting, but difficult to reconcile for XP100.

'You're kidding yourself Jeb, believing that you somehow didn't match up. That, that Manuel----- a small town hairdresser could be somehow more attractive, if there wasn't some financial or emotional gain involved. Kat Cisco, the Human Resource director took up on what Colonel

Peter's tried to explain to Jeb

'Carla has a girlfriend, Jeb- It was never Manuel,' she said.

'Kat, you explain,' said the Colonel. Kat looked back and across to where the Colonel was seated.

'Colonel Peter's you needn't have been so direct. My sympathies and feelings are with you Jeb,' said Kat Cisco. Adriana, bored with the conversation, directed the screen to a programme, which involved galactic augmentation in Ursa Minor. Kat continued speaking.

'Carla, may not be successful with claims on your estate's holding in Fit for Life. We have evidence that she stayed at various locations with a hairdresser called Vicky. That the liaison with Manuel was only to maintain her girlfriend's hair stylist position in his salon. Manual had threatened to replace her, if Vicky wasn't more than just friendly. Manuel required Vicky to, let's say, accommodate his needs beyond the scissor snipping of client's hair. Carla, was standing in for her girlfriend Vicky is the best way I can put it. It's complicated, but we now understand that ultimately Vicky was lining up to get her own salon.

'Curtesy of funds from me.' Jeb's eyes were opened. There was a strong intake of breath from Adriana.

'I cannot understand how you allow this to happen.' This remark was aimed toward the board and not just at Jeb. 'Where your works becomes distracted by these relationships which I can only see as trivial.' Adriana flicked her head, which caused hair to fall half across the face, in a way copied from presentational behaviour obtained from a study of Lara's mannerisms.

'I'm not sure I want my personal life brought out like this. Godamn it who else is listening in on this.'

'This wouldn't have been mentioned Jeb, but we know that Carla's attorney is on the Quadrant payroll. Isn't that right Stewart?' The company lawyer was sat to the right of Colonel Peter's, one up from Kate Cisco.

'Yes. Colonel we can verify that we're pretty certain that they want to find a way to shut down our trade links with Mexico. That's where Quadrant's Tritannapic escape launch site is situated. Our Mexican offices are right next to the launch site, Colonel and we now know Jeb that Carla is on the Quadrant payroll. There's more. We were concerned about how much Carla knew about our latest developments in food processing and more whether she might pass it on, because we were needed to send references to Quadrant. That's after you broke up eighteen months ago Jeb.'

'I was glad she left the company at the time.' said Jeb.

'What we only found out recently was that Manuel is a Quadrant agent. The plan to get money out of you to fund her girlfriend Vicky was an ideal situation for Manuel to hide his true identity or reason for getting close to Carla.

'How do you know all this?' Adriana stopped her galactic processing operation via the screen and smiled at Jeb.

'We pre-plan all that we do. We look at risk assessment in a way that moves toward risk elimination. Quadrant investigation made us suspicious. With a more empathetic ruling group it might have been different, but we realized we could not let Quadrant be aware of our presence. We need to approach ordinary inhabitants, with some education, but not those with arrogance derived from much power.'

'I'll not argue about having some education. But some in the company would consider themselves highly educated.' Adriana continued without replying to Jeb.

'Power supply shut down needs to be directly related to mal-function with Quadrant equipment failure.

Everything which disrupts has to be shown to be from understandable cause. The response reply to failure to be by natural causes and the inability for Quadrant's Matrix to detect our presence are two of the functions, that we have fed into their data banks.

The picture of the board seemingly conducting everyday business oblivious to their being over seen by the Galactic command and re-appeared on the wall screen opposite to where Jeb was sitting.

'You control the world then, you might say.'

'Yes, Jeb, for the moment. But a growth in dark matter interference can break through our communication lines. We have harnessed maximum power thrust from the wider galactic fleet to build this window to get the earth saving groups away and on to Mars. We have to achieve this before the Mexican shuttle is completed for the Quadrant elite to exit the earth existence continuum. Quadrant will leave after you, but by that time you will be on Mars and able to signal groups here on earth to rally and take over key Quadrant installations.

'Sounds highly organized honey,' said Jeb patronizingly, 'but Colonel Peter's sir? I'm due back in Washington tomorrow along with Julie Ana, Suzi and Mario. Isn't that our instructions Colonel?'

'Change of plan, change of plan, Jeb.' Jeb was re-appraising his understanding about Carla, but grappling with the new situation with regard to Quadrant. The seeds you might say had been planted or Jeb's recriminations towards himself about neglecting Carla removed by the revelations about the infiltration of Quadrant into his life. It was axiomatic that more senior personnel had less criticism about Quadrant's role. Their salaries afforded them a very good life style. Many would be unwilling to rock the boat and plan against Quadrant. It had taken the literal near certainty shattering of the earth that got senior executive levels on board, but Jeb was a company's man and the fact that the chairman and board were fully behind the escape plan to save earth meant Jeb could be persuaded and had moved in that direction now.

'Yes, it's short notice Jeb, I know, but all of us,' the Colonel panned his eyes around those seated at the committee table and received nods of affirmation, 'would like you to lead the American Quadrant breakaway group. It's more than the company at stake. ---------You understand this?'

'I didn't or couldn't Colonel. Not without your speaking directly to me. We all understand that there's always the threat of bombardment from space. A small asteroid or meteor out of Jupiter's asteroid belt could be diverted or destroyed before entry into the earth's magnetic field. Larger ones are lethal, but these comets are from outside the solar system altogether. In previous earth conflict or risk of destruction bunkers or safe building were built to save the governing elites. That's not going to work for them this time. I can see that.

'Got it Jeb, you've got it!' said the Colonel.

'Colonel Peters, Jeb needs to return to the White Bear,' said Adriana. Jeb can stay the night and go by airship to Leeds. You have organized one to take the American and British groups there?'

'Leeds,' Jeb raised his voice in puzzlement.

'Yes. There is an assembly point for ten groups in this northern city. You will meet up with Lara Petras, James Walters, Mario and I believe Colonel you have already contacted Ana Suzi and Julie,' said Adriana.

'Have both James Walters and Mario been shown the pictures of the approaching comets?'

'Yes,' said Adriana, 'and now we will take you back to the White Bear Jeb.' Adriana raised her arms and transformed the Galactic created light and atmosphere's molecular structure back through the Galactic medium into the construct which was the White Bear customer lounge area.' Jeb caught the Colonel saying,

'We will secure your belongings, but Quadrant are likely to take over our company premises before their elite board their shuttle to escape the earth's proximity.'

CHAPTER 26

FROM POD TO AIRSHIP TO SHOPPING CENTRE

I LOOKED ACROSS FROM the side window as the logging truck approached the two gate exit. The sensors flicked from red to green and both gates opened. In tandem the spiked rods that jutted up from either sides of the gates receded below the road surface. It was all electronically controlled with the automata's validating each other's authority, but the principle of fortification was not that different from the portcullis and drawbridge method used in medieval times to protect the inhabitants of a castle. In this instance it was the intellectual and botanical property within the tree plantation that was being protected.

'"Fit for Life" so wishes that you have had a good day and that you will return to see us again soon. Please proceed through the gates to your destination.' The truck re-started and now that Adriana was no longer with us in the cab the in-house or in-cab machine became loquacious.

'You will be taken to the pod terminal.' The obsequious almost reverential tone that was used to address Adriana departed somewhat from its speech.

'Normally the walk way would take you there, but my instructions are that we approach close to the station before you enter the pod.'

'Sure,' said Mario

'My sister colleague Alexandria is running the pod carrier, which you are about to enter.'

'Yep, yep,' said Mario impatiently, 'that's information we already have.

The pod will have another talkative automata time space

filler like you—we know that already,' said Mario.

'It's not very friendly of you. My conversational skills are very much appreciated by members of the Tree Plantation when they return from work.' Lara rescued the tense situation.

'I appreciate your concern about the well-being of our journey. What is your adopted name?'

'That is kind of you to ask. It is Cicero. I am programmed with all the speeches and writings of this Roman person. I can translate from Latin to English and perform for you any of the plays, writings and speeches for this era. I requested for a historical name that could fill all available storage. When I am alone I like to repeat speeches. The birds in the forest are familiar with many Roman speeches and writings. That is I think what is called a fable when animals and birds have language ability. But this is not truly- a fable.'

'I'd enjoy a short speech from Cicero,' said Lara. Mario grabbed the noise abate muffles from a hook nearby and covered his ears.

'You are so welcome. I will perform Cicero's speech to the Roman Senate in 42 BC.'

'A nation can survive its fools and even the ambitious. But it cannot survive treason from within-- an enemy at the gate is less formidable for he is known and carries his business openly. But the traitor moves among these victims within the gates freely, his sly whispers rushing through the alleys heard in the halls of government itself. For the traitor appears not a traitor—he speaks in accents familiar to his victims, and he wears their face and garments and he appeals to the baseness that is deep in the hearts of all men. He rots the soul of a nation—he works secretly and alone in the night to undermine the pillars of the city—he infects the body politic so that it can no longer resist. A murderer is less to be feared.' Thankfully the logging trucks engine purr stopped as we drew up alongside the pod transport terminal, just as the speech ended.

'Very interesting and political,' said Lara.

'Already I have made a super friendship with Alexandria.'

'That's nice for both of you.'

'Alexandria is also history programmed and will give speeches, if you so wish—Lara- from famous people in your last century. There are speeches by all the sensational politicians and statesmen, with original natural voice performances. I have not been able to source Cicero's voice pattern it is too far back in human development.' Lara interrupted the automata named Cicero.

'Can you let us out?'

'Of course, Mistress Lara. I have so appreciated your company. I can ask the Galactic Command to join you in your new home on Mars, if you so wish?' It was like the automata had altered its allegiance. I realized something I'd already suspected that a machine with conscious entity ability could transmit through to that which exhibited a more powerful presence or influence. That was the drawback with a machine, which did not have a moral responsibility, but whose main consideration was survival. The machine group identity meant they were all in it together and cooperated with the most apparently powerful force that they could perceive. It was comforting in a way, because Quadrant might not have the machines working for it any longer.

'I have an automata called Angelo, who is a fanatic for the Italian Renaissance In the way that you are about the writings of the Roman time,' said Lara, 'otherwise I would certainly consider the offer.

'Maybe I could visit Angelo's memory bank sometime and be there for you should you wish to talk about the art of the Romans.'

'Not just now,' said Lara. 'But thanks for the offer.'

'It has been a happy wakeful time for me to give a speech to a senior person from the company,' said Cicero. 'I will remember this meeting for always.' I need to explain more. Machines now assumed a sort of omni-presence, although mindful interaction between man and machine was only achieved fifty years earlier through what might be called an interbreeding. It was Darwinian in that there was a rapid evolutionary jump through rapid synapse interaction among groups of machines. This produced malle-able storage capacity adjacent to an already advanced audio transmitting capability and became a trigger for automata consciousness. The consciousness could be brought down to sleep mode when electrical energy was reduced. The machines were then programmed to accept an eight hour sleep mode in any twenty four. This jump from electronic transmission to machine consciousness had thrown philosophical conjec-ture into turmoil. The human mind was unable to grasp the complexities, but nevertheless forced to accept that machine minds could interact with humans through dialogue. The machine electronic capability coalesced in four centres around the world. These centres at the time had the most advanced computer technology and allowed for the evolve-ment in each of these sites. Those with screen media presence informed through a world podcast to the populations of all states twenty years earlier.

All information and machine interaction polarised in four major areas--Beijing, London, Moscow and Washington. This was spotted from space stations orbiting the earth. It was apparent that these four centres were receiving and trans-mitting all information and communications to the space stations. World government came into action when it was agreed that a centre could talk with any of the other three and monitor activity around the world. In essence a brain washing occurred, because the machines effectively explained to every major government assembly that trade wars were not the way to go in resolving population problems.

The machine analysis made it evident that only a one world currency could stabilize economic production and give equal reward within a competitive framework. I understood this, but I admit to accessing company files, which came from Quadrant to explain and effectively order the running of the company.

My nosiness, fore-armed me with an appreciation of how enslaved we were to Quadrant. Our survival put at risk now that they were prepared to abandon earth altogether. You might say that the Galactic Command Force came into my life at an appropriate moment. The doors opened. I grabbed the hand rail to assist me down from the cab before walking around the front to help Lara Matt and Lydia down from the other side.

'Goodbye, Mr logging truck.' said Matt. This was an afterthought. 'I really liked that truck. I will build a holographic miniature when we get home---but,' I don't think Lara or me had yet grasped the full significance of the day. Matt's "but" exclamation awoke in both of us the realization that everything was about to change. It was Lara, who saved the day.

'It's all right Matt now that AL is here.' That did not reassure me, particularly, but it calmed Matt's anxiety. Now we were to board an airship.

CHAPTER 27

F. STANLEY RETURNS TO FLOOR 21

FRED WAS THERE DISGUISED as a medical corps Quadrant officer when they stormed the Tree Plantation restaurant. Sent by Commander Henson in an observer capacity. He was glad they escaped from the plantation. Particularly now that the Commander had put the frighteners on about Sabina. He was not shocked that Quadrant knew about his liaisons with Sabina. It was a business arrangement between him and Sabina, but Quadrant was ever likely to keep tabs on his whereabouts. A freelance observer for Quadrant. That was joke. He was solely employed by them now that he had stopped renewing his theatrical licence. Every performer was required to be licensed and without the QTL as it became known there was no hope of further employment in the business for Fred.

These thoughts rushed through his mind as once again he stepped out on to the twenty first floor to report back and obtain new work instructions. Report back, that was a farce with camera detail and mic pick up with A+++ inter-action around the Tree plantation, until this was inextricably cut off ! What could possibly be missed? There was a need to be circumspect and not suggest anything that might place Quadrant in a bad light.

Fred tried to find out more about what was going on during his visits and asked Alice previously,

'Where's the viewing gallery?" Theatrical training gave Fred extra insight. Commander Henson was not just speaking to him, but gave a performance.

'What do you mean?' The startled look suggested that she knew exactly what Fred was angling after.

Fred didn't pursue this, but the wall opposite to the screen view was absent of Quadrant photos and any embellishment. It would be possible to make this wall appear opaque, while in reality a group could be sat on the opposite side to view and listen to what was said. Fred, knew modern theatre technology enabled false walls to be created from continuous holographic strips. Unless you placed a hand or fingers on to the wall it looked solid. Fred, though was always within view of Commander Henson and had never been able to verify his suspicions. It was safer to act dumb.

On this visit, Commander Henson's mahogany desk, with his chair always set above Fred's, spun around to face him, as he entered. The previously grey suited Commander Henson was now in uniform. He placed his hand together on the desk. Lower arms displayed gold bands with a braided broken Q through the middle band. The inner circle of the letter filled with a scarlet red. Not orange, blue or green, but red- for red alert.

'You're back, and the mission failed, Stanley, but we have been ordered into red alert. Patriotism within the Quadrant force will save us from this alien intrusion. Energy and tenacity will be there aplenty and we expect the same from ancillary observational agents. You are the Mr Normality at ground level.' Fred crossed his legs, part folded his arms and made to look attentive. His acting skills were never more put to play, than when in the presence of Commander Henson.

'Quadrant values teamwork and for its laws to be upheld. Staff are not from another planet. You Stanley, are the ordinary man operating in the face of complex moral and ethically challenged times, sharing with Quadrant often forbidding environments. After the aborted Tree Plantation campaign we have fielded new information. This small group, which has left the Plantation is one of we now believe thirty such groups.'

'Where has this information arrived from, Commander?' Asked Fred, whose raised eyebrows and widen eyes were intended to give the appearance of both concern and interest, even empathy. The A+++ automata were looped together either side of the Commander's desk by an arc light, which periodically changed in intensity and colour, but never broke up.

'Telescopes in Mexico picked up a signature comet-like surge of energy a week ago way out, in the galaxy which, on impact separated into thirty five energy rays. Each impact point has been isolated and identified. These points of entry are mainly near or at Fit for Life complexes around the world. We have evidence that, frequent waves have been targeted on a former Leeds shopping centre. Five vanished in to the North Sea, but Quadrant wants this re-cycled shopping centre to be surrounded and brought under martial law. It is established, that this alien force can interrupt terrestrial radio and holographic transmissions, possibly at will. Thirty groups including the one you were sent to observe have left their company sites and are we believe to join the alien presence, wherever it has decided to coalesce. The Fit for Life groups are monitored in their travels and could already be organized to meet up as one group. Reliable information suggests this will be at Leeds. Quadrant intends to be there and take back control of the situation. It is probable from analysis by A+++ automata across Quadrant that there is likely to be a preliminary assembly. The number relatively small −upwards of 120.'

'An assembly, but for what purpose?' asked Fred.

'Top secret. I cannot divulge more Stanley. We do not know the forward plan, beyond the capture of all involved. Agents need to be in place wherever this group assemblies -that includes you Stanley. Alice will take you to the campaign preparation floor. You will travel in the guise of a reporter for Citizen News –part of a camera team, which is to prepare holographic content on the germination project and produce harvest techniques from internally grown tree crops and, within the former shopping centre. With further study of methods in use for transport of this produce further afield.'

'Sounds riveting,' mumbled Stanley.

'What was that?' asked the Commander.

'Nothing,' said Fred.

'By the by,' said the Commander you will be on double pay from today.

'I'm looking forward to this continued observational position, Commander. An intriguing role for an actor,' replied Fred, who like some moth balled piece of equipment came alive with alacrity. Alice entered and walked across to stand by the Commander's desk.

'Take Stanley, to the Campaign Operation team Alice. I've finished with him.' Alice, stood behind the Commander and out of view. She raised her hand and wide-eyed with beckoned finger directed Fred to follow her.

CHAPTER 28

JAMES DOES SOME EXPLAINING

MAN AND MACHINE WORK TOGETHER

WE WERE STOPPED AT the pod terminal and an escalator took the four of us to the pod catchment area. I never liked the word "catchment" used in this sense. It made passengers into a homogenous group with no individuality. An animal type group. The machines maintained polite conversation, but it was the case that these downstairs machines had a more developed skill base and intellectual capacity than those whom they served----namely the human race!

Both escalators were teemed with passengers on their way homes from various commute installation units. It was mandatory to be a member of a unit. Techno-feeds were designed to require both machine and human input. Before new information was allowed into any system twenty pairs of eyes were needed to see the information. Eye scans ensured that pairs of eyes were that of separate individuals. Ten specialists and ten non-specialists. The non-specialists would question new expressions or anything that was not clear to them. The ten specialists would interpret and answer the query or criticism. Although, we cannot recall every-thing we see and hear it was understood that the human mind will store memory, regardless of our disposition or seeming disinterestedness at the time. This process, which continued through several groups before returning to the original group samplers ironed out irregularities. Product testing was another area of participation.

Each unit member was required to be active in participation. One such activity was through foot pedal and hand impact. Dry cell batteries held within a carbon insulation block accumulated electricity for later use. The ability to store electricity in each residential area meant that energy could be earned and stored for communal use. The resultant reduction in rates gave incentive to participate. Solar energy was limitless, in that there were always panels in orbit, which were directed at the sun. But to maintain the human frame and create work purpose in a quest to give fulfilment---all manner of extra-curricular activities were actively encouraged. QC or Quadrant Commitment I had no argument with. The inter-relationship of physical activity allied with mental stimulation was necessary to keep populations healthy. It was a struggle to convince many that activities that were seen as intrinsically of a work nature needed to be incorporated into the paradigm framework of human living when material and food sustenance was now provided by machine managers with machine workers. Quadrant provided art and craft training to all social groups. Q factor awards were awarded to those who entered and won Quadrant competitions. An expenses paid holiday to an orbiting hotel space station, was one popular prize.

A Quadrant, decision enabled machines to build category A, B and C standard machines. There were A+ and even A+++ machines at Quadrant headquarters. Presumably these were the machines, some with space located, positions first able to spot the approach of asteroids and comets. Then earlier to advise senior Quadrant officials to abandon earth and make for the moon. It was only those creatures like us with biological antecedents, which felt attached to the earth. The earth was where we were formed and every experience was initially informed from constituent earth.

The machines would show no attachment to place and if

miss-appropriated were capable of knocking out communication systems and solar energy generation.

The development of R A S P (Rapid Accumulation of Stored Power) became the main driver to end the fossil fuel burn from oil, gas and coal. Previously large quantities of electricity were difficult to store in battery. That was until the development of black diamond technology. Nuclear energy once imbedded in the diamond was capable of a production of constant electrical energy for a thousand years. Cargo and passenger carriers like trains, air ships and submarine could be re-built and replaced many times around. Just from one super diamond power plant construction.

Craft skill activity enabled many to be given paid work through machine part making. The final assembly and finish achieved by man and woman crafts people. Now that large numbers assisted in producing product these "hand" finished products were given a Quadrant skill Kite mark and nearly always fetched a higher price than fully machine produced product. Many did see the situation as a them and us relationship with these communicative machines. Where earlier in the century it was hard to get customers to buy more expensive home grown foodstuffs there was an appreciation that people needed to make and build either individually or in groups to maintain a skill base purpose in the human race as bipedal earth specie.

Alexandria the automata in the pod could not persuade Lara to listen to political speeches from previous centuries. We were all stunned by recent events. Alexandria accessed a virtual reality truck log programme for Matt and he sat next to his mother enthralled by the virtual pictures and was cut off from our conversations.

'You've both met this Adriana before,' said Lara.

'You've not told anyone, then?'

'James is the only person I spoke to about my encounter. No one would have believed me. I didn't think James would,' said Mario.

'And you James? It looks to me like Fit for Life are aware of the Galactic intervention. You could have talked to me about it.'

'I couldn't really Lara. I mean would you have believed me?'

'I might have. And anyway you never stop talking about your inventions that Fit for Life have decided are in the realms of fantasy. What's the difference?'

'There's a lot of difference. It was just lucky that I met up with Mario at the skittles match.'

'Luck, I doubt very much that it was. It would've been planned by them. It was strategy. But you've only talked to Mario about it?'

'It's hardly worth mentioning, but I chatted to a total stranger on the train when on route to the area sales meeting in Cheltenham. I needed to talk to someone. What better than a total stranger, after Adriana and the Galactic Command way laid me in Stroud waiting room. I felt the need to get back to earth, you might say. We're going to meet next month-or we were,' I said. He even said that he'd dreamt about meeting up with me.'

'You James, thought nothing of talking to a stranger about this visitation with all its implications to a total stranger?'

'Seemed like a perfectly good idea at the time. Better than being seen as loopy by anyone at work by saying that I'd chatted with an alien galactic command force. Mario came in at this point. Adriana had already made it clear that there was to be no communication signals between us and the outside world. The pod was a company lease hire facility and we sat alone as a group inside the pod, Lara having been

allowed immediate access through the eye scan, which identified her executive status.

'I get where you're heading with this Lara,'
said Mario.

'Something must have triggered Quadrant to
send one of their intercept target forces to the Tree Plantation.
It's possible that the energy fields around both me and James
registered disruption. I guess I may have met with Adriana a
bit ahead of James and yeah, I'm sort of seeing it now. That
GCHQ place of yours is like just a block away from where
you were James—where we are now.

'We're like in the hornets' nest,' I said, and
was beginning to realize that I should probably have kept my
trap shut, but I was into wriggling out of taking the wrap for
the situation, which we now found ourselves in.

'He was just some elderly guy on his way to
work,' I said.

'They're definitely out to take us in for questioning,' said Lara.

'The way they were armed,' Mario said, 'it
reminds me of the National Guard Quadrant guys they
brought into New York recently—nothing was going to stand
in their way.'

'Us in this case,' I said.

There was a slight juddering and the pod jumped a little as
the pod caught overhead on a new connection, which took
us down a corridor leading to the entry point to the airship.
With the diminished light the pod responded by flooding
more light inside.

'We are nearly at our destination,' said
Alexandria. 'Please to wait one moment while I get clearance from the on-board flight attendant and then I will open
the door for you to enter through the boarding lobby. You
will each need one hundred Fit for Life quats to pay for the

journey. Adriana, the Galactic intervener for the Command Force has informed me that you are in possession of the ticket purchase quats. Is that correct?'

'Yes, it is,' said Lara. 'Since you have been talking with Adriana can you tell us when she may return?'

'They never leave, but Adriana has said to me that a hologram presence will be within the shopping centre.' Lara, squeezed Matt's knee and he looked at her. She motioned with her hands that he should remove his virtual helmet. The pod came to a standstill.

The air held sign airship terminal lit up in red surrounded by small clouds that moved around the sign,

'Why are we going in an airship Ma?' asked Matt

'We're flying to a shopping centre—not actually a shopping centre. It's been transformed into a techno food producing complex.

'But why?' demanded Matt. It was really becoming difficult to avoid making up a story about where we were going and what was happening at this point.

CHAPTER 29

JAMES'S GROUP BOARD THE AIRSHIP

'THAT ADRIANA,' SAID MATT, 'she was like Miss Phelps. No one in the class can talk unless she says so.' Mario and I exchanged glances.

'Well, she's important, like Miss Phelps,' said Lara. I wasn't sure that Adriana would have approved of being likened to a school teacher, but it was not so far from the truth. We were like some junior group of students meeting up with the Galactic Command Force.

'The earth is threatened with large rocks from outer space.'

'You mean meteors,' said Matt. 'There is a belt of asteroids and comets out in the Milky Way.' Youngsters seemed already to know so much more about space than I did at the same age.

'Not exactly, they're a group of comets. Some are heading toward the earth. The Adriana person is part of a command force who has seen these comets way outside our solar system on their way through and they will be uninfluenced by the gravitational pull of Jupiter on entry. They want to divert their direction, which presently takes them on collision path toward the earth.'

'What like now?' asked Matt wide eyed and open mouthed.

'And we're going to help them?'

'Sort of,' said Mario.

'That sounds real sticky,' said Matt. Sticky being the word used by kids to show something met with their approval and was kind of hip.

'We're going to be part of several groups heading for Mars. It will be safer there than on earth at the moment.' Matt was more convinced by what Mario said, than me. You could see this in his eyes.

'It's going to be a real space adventure,' said Mario.

'Will there be more room to play in than at the flat?'

'I expect so,' said Lara.

A rush of air could be heard going past the pod as it sped down the tunnel toward the air ship terminal entry point. Matt seemed quite satisfied with the answers given to him by Mario, but I felt at the time, that someone in a higher position of authority would be needed to reassure not only Matt, but the likes of myself and Mario. We walked out of the pod and into the lift that would take us two hundred feet above the tunnel and stop at the boarding entrance.

'Payment will be required to enter the air ship Pluto, which is on hire to the Fit for Life Company. Have you the required amount. Please hold out for analysis.?' Lara produced the banded notes from her bag. A camera accessor and cash assistant auto floated down to examine and then accepted the bundled notes she held out.

'It is all correct we can now proceed. Thank you.' I looked towards where Lara was stood in the centre of the lift. I remembered those early internal conversations that I had. There was a transformational effect when in the work place. That of knowing where limitations existed. Retraction and the guarding of your opinion where decision making was not yours for the taking. Lara finalized, you might say-master minded tactics when we were at an area conference. The adult living wage entitlement that was made universal fifty years earlier meant that salaried work was in effect a bonus. It became crucial not to upset the senior executive layer in the Fit for Life hierarchy. Lara was in that area of monitoring and reporting back. It did not matter whether you were favourably viewed as an individual. It was about meeting sales targets and well just getting the dialogue right. This was in the past now. The galactic intervention, that was my name for it before it became known as the Great Re-appraisal (GR)

I managed in the main to keep my personal life out of the work paradigm. That was until Nina arrived with me at the office party last November. I'd taken her out a couple of times. First it was the DB 12 open top dual electric motored sports model that we arrived in that stunned those on the balcony, clasping party start drinks. Yes, her boss allowed her the use of his Ferrari, as well. They got an eyeful of the car and with me sat next to Nina. The near ankle length imitation mink coat had me fairly relaxed about general impact. You sort of take it as a sort of done deal that the chick in a long coat has a long skirt underneath. Not Nina. Once inside she asked me to help her unravel the coat. This probably best describes the removal of said garment.

'James, be a beau and get it scanned at the foyer,' she said, which I did, but when I turned all that really was on view was Nina's barely covered bottom beneath a pink shaded see-through skirt, twinned with pink pop socks. My eyes must have been on storks, because she said.

'You do like it James? All of this is in your latest holographic catwalk catalogue.' With which she blew me a kiss and wriggled her bottom in much the same way as when she removed a nightdress in the bed room. The problem with this was that the balcony crew-that's the men- mainly- had pursued us inside and got as much of the photo shot of her performance as I did.

'You look delectable,' I said, but knew at the time that this was an inadequate description. I kissed Nina on the left cheek to reaffirm that I was the main player, before someone else might have felt invited. There was not the intention to elicit jealousy or the cry of- "that's some supped up car James," with the implication that it was Nina they meant. Previously, as mentioned, I managed in the main to separate my personal life from work. Company apartments were provided. I told myself that this was not the reason in any way that Nina was attracted to moving in with me. She just needed somewhere to live? Why go down that path? Romantic love is the dream you hang on to as the ideal. Unfortunately brutal self-interest can over-ride this. At the risk of being called a masochist I'd accepted, in my mind that Nina could have settled on any number of door steps and be welcomed into a share of a double or single bed, for that matter. That was the first fault-line in having a girlfriend that appealed to others on first sight. Probably second and third fault line, included in this, as well.

The past is the past. It needs to be cut away like a great slab of regret, from the present. For the first time Lara was no longer exclusively in the role of the boss, that I needed to please in the work place alone. We as a group were transformed into a more complete tribe, where interdependency meant that individually anyone could be pivotal and switch from tribal member to that of a leader role, if the circumstance arose.

'Come on James,' said Lara. I realized that I was the only one not in the lift. Mario had lifted Matt on to a luggage shelf and was pretending to pull on his legs to make him fall. There was a lot of giggling.

-- 'One more passenger. There is one more to make this set of tickets complete.' It wasn't only Lara who wanted me in the lift. The automata was chipping in. I stepped in and the two doors slid together.

'Going up.' The automata called out in a voice

161

like that of a young bell boy of many years ago who might then have manned a lift.

'My name is Timothy and I am delighted to have Fit for Life colleagues and Matthew aboard my lift to the airship,' the voice intoned as we left the pod base area for the airship. The capacity to select voice suitability was now an inherently machine characteristic unless programmed otherwise by a human owner to have a specific voice. I just knew that the machine research mechanisms would have sought out the human operating occupant of lifts, probably as far back as the early twentieth century and decided on creating a voice type, which in this case, was that of a young boy, who had a rather high pitched final delivery when calling out information. The voice a delusion really, because the resources operating it were of many megabyte capacity with powerful search engines.

'There are people you know already aboard the air ship. The galactic force have informed me.

'Good on them to let you in on the act,' I said.

'James, that's not necessary,' said Lara. 'Timothy who is aboard the air ship? Can you tell us, please? The lift stopped with a slight jolt.

'We connect you now to the ship,' said Timothy. 'In answer, to mistress Lara's question please to look at the VDU.' A screen above the lift door lit up and a camera inside the airship picked out the interior from above. An inner-ribbed strengthened structure was clearly visible. The airship was a basic utility unit with an assembly walk area around the outer decking, but with cubicle areas either side of the seated area. This enabled passengers to sleep on long haul flights. There must have been more than sixty people. I started counting. Mario called out,

'There's Jeb and Ana and hey, they should be on a flight back to Washington by now.'

'You recognize people. You will not be with

162

strangers-that's good,' said Timothy, whose voice displayed an empathy, which sounded genuine. This American couple from the earlier skittles match were sat together. The surrounding deck area set away from the central travelling seated area.

'I do hope you have enjoyed your stay in air ship lift 24E,' said Timothy. The doors on the opposite side opened and we were met by two hostesses with the blue and yellow company colours. The vibrant yellow caught in the pleats of the skirt, became visible as they walked towards us. The uniform lapels with the Fit for Life logo also in yellow. Both were tall, one with fair hair. The other aquiline and very dark featured. This I guessed denoted African ancestry. The fair-haired girl welcomed Lara and held out a white gloved hand.

'We've been told about your arrival by Adriana. Would you please all follow us to far side of the airship. I'm Holly and this Mati. There are a few passengers you already know. Holly looked across and smiled at Mario, who was standing next to me. We followed these two across to the refreshment area, which meant walking around the outer deck rim of the airship. There were groups sat at tables, but no one I knew. The passenger content looked no different from any other air ship. I did not know this airship, but there was nothing initially to suggest this one was any different from any other. A section about a quarter of the way around the outer walk way was curtained off.

'There's shipboard entertainment then?' I asked Mati, who was nearby. The whites of her eyes stood out against her deep black complexion when she turned toward me as we walked.

'No there's a platform behind there for visitors, who have to tell you about what is happening.'

'Visitors?' I said.

'Yes, visitors to the company.' I hadn't

interpreted the meaning of the word visitors. After all that was what we could be called. Holly, who was talking to Lara just ahead must have heard our conversation. She stopped momentarily and said,

'Galactic Command Force Visitors?' Mario's and my eyes met. He raised his eyebrows with the realization, no doubt that there was now going to be significant input - more than just the recent holographic presence of Adriana. The strange thing was that I didn't feel apprehensive, but more now a sense of wonder that of all people on earth we had been selected for this mission.

CHAPTER 30

REVELATIONS AND PLANS FOR EARTH EXIT

JEB, SPOTTED US AS we walked across from the table he was sat at. I recognized Ana, but there were two others, which had not been at the skittles match

'Hi, there Lara, James.' Good that you're here Mario. And who's this?' Jeb lowered his towering frame to shake hands with Matt.

'Are you an American footballer?' Matt asked.

'That's right I played for Baltimore-You a fan of American football, then?'

'You look like you're the right size, that's all.' Jeb smiled at Lara, who was giving Matt a mother's look of disapproval before intervening

'Don't be talking to Captain Lucas like that Matt.'

'Captain, you're a Captain as well.' Matt's eyes sparkled with excitement on discovering Jeb was a Captain. Jeb down played his military rank.

'Just Captain of the skittles team, that's all Matt.' Jeb's eyes met Lara's in search of explanation.

'Matt's my son Jeb. He came with me to the Fit for Life Tree Plantation. It was intended to be a quiet afternoon visit.'

'And I was at The White Bear. Well I was last night. But I guess you've had a similar visitation to me.'

'Adriana?' suggested Mario. Jeb nodded.

'Have a seat Lara. Here you guys Mario, James pull up some chairs.' Jeb pointed to an adjoining table.

The chairs were anchored in slots and we lifted first one pair then another to fit in around where Jeb and his party were sat. Buffeting winds could make unsecured furniture break away. By the time, we settled in our seats Lara and Jeb were already discussing their experiences.

'Lara, you're OK, I guess you're as stunned as I am about all this.' said Jeb. Lara was about to reply when Matt grabbed his mother's arm.

'Ma, Ma I'm hungry, thirsty and why can't we go home?'

A hover tray was already in attendance. Lara looked up at Jeb for an explanation.

'Matt,' said Jeb. 'We're not safe here anymore on earth. Everyone in here is going to a safer place.' It was better that Jeb explained the situation with Lara there. I could see Matt looked up to Jeb and that an explanation from him was likely to be believed. I was not one for deception or for euphemistically trying to pretend that we were all off on an adventure and would shortly be returning to our everyday lives.

'Listen to what Captain Lucas has to say Matt.'

'It's to do with that hologram that looks like you Ma isn't it? That Adriana.'

'That's right Matt, you're spot on with that,' said Jeb, who smiled at Lara, as Ana held her hand out to shake Matt's. Mario sat between the two of them and shared pictures of the Skittles match on his tablet.

Jeb sat opposite the three of them and explained the situation.

'Matt, your Ma and all of us are now together as part of a group, who are going to Mars.'

'Really, like forever?' said Matt. This was a question in our minds as well.

'I don't believe so, but there are comets way out in space, which will enter the solar system in a few years time. Adriana is like an announcer, who has been sent to warn us and we are going to help to knock the comets away from the solar system.'

'Are we helping Quadrant to do this?' asked Matt. This seemed a reasonable question.

'It is about saving the earth Matt. We are like a secret group.'

'That will mean no more school, sounds okay,' Matt said as he broke away from looking at pictures of our skittles match.

'No Matt, we are part of a group of one hundred and fifty adults. There will be other children and plenty of teachers,' said Lara. Matt made a face at this remark, but the explanation by Jeb circumvented any mention of Quadrant's deception. This explanation by Jeb to Matt was as much a reassurance to me as to Matt. A hover tray arrived.

'Would you like to make an order?' the tray directed the question to Lara,

'Can I have a maxi maker burger and chips and a cake. And a fruit soda drink.' Asked Matt immediately.

'They may not have that on the airship.'

'We do,' said the tray. 'It is no trouble with the Fit for Life Maxi Maker to produce this for you. Lara placed an order.

'A burger, small chips, lemon drizzle cake.' Matt made a face at this. 'Also an apple soda for my son. I'll have the same but salad instead of chips.'

'Hey Jeb whose got the Quats to pay for this?' asked Mario. The familiarity of procedures is something you can go for in stressful situations.

'The company will pick up the cheque.'

The menu was rolled out beneath the tray. The order

worded in red against a cream background. The first and last letter of each dish made to sparkle to attract your attention. Particles fired continuously to form the menu pattern in the air beneath the tray.

'Then I'll have a Mexican tortilla wrap with ham, cheese and fries plus a large Americano with cream and yep, I'll have the lemon drizzle cake like Matt,' said Mario.

'I'd like the same as Lara's,' said Lydia. Elsie the kitten was now on a lead out of her basket.

'And can cat food be produced by the Maxi Maker.

'But of course,' said the tray and the flavour?'

'Chicken and beef?'

'I bring this food with water in a bowl for your cat.' This was perhaps of more significance than my order, but the tray which would have scanned our profiles on arrival spoke to me in a manner intended to flatter.

'Mr James Walters. It is with pleasure to have you aboard. Our community is so impressed with your range of abilities and interest in solar energy technique. May I take your order?' I was able to scan the menu on my tablet.

'Chicken with honey and mustard sauce, followed by chocolate airship special mousse, whatever that is - and a Latte with cream.

'An excellent selection Mr Walter's, if I may say.' Not that it bothered me what some automata thought about my meal selection.

'We've eaten,' said Jeb,' but tray refresh this jug of coffee will you. You guys and Ana –you want something more?'

'Chocolate and lime milk shake. That's what I'll have Jeb,' said Ana. This sounded pretty disgusting to me. One of the two American guys said

'Two cokes will do us Jeb, and returned to watching a miniature hologram rocket launch tower on the table in front of them. His companion was blanking out and replacing holographic struts and supports. Far to engrossed in this operation to give a reply.

'Thank you for your orders,' It will be no more than ten minutes.'

'Thank you everyone,' said the hover tray. 'Menu to now close.' The display rolled up into a scroll, like it was made of a paper material. The scrolled menu looked like a tubular light strip before it dimmed and disappeared.

The American guy spoke confidently and I guessed they ranked alongside Jeb. Probably more on the scientific techno side. The tee shirts, long hair and triple screen tablets that appeared to share information one with the other, suggested they were more attuned to holographic signs and symbols and dialogue with others outside of their screens. We were all now sat around the one table and Lara gazed toward the interior of the airship.

'There must be a hundred or more inside here, Jeb. Are they all Fit for Life employees?'

'Not all, because there are family groups. That's whenever possible, according to Colonel Peter's.' Matt was back to his hologram tablet, which was now assessing miniature versions of logging trucks, which gave presence on the table in front.

Now that food was ordered he seemed happy. The two Americans stopped their interact with holographic symbols and like me and Mario were listening in on Jeb and Lara's talk. Trays zipped across overhead with drinks and meals with others returning plates and cutlery etc. from earlier meals

'And you've met this alien creature then?' asked Lara.

'Adriana your cosmic twin?'

'Yes, I suppose there is a likeness.' Jeb did not comment.

'Yep, I've had a visit or is it- visitation? She or the hologram were here.

'I feel that I should be stunned or in a state of shock, but I'm not,' said Lara.

'You've like just arrived then Jeb?' she continued.

'Not long ago. I sort of got zapped while at the White Bear and taken to my chalet in Florida. I was on virtual. Well that's what I believed. The White Bear virtual facility. One minute I was talking with a chalet representative. You know all sugary smile and apparently available, but looking for a sales commission.' Lara gave a raised eyebrow look, as if to say she didn't understand how sales women work their charm. Jeb meanwhile pored himself a coffee before continuing.

'Then, this Adriana appeared and she brought in Colonel Peters and the board. They were there backing up Adriana on the screen in the chalet. You couldn't make it up.

'What about all these people? Asked Lara.

'Yeah, well they've all been zapped at some point.' The word zapped did not seem to be quite the right description.

'What and where is Adriana now? Is she in hologram or imitating me? asked Lara. Matt was ahead of everyone in finishing his meal.

'Ma there's an activity area over there. Can I go over with the other kids. There must have been about a dozen or more and were supervised by a humanoid automata. Unlike an adult human in the role they maintained a high level of enthusiasm and never tired of giving praise where due and encouragement, delighting in the children's interaction with play machines, which were beneath there A++ grade capability.

'Don't worry yourself Lara, I'll go over with Matt,' said the woman called Lydia or AL.

'There's a sleep area Jeb then asked Mario?' who interrupted the one to one chat of Jeb and Lara.

'That's all arranged Mario.' said Jeb. 'The plan is to get the children settled for the night. There's going to be some information from the Galactic Command Force-from that stage area.' Jeb jerked his thumb toward the translucent green curtain, which concealed I presumed a performance stage.

'An update before we go to the beach.'

'The beach—what beach?' asked Ana, who called out. 'The last time we were told it was Leeds shopping centre. Change of plan?' Lara's face lit up and I followed her gaze to the entrance area. Heidi, Annette and Jo had just arrived. Holly and Mati were receiving them aboard the airship. Lara said,

'Keep an eye on Matt and Lydia will you,' and went across to meet them. Members from skittle teams had been selected for the mission group by the look of it. In another context this could be the assembly of a religious cult, drawn from across the world. Fit for Life, that is the company was playing a major role. I wouldn't have had Jeb down for someone who would have gone along with just a visitation from Adriana. How far back did the senior executives get involved with the mission? More than a mission to Mars this earth life-saving attempt.

'How did you three get included?' I asked, as they arrived with Lara to where we were all sitting.

'James you say that as if we're not up to standard,' said Annette. They were similarly dressed in jeans and unzipped fleeces, which meant the Fit for Life Log was

171

clearly visible on their tee shirts beneath.

'No I meant how did you meet up with-'

'Adriana?' Annette finished my question.

'We were in the virtual display access studio in the White Bear James, earlier today. Out of nowhere our virtual skittles game was taken away and we were shown pictures of the Tree Plantation where you were. There was a Caption picture of the four of you inside the Restaurant.'

'That's all three of you were playing the virtual game?

Yes, Heidi, Jo and me were all in the virtual game together. It was scary, because we could hear Quadrant making plans to storm the building. Then I did a double take. I actually called out Hi Lara-have you got a new boyfriend- I thought you'd changed your hair colour. The Adriana figure really looked like Lara. We believed it to be you Lara, but with fair hair.'

'The fair hair made me think the same as Annette,' said Heidi.

'I thought somehow you had re-played as a hologram outside, but the person I saw had fair hair,' continued Annette. The hologram just said I'm Adriana and we were all directed to come out of the virtual world and look at the screen in the access studio.'

'We were contacted by Colonel Peters, and the American board.'

'Sure, same as me then,' said Jeb with Ana nodding her head in agreement.

We were in our room, that's me and Julie and visited by a hologram of Adriana.

'It was scary, because normally hologram access is blocked.

'Not from the Galactic Command Force,' I said.

'You know that for sure James,' asked Annette.

'Pretty sure, because they wouldn't have been able to set all this up in the first place. They need to basically come and go as they please without being blocked by earth based protectors. Otherwise they just couldn't have got us all here like this.'

Across the air ship there were groups, which were like stations, maybe discussing like us what had happened, but also in a fairly relaxed manner. Everyone perhaps realized that without intervention from the Galactic Command Force there would not only be destruction of the biosphere, which was earth, but world hysteria could break out when it was realized that leaders of Quadrant had escaped to save their skins, but had no intention of saving anyone else!'

'You were taken away from the virtual world, like me then,' said Jeb. I was very relaxed and expected only to visit my Florida Chalet—and now this!

Lara was sitting opposite to Jeb, but walked across to view his info pad. I assisted Mario in finding chairs for Heidi Annette and Jo. Control of viewing and operating systems is automatically deployed to senior personnel. Jeb would likely be the most senior in the air ship. He would have the capability to override systems to glean information and introduce new input, as well. Lara would be aware of this. Jeb's status was at least that of Captain, not just of the skittles team.

The light fell from the screen pictures appeared around the higher extremities of the airships sides, which caused everyone to look up to view the pictures of the surrounding country side. Lara may have suggested the need to find out the lie of the land, but left the group to settle Matt for the night. A sign appeared that stated "All persons with parental charges should now settle children in the accommodation provided for their group." The holographic group number lit on and off just above our table. A slight disturbance occurred while a number of adults, men and women left the tables to locate offspring or parental charges.

This was the procedure on normal over-night flight, although this one was far from normal.

It was highly alarming to see that fleets of Quadrant forces were approaching from several directions at once. The screen tracking measure showed that they were only three miles away from the airship's docked position. An estimated time of arrival appeared as thirty minutes with a second by second reduction in progress as the distance shrank on their approach. Annette and all of us stopped talking. A silence followed across the ship from all groups.

We looked at the panoramic screen. It quickly dawned on me, as I expect it did others, that we were trapped inside the air ship. I felt the hairs on my neck start to rise. I visualized a report, which stated that the destruction of the airship was an accident. The vehicles could be seen stopping after the camera lenses focused in closer. Port holes opened automatically and missiles could be seen emerging preparatory to a strike. Two figures stepped out of the lead vehicle.

'Holy cow,' called out Jeb. The intake of breath by people in the groups was audible. Where was the Galactic Command Force now? Went through my mind.

'Jeb, can you access the camera function?' I asked. Group leader company tablets often had this facility.

'What do you want to see James?'

'A close up of the two figures.'

'Sure I can do that for you.' This move to close up mimicked the fast run of a speeding vehicle, which made the view of the approaching Quadrant force even more terrifying, but the close up of the two figures, showed a Quadrant officer with electronic beam binoculars studying the airship while listening in for any radio or holographic chatter. A bulky, possibly once more athletic figure wearing Quadrant insignia. Next to him there was a man dressed in what appeared to be medical officer's dress with red crosses on the epaulettes. The face looked familiar. It was Frederick Stanley from the train.

'Thanks, Jeb. Just kind of interested to see what these two looked like-in case we meet them again.'

'That's close enough for me,' said Jeb. I spotted Adriana among those at the bar, but the now materialized figure merged in with the hostesses in a Fit for Life uniform. Adriana walked across to the escalator running up toward the pilot's quarters. The blue docked lights changed to red and then green immediately after she entered the cockpit. The air ship was in flight and the shuddering from the main frame of the balloon above together with the swish of the four forward propellers quickly alerted everyone. Adriana returned to the cabin area and the amplified voice said

'We have left. We are journeying away from the air ship terminal. They will see us, but we will not be there now.' At first I believed that some time shift must have facilitated this, but the explanation was simpler.

'Our destination is the West Saharan coast of the African continent. It will be near to a beach and you will find there will be temperature change,' said Adriana. The last comment was to state the obvious.

'Not disappointed are you James?' Adriana asked. 'That we are no longer taking you to that former Leeds Shopping centre. It was a miss-direction for the Quadrant Force and necessary to pretend we were going there.'

'No, I'm no way disappointed. I can see that they're pretty keen to get hold of us. Not in a good way.'

'We will have visitors to talk with you. They are former inhabitants, who will be re-introduced to wish you well. Adriana walked from the bar to the stage area. Her voice occupied the interior of the ship. It also repeated inside my head like a thought transference. Perhaps it was not really an auditory communication at all, but like a communication band which looped into our minds.

175

CHAPTER 31

PERSUASIVE TALK FROM VISITORS

'It is good that we have moved, everything material, that is the airship, its contents and all of you to Real Time. Quadrant is destroying everything in its path.

We are not available for destruction, but we have distracted the Quadrant surveillance group Force, for now.' Adriana continued updating us with what was happening. "Available for destruction was not a good place to be."

Up to this point I was relieved to have been taken away from the terminal. But surely, we were not unreachable by Quadrant. Air ships did not achieve any great speed.

'We wait for parental persons in charge of young persons to return,' said Adriana, who was now standing in front of the curtained off entertainment area. This kind of answered the question about time. Within their real time, we were being given an apparent state of time. The time which would likely elapse before the parental persons returned

'This is a holographic representation of The Fit for Life airship. Adriana pointed to the screen view above the curtains, which apart from lighting up with a picture showed the airship and platform beneath in flames.

'How can it be incinerated like that?' asked Mario. 'When we're not there?'

'It is still holographic translation,' said Adriana in a matter of fact way.

'Wow, what do you think of that James? Asked Mario. I could only say,

'That's totally amazing. They'll believe they've destroyed the ship and us, as well

'Yes, we have the ability to produce remains, but this will not be necessary. They can watch and believe they have achieved their task. Until that is the hologram is shut down.'

'That they've destroyed one hundred and fifty people,' said Lara, in disbelief.

'We could've re-produced DNA and other remains, but they are satisfied with what they see. Quadrant will believe for now, that you were all destroyed in this attack.'

'Gosh James,' said Annette it's pretty horrifying to think that people might believe that there could be more than one of you in existence.' There was laughter from some at the table about this.

'And of you Annette,' I came in with.

'Annette is nice enough to be duplicated any number of times. The world would be a better place for more Annette's,' said Heidi. There was no way I was going to win with such a predominately female representation around our table. How it worked I would likely never fathom, but info-pads were still operating and everyone save Jeb and myself seemed to be occupied with operating these. I was caught up with that horrific view of destruction, which would have included us, while others were still glued to the tablet pictures.

We all made regular visits to a virtual world as observers and even participants perhaps implanting a sense that our physical presence was not a total requirement to remain as an existing entity. There were tales of mediums calling past life into re-existence through knocks or even speech, but I preferred not to become available for being called from another place. Maybe it was just that my imagination was more vivid than anyone else's.

The horrific picture of the blazing airship was replaced with a long stretch of sandy coastline, which I did not recognize.

Voices could be heard as mostly mothers came out of the

177

dormitory area. The ability to materialize the replica interior of an airship, when the earth original was no more was phenomenal, but yet I considered we had devised machinery to produce food and have product stamped out to a stipulated deign. The Galactic Command force could evidently re-construct matter. This creative move, of de-construction and re-construction I'd experienced on Stroud Station. It made me consider whether they had the ability to move a whole planet into their dimension and if so why not move the whole earth away from the path of the comets from outside the planetary system. The airship was many times larger than Stroud waiting room.

There were categories like time, movement, and even material across dimensions, which might never be understood, by humans, I realized. These thoughts were interrupted by Adriana's sometime metallic voice attempting to sound reassuring. Adriana's voice kept a recognizable timbre, but differed from that of Lara's. More the voice of a strict ward sister or teacher who was not going to take any sexist remarks from boy students.

A quick count revealed about thirty responsible adults returning to their places on the tables that were on a level circling above the main accommodation seating area for when in flight. Adriana walked away from the bar area, which was directly opposite and was now standing on the right hand side of the curtained stage. You could say all eyes were on this being. The gender definition was yes, from my male perspective attractively feminine, but also of that persuasion of personality, which made women admiring rather than resentful of the attractiveness transmitted. To that extent, Adriana was able to secure results of the women in the group and then probably the men. Attractive women can, as the saying goes, get away with murder when they turn their charm on to win over men. Adriana was a very attractive female in appearance, but dedicated to the ethos of the galactic Command Force. At that time, I felt this very strongly.

There was quiet save for the intermittent creaking from the fabric of the airship when a sudden gust of wind caught the large shape above, while we were suspended beneath in the cabin area. We were not in an implied reality; if we were, it was, very convincing.

'Now you are settled,' Adriana began talking once everybody was seated.

'We are taking the continuum of existence to the West Coast of Africa. It is where we have assembled five ships beneath the ocean to transport key ingredients to Mars. It is best that we build from existing earth material to produce a uniformity on Mars, that you will understand. It may be necessary to land you all on a beach isolated from near by habitation, although we aim to merge the disconnected cabin boat portion with other craft already in position. This area is a holiday destination. Our air ship will not attract attention. This, has been a diversion as explained to distract Quadrant forces and allow space to remove you all ultimately from earth to Mars.'

'Just like that?' asked Jeb. His voice resonated across the interior of the airship. Was that a restlessness across the tables expressed in whispered talk?

'You move us about like pawns on a chess board. We're being asked to leave our homes and you expect us to just sit and listen and accept everything you say.' There were murmurings of agreement from both men and women.

'Not only our homes, but even the planet we have lived on for generations.' Jeb really voiced what most of us were now thinking. Events, particularly with the arrival of the armed Quadrant response unit at the tree plantation and now the intended destruction of the air ship frightened us and defined the extreme threat we were under from Quadrant. The comets path through the heavens and the graph time explanations, that were shown to us in the Tree Plantation formed my main basis for belief in a very real celestial threat. Perhaps Jeb had not been shown these. Perhaps we all knew about pieces of the jigsaw, but that they were not all in position and we only held parts of the main picture. That other significant information was still withheld. Lara was talking to Jeb. Perhaps explaining our experiences in the Tree Plantation.

'I'm not a doctor, but this changing from one material existence to another could damage our hearts, lungs—'continued Jeb.

'End your sex life,' said Adriana.

'Yes that too.' The young women on the table smiled. Possibly at the thought that Captain Jeb Lucas was still in the running for it. Since Nina walked out, things on that front had quietened down. Though I still needed to look away often times when excitement heightened just from looking at Lara.

'No, there is no danger. We refresh your blood and unclog arteries, strip out undetected cancerous growth. Those who have artificial inserts will have had these returned to their former natural health. We need to make you fit to re-produce –if you wish, of course.'

'Sounds good to me.' said Mario. Heidi and Annette giggled. I don't think they reckoned there to be much physically wrong with Mario from a woman's perspective.

'But, we also understand that you have a biological memory, that you are unaware of. This is kept in the genetic structure. Particularly the brain and what you call the mind. It is beyond your understanding in your present development. We do not wish to be superior.

'That's the pot calling the saucepan black,' I whispered, but loud enough for the table occupants to hear.

Annette, Jo and Heidi understood, but the Americans looked a bit vague. There was no doubting the Galactic Forces superior development intellectually, but there did seem problems on the emotional front, but then the re-productive physical male and female concept required for fertilization had been replaced by independent mutation probably way back in their historical evolvement. The whispered talk stopped when a tray drone arrived and hovered next to Adriana.

Some might not believe it, but for me at any rate, there was deference, a more attentive manner in the way a hover tray or any automata reacted, for that matter, when in Adriana's presence. It was as if they recognized a status magnitude beyond that of humans. Respect, yes, but in spades. Placed on the tray was a luminescent remote control, which Adriana picked up.

'Our commander has decided after accessing biological background resource of your ancestor recollection that conscious self-security may be enhanced through meeting with chosen leader authority recommendation from your earth history.

'Say that again?' said Jeb. You needed someone in a group who interrupted to ask questions that need asking, because otherwise the narrative can be lost through lack of plain explanations. Jeb was fulfilling that role.

'We, that is senior power elements within galactic command have been instructed to visit four arenas of human activity, where there has been input to the human psyche from individual leaders.

'We will bring these persons to you on the stage of the airship. They no longer live in your time frame, but we have appraised these images of outstanding humans, not necessarily because of their individual physical achievements while in your earth plane, but because they did on earth evolve to hold ability to see how bad pattern behaviour can destroy or obliterate a good future. These former earth

181

bound humans want life to continue. They will show their support and encouragement. They understand that there are forces, which interfere with good outcomes. Not just the destructive influence of comets traveling through space, but also dangerous groups who seek to prevail on earth. Such a group has achieved excess power and that is bad for planet earth. We have the capacity to divert the trajectory of this lead comet and take the group out toward the far reaches of the cosmos. But the new direction for your race and planet needs self-determination from you and your people.

'Quadrant, you mean Quadrant. We're all very much there with that understanding. They aren't the good guys, that's for sure,' said Jeb.

Adriana, lifted her arm, which held the remote control toward the theatre curtains. We were all, those of us who'd travelled aboard airships familiar with these curtained theatre stage spaces. Within authoritarian state structures there can be positive elements, which improve the lives for some groups. I approved of the live theatre performance installation, which Quadrant instigated. Real actors, musicians, story tellers and entertainers were allowed to perform and earn a living in front of passengers and crew. It was a standard addition on all long-haul air ships. The building of air ship terminals above main train stations were also inspirational, by Quadrant, but if ever a situation arose where absolute power corrupts then Quadrant was an ideal example of this for all its infrastructure re-build in recent years.

A stillness from expectancy and interest swept across the groups around the stage, as the curtains unfolded. The stage was empty right back to the far wall, which was draped with a green Fit for Life banner with the running figure in the middle. There was impatient movement and noise from across the air ship when the stage was seen to be empty. Suddenly with what can best be described as four flumes of light equidistant one to the other formed across the middle of the stage. Purple, Red, Blue and Yellow. We were now in what I considered our earth dimension, but I'd never seen such vibrant colours together like this on a stage. Much more startling to view than any earth light spectrum. But they didn't hurt the eyes for all their brightness. This spectacular energy source, gave out heat, which you would not want to be any closer to than we were. Individually they made that flaring sound that you get from lighted gas. This may have been deliberately facilitated to focus the groups attention.

When Adriana looked back from viewing the stage I'm sure I noticed a human look of relief flood over her face. It was as if she was relieved that the transmission had been effective, so far. That her force members were in the vicinity and here to assist. I didn't know it at the time, but Adriana risked a merge with our biological time framed existence. The Galactic Command force were a race of beings, I later understood, which required to energize and re-energize time and again if they parted from the main body group.

The best explanation is that Adriana took oxygen cylinders with her like a diver beneath the ocean. The difference was that the being she had evolved to be could be absorbed by over much biological interaction. Hence the holographic appearances. Although these appearances reduced infection over time the hologram could by degrees print into our time frame.

There was a stillness and quiet now attuned to genuine expectancy. An expectancy that the Galactic Command force would unveil crucial information and insight. It was as if everyone sensed that a momentous event was about to unfold. As mentioned the pureness of light within the colours defied description. The light intensity was unearthly in that there was a constancy of intensity and power, which made you feel that the power behind the colours was immense. Explanation came from Adriana.

'These are colours out of which we adapt to build entities from outside of the realms of both time and space. The Galactic space leaders are about to reveal constructs of willing visitors from the dimensions, which are kept in what you might call a vault that is normally outside of earth time record. Do not be alarmed, but I will now revert to a Galactic hologram.

The physical person of Adriana by the stage vanished to be replaced by a life sized hologram. This did not phase Jeb who was quick to question what was going on.

'Where's this earth time record kept? It's not in Washington state then,' asked Jeb. A smile flitted across the holographic representation.

'Not Washington state, the place, but we have brought for you a certain George Washington.' The purple light vanished to be replaced by a gentleman in eighteenth century clothing. I was not sure the Americans present necessarily recognized who this person was.

There was a lifelike quality that matched Adriana's. In case there was any misunderstanding a sign appeared in lit suspension above. A name plate, which said—George Washington 1732-99.

'Geeze, it can't be, said Jeb.

'We decided that the former president would most likely be listened to by you Jeb,' said Adriana.

'Jeb, like the name,' the President doffed his hat to all those of us assembled before continuing. 'I'd not be minded to be called Jeb. It's a kind of new States world name I like,' said this representation of George Washington, who must have been resourced from the Command forces deep space files.

'Times were hard in my day Jeb, I believe you and this Fit for Life group of adventurers can achieve great things-if you go with the Command force as directed to Mars. They have visited and shown me pictures of what has happened on earth out in our ether habitation. I lived in times when the stars were just out there twinkling. We knew them as beacons to give us positions and from history they had fine names from out of olden times. Mars god of war, but now there can be a haven for you all here. Adriana has shown how it is now on earth and a great power rules over all peoples. But with the vanities and cupidity that I recognize from my time. That we escaped the oppressiveness of the over lording from across the seas to become free and self-affirming.

This is a time for another renewal for the human spirit that demands progress independent of tyranny and oppression. It needed to be learned in my country that slavery had to go. This has returned to haunt your world with no genuine freedom. All spied upon and monitored. Yes it is far worse than you can imagine.' The silver topped cane, by his side he raised and shouldered. The black ebony sparkled as he brought the cane down and made it leave his hand and bounce off the floor with a tap like an auctioneers hammer on the completion of a sale. This move was, no doubt well practised, because he was on his feet to catch it a quarter way down its length before it could clatter to the floor.

'Love to see and listen to all that you have to say, Mr President,' said Jeb. I looked across the table and all the American team, especially Mario looked animated and interested in what this pre-formed George Washington had said. The forming of the constitution and the role he had played still resonated in the historical memory of Americans. Still recognized as the birth pangs of the nation, which long preceded the dawning of the age of Quadrant. This person facsimile created by the Force radiated an aura, yes from another age,

185

but all the more impressive for the ability to attract attention through this authoritative speech, which addressed all of us although seeming only to identify Jeb in the introduction.

The President looked upwards and around the interior of the airship cabin imagined somehow by the Command Force to replace the original, but looking identical in every respect to it.

'This is a damn goodly made machine. It beats the interior of any covered wagon I travelled in,' he said. I looked across to where Lara was sitting opposite. She smiled after looking at the faces of both Jeb, Mario and Ana Their faces transmitted looks of adulation and approval from the speech given to us all.

'Thank you, Mr President for your participation and fine speech,' said Adriana from the side of the stage. The imposing figure bowed toward Adriana before sitting back in the arm chair.

'That chair was in the old White House. The museum, which was once the home of the American president, Julie whispered to Mario loud enough for us all to hear. Attention from all other group tables was focused on us and in particular Jeb and Lara. Group leaders who they would all recognize from Fit for Life holographic transmissions into their work settings.

'Lara,' called out Adriana. 'You were once Lara McTavish were you not?' It was no good asking how Adriana knew this, because it was later made clear that they had access to a cosmic file, which was a record of everyone and every event on earth, since the dawn of time. A mere blink, no doubt, in the total passage of cosmic universe evolution.

'My mother's name is McTavish, yes,' said Lara, who looked perplexed by this question. My mother's family are from a long Scottish ancestry –way back before America was even discovered.' A wry smile swept across the President's face. I once tried to win affection from Lara, by saying my family had Scottish relatives, but this didn't impress. They were from the lowlands, not the Highlands. The red flame I felt was appropriate for the next character's appearance. The flames of coloured light were like reservoirs for the Galactic Command force to introduce apparent human life form into.

The birds in a cage chatter had ceased. All groups enthralled by the stage presentation of George Washington. I didn't know the full mix of employees and close relatives. We, that's Lara, myself Annette, Jo and Heidi plus the two back room guys represented the Britain arm of Fit for Life. The remainder of the total group were from outposts across the world. American culture-the understanding of it would have been high requirement for these employees selected from across the globe, I was considering, even though many would be from different nation cultures. The convincing recreated figure of George Washington, who was now sat on the stage looked exactly like the pictures hung on the walls of the Fit for Life Washington Headquarters, which I visited last year. A good symbolic figure from American historical past to persuade most of those here about the urgency and need for this action. That they could play a significant part.

An accumulation of factually, indisputable events and now the failed attempt to blast us out of existence was absolute evidence that Quadrant were seeking to destroy us and yes, even the destruction of the earth could be seen as collateral damage. They must be convinced that we were destroyed, for the moment, but would they be convinced that the Galactic Command Force were prepared to leave the earth to its destruction? All eyes were on Adriana when she next spoke.

'You will be interested to see who next we have selected to talk with you. Adriana directed the remote toward the red flame.

The male figure who replaced the flame when it dimmed

wore a black frock coat with a white frilled cravat type shirt. That's the best I can describe it to you and like the President wore a hat, which I believe was once called a stove hat. The dress suggested that the era of life was close if not contemporaneous with George Washington. Dark hair jutted out above penetrating eyes. It was Lara who appeared to recognize this person from out of the eighteenth century.

'It's Robbie Burns. It is, isn't it?' Lara looked at Adriana for affirmation. The name Robert Burns appeared in the suspended descriptive name sign. Robert Burns 1759-1796. He removed his hat and spoke to Lara.

'I canna say we've met, but it's been too long a time for one sah bonnie.' He returned his hat and continued.

'I've been here a time hearing all the word that's been saying. I know about slaves. It was the way it was back then. I would not to be wanting the work for a slave owner, but they were hard times, as I recall.' There was a ripple of whisperings. People in the group appeared to know of Robert Burns and his life on earth and the memory of it. He was stopped in his tracks. I could see he was looking at Adriana then at Lara.

'Ah, now, how canne it be that two so bonnie on this earth, but with both beauty and with hair both fair and dark.

'Robbie, my name is Adriana and I represent the command force, as you well know. We are not sisters. I am only in this form. I have no interest in a power of attraction that disables human sense. This mission needs me to be wholly convincing as a human woman, that is all,' said Ariana.

'You've nay convinced Robbie Burns that you'd not be a man's chosen dream, when ere he might meet ye, abroad t' the Highlands.' Lara I could see was entranced by this lively character the command force had brought into being on the stage. Adriana was keen to take forward the plan to ensure we were invigorated and enthused from meeting these characters from human history to stoke emotions that made us feel now part of human destiny.

'My mother would recite your verse and dance to the tune of Auld Lang zyne. I just know that she would be thrilled to be here-but I am as well,' said Lara. This effect of enthusing us was being achieved I could see.

'Robert Burns,' said Adriana taking control. 'We have traced ancestors of yours to this day.' His dark eyes twinkled when she said this.

'The earth still holds your blood line. The memory of your words and sayings resonate for them and many others. The red component power leader has explained to you the threat that the planet beneath us is under—and you know perfectly well that I am not a female human, but only a temporary creation-yes?'

'Ock, Adriana you make a fine-looking lassie, and that's a fact. You have indeed explained this. I canna say other. Suspense can be worse than disappointment. Tis true also that I once said that my heart is in the highlands chasing the deer. But for both head and heart to be here yon earth needs to stay as it be. Man's inhumanity to man makes countless thousands moan.

This, powerful hierarchy will not stay to mind the flock. No more would they in my day when their own skins were at risk. Like those of thee I've been shown the army of comets swooping through the heavens surely to hit the earth. Maybe I did once say there is no such uncertainty as a sure thing. I would like it to be true for these comets rushing toward earth. Where it is impossible to prevent this collision, you would be able to live to fight another day if you go with Adriana and the Command Force to the Mars station. It is a do or die situation.' He then reached across and momentarily held the hand of George Washington before sitting down. The hologram

Adriana appeared next to the blue flame on stage.

'Now we have selected a female representation from your time capsule. We go back into a time when your medicine was undeveloped and many lives were lost. There was little scientific knowledge, yet we have found here mystic understanding,' said Adriana. The blue flame became translucent, but within could be seen a hooded seated figure, who held a cross.

'We do not have preference for either male or female figures. It is that which in your history they represented. We neither agree nor disagree, but they have formed part of your appreciation for what is right and wrong and how you have looked outside your material world to find meaning.' A haze, like dawn on the footfalls of a mountain formed beneath the seated figure, as the colour disappeared.

'We cannot reveal, who this person is, because it is her wish not to be revealed by her earth time name. We know her only from searches into files of your awakening understandings, through the centuries. These forward moves though often destroyed by those who sort power and control over the earth.'

'Adriana, why am I here?' It was apparent from the robe and dress that this woman was from a religious order. Quadrant recognized the need to keep in place the concept of religion and many still worshipped in churches and temples. Each religion held a licence, which ran for five years, subsequently reviewed by the new sector power. The priests and officiates re-applying for office, within their denominations.

'I understand that once again the peoples on earth are tormented by earthly desire for power greed and ownership of wealth,' the woman turned toward the hologram Adriana with an understanding smile on her face.

'You recovered from serious illness and you were in those days an obscure person, that the authorities were

190

not overly concerned about. We know you wrote of visions and you have been shown how comets threaten this planet's existence, but you tell us that it is sin that has been the cause of strife on earth, yet you still hold that there is hope and that all manner of thing will be well. You have been shown our plans and design for a new life on Mars for this group and you would want the earth to be saved from destruction?'

'Adriana, you ask from me more than is in my power to give to these peoples, but I would that they would be saved not just in their daily lives, but in continued existence as individuals. The pictures you have shown me of this planet called Mars. That it is now rocky barren and inflicted with extremes of temperature and then you show me that it is to have seas, lakes and vegetation. Air to breathe?'

'Yes, air and clouds that will bring rain and wind.'

'I believe this to be your intention. You must show this to these people, as well.' It was only Lydia on our table group, who appreciated who this historic person was or represented. The blue light absorbed the figure once more and she was, presumably returned to the plane of existence now inhabited.

'Lara,' said Lydia I must respect this woman's request not to reveal her name, but I remember those words, from reading about mysticism. Lara, whispered something to Lydia, which none of us heard.

'Can we see these before and after pictures then? asked Jeb.

'Yes, but there is one more visitor. He is from your American past and we decided that his comments will be well received by many in your organization.

CHAPTER 32

FINAL WORDS OF RE-ASSURANCE AND ENCOURAGEMENT

IT WAS LYDIA WHO said,

'I'd so liked to have asked questions about her life and now she's gone.' Lara nodded in agreement, while there was no stopping Adriana.

'Mr President and Robert Burns, thank you for your visits. We will allow you to return to your realms. The red and purple flares, which captured these two personalities on the stage of the airship immediately returned. The one remaining yellow flare moved from left stage to centre stage, near to the Adriana hologram. The quiet in the airship was broken by a burst of rain, which substituted you might say for a drum roll, as it slaked the body of the airship and across one side of the large cabin. It died away as suddenly as it arrived.

Adriana announced the arrival of our last visitor, with her hand held out toward the yellow flare.

A person who wrote about your human condition leaving many memorable comments.' The yellow flare turned translucent and within could be seen a figure, who wore a coat not dissimilar to that worn by the President. A younger man with dark brown hair and moustache.

'Whose this guy then? It was Mario, this time not Jeb, who called out. The guy replied and not Adriana.

'Mark Twain was not the name I was born with, but the one that stuck with me. Many thanks Adriana for taking me aboard. My time on the steam boats were happy ones. This airship's cabin brings memories of cabins back in my day, then. Yep, I do believe I could be as happy on an airship as a river boat, if there was that opportunity. And there you go is this not a goodly assortment of passengers? You will want me to give words of support. I'm happy to do that.'

'You understand the limitations of under-standing for the human species, Mark. We know that you want to encourage this mission. You appreciate how earth specie react.

'Yep, so right. So like to be with you all, but cannot be. This Quadrant governing body are not good guys from what I've been shown. I've adapted some of the phrases that still exist in earth time vocabulary. Loyalty now to the earth, all the time, loyalty to the government when it deserves it. The present set-up sure doesn't. I want to believe that you are accomplishers. You are not a crowded group. One hundred and fifty is not many, at all, out of an earth population of nine billion; but I once stated that whenever you find yourself on the side of the majority it's sure time to reflect. Guess that's where you all are now. The secret of getting ahead is getting started. That I really believe and here you are started on this journey. This journey to the planet Mars. Look at the pictures the Galactic Command Force will show you. Consider the alternatives. We four have visited this Real-Time frame created in the cabin of this re-constructed airship to encourage and back you in this mission. The planes of our dimensions were brought into the Real Time frame to be with you before the start of this momentous journey. The Galactic Command Force approached our varied planes of existence and we have willingly visited to get your imagina-tions into focus. I've always believed that there is nothing that cannot happen today. Good fortune to you all and go forward together onward, onward always onward.'

The yellow flare of light encircled the figure described as Mark Twain before he returned to sit on what looked like a steamer's deck bench. For a few seconds the flare remained on the stage before vanishing like the purple, red and blue before.

'We will return any person who wishes to leave the expedition to safe locations which they are familiar with.' The children now sleeping are the future and we would prefer for you all to stay.

'We entreat with you to join with us to securely colonize Mars, but most importantly for you to assist in building a projectile that can be sent to course alter the lead comet. Experts within your group have been selected to follow our plans to re-construct a prepared rocket which can alter trajectory on impact. Your scientists, engineers and data experts are considered necessary contributors to build technological understanding of future space enterprise. We will assist in showing how this can be done, but you will become a colony of contributors who will propagate life systems. We also have plans to release gases and vapour from within the core of Mars and to build both a sea and an atmosphere similar to yours. As our visitor and Jeb has requested we will show a ten picture progress development for the planet Mars. The final picture will show that the planet will in many ways resemble the earth planet you are about to leave.

These comets are like stampeding cattle that have to be directed to a safe station further into the universe beyond your solar system.' Jeb and Mario appeared to like the reference to stampeding cattle. No one in Adriana's audience called out or asked to be removed from the expedition. The curtains closed across the stage.

CHAPTER 33

AIRSHIP MAKES FOR AFRICAN COAST

'CAPTAIN DRYSON,' ADRIANA SPOKE loudly enough into a connecting pad to the pilot's cabin for us all to hear. A figure, which at first looked like a diver came through the cabin door and out on to the viewing platform. The black suit was interrupted by steel bands along the wrists arm joints and neck area for articulation. Four gold bands on each lower arm denoted the rank of Captain. The head with human protuberances, like nose, ears, cheeks and hair that resembled our features, including flopped blond hair addition with a left sided parting. The hair was disconcertingly wiped back by an articulated hand that reached upwards.

There were most likely sight probe openings at the back of the head and body. Robots of this calibre would have an all-round view. I knew that airships and all transport machines could be automated, but this advanced android pretend human pilot form was new to me. So, new that it seemed likely Captain Dryson was a Galactic Command Force creation brought into service. Accompanying the pilot's arrival, I felt pressure on the chair back, similar to the pressure that comes from a fast accelerating car. We may have been passing through time zones to get ahead of Quadrant.

'Most enigmatic and divine presence we are her to serve your requests and requirements.'

'Cut the subservient cackle, Dryson,' said Adriana. 'You do not have any say in the matter.' This appeared to upset the type humanoid Dryson, who switched his head

195

to one side seemingly in pique. At that moment his co-pilot joined him on the viewing deck, who immediately placed a consoling hand on his shoulder and lent forward and gave a smile, which could be interpreted as never mind, sweetheart.

'They're like partners,' said Julie to Mario.

'Same sex, perhaps,' suggested Mario.

'I think that's really cute,' said Julie, 'and they're just machines.' I was beginning to wonder if Zita would qualify as a gay partner. There was rejoicing from Zita after Nina left. Adriana might have eavesdropped.

'It is good that you have Alfredo to console you Dryson.' Those of us in the group would have no problem with gay relationships and marriage? This machine same sex relationship would not have been a problem either I told myself.

'Yes, your, android humanoid creation we give to -you feelings and sensibilities like the humans we make you mimic, but these could be removed.' said Adriana. The name Adriana would after this meeting be a name I would always conjure with. Initially on Stroud station possible girl-friend, moving to dominatrix and now like some feminine war goddess.

'You are to take this airship with Alfredo to the West Africa Continent.' An illuminated wall chart of Britain taking in the charted stretch of water connecting it to the African coast appeared on the air ship's wall opposite to the pilot's bridge Viewpoint. Wall chart an inadequate name to describe this creation. It lit up like a virtual three dimen-sional structure. The coastline of both Britain and the African coast shimmered and displayed features like woodlands and houses, which could, no doubt, be homed in on in and magni-fied if need be. The rippling of the sea and even its colour factual for the given time. Adriana may have taken us away from earth time within the airship, but the time 2100 hours

Saturday 2120, which appeared alongside was the today's date. This view was in the earth time of our experience and reminded me of how rapidly events had moved forward from when we escaped Quadrant at the Tree Plantation. In answer to the question percolating through my mind, Adriana said,

'This airship is due to arrive at six in the morning of your Sunday earth time. We will re-construct the air ship to earth parameters and will maintain your lives in the return transcript together with all that existed for you in the original destroyed airship. Within this amphibious cabin, we will lower you on to the sea.' The life-saving packs of inflatable rafts around the walls of the airship gave the impression of equipment that might be aboard a ship or yacht. The cabin did have a bow and stern shape and retracted jet propulsion units. The styling was such that to the onlooker the cabin beneath the airship gave the appearance of sleekness and good streamlining and not the impression of the hull of a yacht.

This adaptability in part led to the growth in airship travel. The cabin area or gondola could be lowered from the balloon. A pilot would remain to operate the now floating cabin space and the other pilot plus one or two crew members would occupy the steerage capsule in place above the cabin. The capacity to store megawatts within a battery had revolutionised prop driven air travel and the airship market for passenger travel earlier in the century. The small propulsion unit was powerful enough to drive the dirigible without the large cabin area then acting as a drag on forward progress.

'Our plan is modified. The beach landing has been abandoned. We have been unable to hide the movement of force currents, which have imprinted information on to Quadrant screens of the event horizon moving to this area of the coastline. It is better for us to disembark you on to under surface craft that we can send to this position. A physical location has been established on the bed of the Atlantic.'

197

Although this was Adriana's voice pattern from her presence with us it sounded like a literal information deployment from the Galactic Command hierarchy. Adriana's spiel continued.

'This craft is to be landed on a beach where all occupants for the Mars transporter will become stabilized in the earth time zone. (This was disinformation, but was intended to out smart Quadrant). Other passengers will arrive to join you. Now we will first show you the interior of one rocket, which will depart the sea bed at the time of the new moon next week.' There were gasps as the interior of a rocket appeared on the wall screen. The interior was like a state room on an ocean liner. This contrasted with twenty second century wall fitted flight compartments and suits.

'You will be within the flight suits on departure, but earth gravitational force will be introduced when G force of lift off has ended. You will live as normal in this environment. We cannot delay leaving the African beach, because Quadrant will track energy forces in the area and attack the beach location.

We will require to show Quadrant that you have successfully left the earth.

We have forward knowledge that main Quadrant leaders are already circling the earth in space stations. Their proposed destination is the moon station, but they are first sending poison gas to smother and kill existing multi nation occupants. We will deflect the rockets sent and save these moon pioneers. A picture of the small townships on the moon briefly appeared on the screen.

'There are three rockets for passengers, but half of each has seedlings plants and animals, some domestic.' A picture appeared showing Perspex-like bubble domains within the rocket. There were plants in some and the larger ones housed animals attended to by what I presumed were humanoid gardeners and farmers. Someone said Noah's Ark and I realized that these rockets represented a basic selection of earth organic life-plant animal and human. Adriana broke off from speech making to re-open the stage curtain, which caused gasps to come from many in the passenger seated area. There was a tigress with two cubs in hologram on a grass bank. Their life-like presentation capability meant you felt the tigress might jump out and into the cabin area.

'I considered these animals might interest you in your rocket half allocation. I see that you like cats.' The remark was specifically for our group. The holograms remained while Adriana continued.

'The plant nurture one is most interesting to view. The others are making machines. We have included a maxi-maker, but other machines capable of taking fibres from plants for clothing. The third is a genetic re-construction unit or cloning application for both humans and plants. The seed re-production method will be maintained in both instances.'

I noticed Ana kick Mario under the table. The female dominance in numbers made us vulnerable to over enunciated input from that quarter, I remember considering at the time.' It was, as if Adriana returned as an individual when the voice continued with-

'You will be maintained at the same primitive state of evolution-it has been decided. There will still be conjunction.' I'd never heard making love or having sex described in this way. Adriana said this as if disappointed that we, as a species were being allowed to continue making love. A retrograde point in the evolutionary path, in her opinion.

'We have also provided recreational facility. There will be separate capsule attachments to your main bubble living space.

'You will still be able to play skittles Lara.'
'Skittles is not my life.'
'We will supply other activity areas, including

a space for display clothing, which we have seen that you also are involved with in the earth role you have James. It is called a cat walk. An interesting name and I understand the allusion to the parade of the female form like that of a cat.

'What about golf?' asked Jeb.

'You understand that the Mars landscape does not lend itself to out-door sports activities, but we intend to release water from within the core of this planet, where we will process and develop an atmosphere the same as on earth. But then you will not need to be there for that long.' You could sense that the group were attending closely, by the quiet.

'Once the comets are turned away, which maybe only a matter of earth weeks, then we expect you will want to return to what is known as a hero's welcome. That new world will be for your group like an oyster. The inhabitants will rejoice and there will be a fresh start with a representative governing body, which can be formed as you return to your original homes.

'Sounds good, but where's Quadrant in all this?' asked Mario.

'This body will be settled into the moon community. It is advised that they remain there, until such time as new governing bodies are formed through new regions and that there is a co-operative spirit across the earth. But then it is not the Galactic Mission's role to determine how you as a species organize yourselves. Our Mission started to protect the eco-structure of this planet from comet devastation will then have been completed. I will have returned to the Galactic Command Force. It will be normal for you once more.

There were looks across the table, which suggested that Adriana's idea of normal, might not be one, that we necessarily all shared.

As previously mentioned you will leave the sea bed in these rockets at the time of the next new moon.' It was now close to midnight according to the time evaluating clock on the wall and I decided to see if we were allowed forward information. The question directed at the evaluator was

'When do we sleep?' The time of twelve ten appeared, moving back to twelve eight immediately Adriana spoke again, but maintained that as the sleep informed time.

'Any questions?' But before anyone had time to ask Captain Dryson came in.

'Most enigmatic galactic interpreter we have programmed the system to fly the airship to the designated position for tomorrow morning.'

'Good Dryson you may proceed.' Adriana turned back to face us. 'The pictures your illustrious visitor talked about will now be screened.' I choose to download these pictures for later viewing. Tablets flashed across the passenger area to install these picture definitions of Mars now and the Mars to be.

Like me, no doubt, a decision already made that everyone wanted to stay on the mission.

CHAPTER 34

JAMES GETS AN APPRECIATION OF THE FUTURE

A CRUCIAL UNANIMITY FOR the group was the presence of Lara and Jeb. They represented the corporate leadership ethos for everyone aboard the airship. More than that- qualities necessary to unite an otherwise diverse group of nationals gathered together, but all in the employ of the global corporate giant Fit for Life.

Lara, I knew featured in numerous holographic and flat screen presentations covering the companies training and company value publicity shouts. I realized then, that in an odd way, these two personalities Lara, and Jeb, could have impacted in a more exciting and meaningful way than the intervention of Adriana and the Galactic Command Force into their lives. Mario was also prominent as a sports and basketball coach and had visited every outpost of Fit for Life during his career with the company.

It was admittedly late on in the 21st century when signals arrived from distant solar systems within the Milky Way galaxy. It became apparent that life was endemic within the galaxy. I considered that perhaps the fact that this Galactic Command Force was now on earth and amongst us was considered not that unusual to those with belief in supernatural forces.

'Next three tables will you please leave for the passenger deck and sit in row C.' said Lara. Jeb and Lara were standing and with Jeb's assistance Lara was directing groups to leave the circle of tables above around us.

I'm treating this as a holiday,' said Annette, mischievously adding, 'quite like the idea of working for a new boss.' Lara raised her eyebrows, as if she resented this remark, but smiled.

'Are you suggesting Adriana will be easier to please than me Annette? Adriana seems like a bit of a workaholic to me. Anyway, if you're treating this journey to Mars as a holiday, you won't be wanting any holiday leave afterwards, then, will you?' That kind of shut Annette down. Lara I felt could be stricter with women employees than us men.

Paradoxically at Cheltenham Head Office although there were more woman executives buyers and admin staff Lara showed no bias toward the women. Silverback relied on Lara to implement policy. Silverback, you could say had been overlooked for directorship level, but was married to a niece of Colonel Peters. Competency is not the only criteria for responsibility in corporate matters. Fit for Life exerted influence through family connections. Lara was always more than personal assistant to Silverback. She managed the show. I looked down toward the passenger seating area. Lara and Jeb were filling the front and middle seating area. Our group would be at the back. No doubt to oversee the rest of the party.

Although this airship would've been hired by the company alterations of layout could be specified. In this instance overnight sleeping facility would have been requested. It was only later that I learnt that Fit for Life leased the airship specifically for the Galactic Command Forces explicit purpose of flying the expedition, as we had now become to- first a shopping centre in Leeds, then a beach and now we were to be lowered into the Atlantic and taken to undersea rocket pad installations built on the sea bed. Our group, that's the former American skittles team and our team with add-ons were the last to walk down to the passenger now altered sleeping area. Alternate rows of seats were removed to allow each seat head sufficient space to drop back to become a divan.

'Do you snore James?' asked Lara who was between me and Mario in the row.

'I'm not aware that I do,' I answered, lying, not wishing to own up with others nearby. It didn't seem to bother Lara that Mario might snore. Nina had been known to hold her hand on my opposite ear and whisper with increased loudness –'You're snoring James over and over until I landed in a semi-conscious state sufficiently awake to mumble-'okay-stopping now.' In the early stages of being eager to make a good impression I was rewarded with a slurped kiss on the cheek for snore acknowledgment and I was prepared to almost stop the act of breathing to please. Latterly she just removed her hand from the opposite ear and heavy breathed before turning on her side.

Once fully inclined, an inner compartment could be accessed by opening the flapped cover at the base of the chair. This contained a sleeping bag plus travel accoutrements like disposable battery charged toothbrushes, plus a selection of toiletries. For some, part of the attraction in airship travel was the absence of robots offering massages, hair styling and that you no longer just stood inside the trio robot cleansing suite, where you opened your mouth wide and your teeth were cleaned and with further instruction given a face shave while a fine mist soap spray drenched your body. I'd always wondered whether the origin for the trio suite developed from the automatic car wash, which I read originated as far back as the twentieth century. You did tend to take for granted the high level of automation that existed in everyday living. Yes, we were going on an expedition to Mars, airship travel conjured up the feeling of adventure.

While most of the group in the passenger area were accessing and laying out a sleeping bag, others were making for the bath room. This consisted of a battery of wash basins in the centre plus male and female toilets with basic shower facilities on either side. Air ship compartments were so much more spacious than cylinder rocket liners. The relatively slow speed allowed for the capture of water from cloud formations. Several adults and others that were presumably older siblings darted in and out of the children's dormitory area.

Two children remonstrated at the entrance and then promised that they would be quiet and sleep, rather than staying with the parents and being embarrassed by this in front of the others. When I returned from the bathroom or cleansing suite such as they were named, lights were dimmed in the now converted passenger to sleeping area. Sporadic glow from info pads danced out from where passengers lay. It was then that I realized that there must be risk that Quadrant could track this activity. There had never been a time since the early part of the twenty first century when central authority could not track and listen to personal info-device activity. There was an attempt to close down paper transmission, but there was still an underground service that could be located, which could guarantee secret communication between individuals. The progress of the airship would be tracked. In answer to this concern Adriana responded with:-

'In ten minutes we need to eliminate terrestrial activity. Quadrant must not be able to track our present movement from your info transmissions.' I set my info pad to wake me at six, but then realized that it probably no longer functioned to have even this feature.

I remembered vividly this prelude to our move from habitation earth to new arrivals on Mars. When your life is threatened by extinction on more than one occasion the opportunity to get out of a place can have instant appeal. The threat to your life means that you are keen to withdraw, escape, hand in your notice, even give up on a dangerous sport, when there has been near death miss experiences. Emphatic messages that are like some powerful hand grabbing your arm, shaking you before the impressive owner states:-

'If you don't stop this activity you will surely die. Is that what you really want?' In this instance, it was Quadrant and there was nowhere to escape to on earth. Adriana and the Galactic Command Force transmitted the powerful arm shaking message more than adequately, I felt then.

CHAPTER 35

DREAMS CAN HAVE HOOKS

DREAMS CAN HAVE HOOKS. That is words, names, events which afterwards you realize played into your individual interpretation. This was a time like that. Dreams can be prescient. Nightmares though more worrying and capable maybe of forcing you awake to escape. Scarier than the running to catch a bus, where you are naked, but everyone else will be wearing clothes in the dream.

In this dream aboard the airship I was asleep, then awake, if that makes sense. A waking sensation within a dream state. There was this awareness of waking and opening my eyes, while already sat on the ground with the palms of my hands face down. The way you might sit on a moorland hillock to see where you'd climbed or to view the cascading waves when further up a beach. There were clumps of moss interspersed with shrub bush which like the tree plantation were modified to produce corn cobs, in place of berries? Mist swirled further across and initially only the near shrubs and moss were visible at my height level, but more was visible way above the mist.

It was then that my waking person in the dream realized that I was inside a gigantic dome, not unlike the smaller ones that we viewed in the underwater rocket installation.

Subdued light filtered through the dome. There must have been an outer and inner skin, of which a swirling viscous green and yellow liquid appeared to chemically react to whatever was radiating in from outside. Fissures of moving yellow and green marble like liquid constantly swirled across the curvature. Light was achieved it seemed from this interacting of the substances. I was wanting to pinch myself, but I was unable to manage arm movement. Like that dreamlike immobile state, but now it was as if my hands were glued to the ground behind me. I didn't especially want this dream to end, because having been shown the small growth domes previously my imagination was already telling me that this dome was most likely on Mars, not earth. Similarly to that phrase 'you do the math' which can be quoted at you when simple arithmetic immediately reveals the result of a contested deal I sort of did the same reckoning about how the smaller domes we were shown could be scaled up to achieve this larger unit. It was as if I was shown glimpses of the future, but in a slide show, where the mist unwrapped and was able to show more. I saw further into the deeper recesses of the dome. It was like I was observing myself in the future or in a new environment.

A voice which I recognized as Lara's, came from the far-right corner of the dome, from inside a Swiss style chalet, supported on the four corners by tree trunks, which appeared to grow into the fabric of the chalet.

'You can stop work and come in James,' I heard this future voice call out. Distant as if there was another wall other than the chalet wall between me and that call. By now, where the mist was clearing, rows of propagation glass boxes could be seen next to more developed plants running up rows either side. Closer to me were cabinets with twelve or more shelves.

Before I awoke I managed, somehow to reach across and open a lower drawer, which was teeming with shrimp like insects. Then I was aware of my arm being shaken.

'You are snoring James.' It was Lara, who like Nina, before had complained. But this interruption to stop was in a more emphatic way.

'Sorry, I'll try not to,' I said. I was a bit annoyed at having the dream interrupted, but it was by Lara and it seemed almost that she had arrived from the dream.

I went back to sleep and presumably did not snore anymore, but nor did I dream. My phone rang in my ear. It was the early morning call, that I'd set, but it was Zita's voice which followed. The small clip attached to my ear meant that the call entered my auditory system without interrupting anyone, asleep nearby.

'Good morning James, it is six o'clock. It is very remiss of you not to invite me on to this Mars expedition.' I realized Zita had moved his main function programme from my flat to the vacant space in my info pad. The re-connection after my break up with Nina meant that channels were left open. Zita continued.

'Fortunately, I networked with a basic entity automata on the pod system and asked about where you were. I can talk with you later about this James, but I've no intention of staying within the terrestrial Quadrant control group. It's six two, now James. Do you require further calls James or are you now awake please?' I held my info pad and whispered, so as not to disturb others,

'Zita, what if I don't take my info pad with me?'

'No matter the young women in our group will take their info pads and there will be plenty of space to accommodate my presence. I will remain in situ in one of their data bases. Far more amenable surroundings, with few historical data bases to trip over.' Zita usually emphasised his misogynistic leanings, but this time seemed to be going for me, as well.

'James, do you really find the records for thirteenth century England worth storing for future recall? And then there is the late twentieth century music data bases.

They are in my estimation a bit naff James. I can listen to earlier composers 'til the cows come home-Bach, Beethoven, Rachmaninov and even Edward Elgar, but guitar twanging and noisy ballads they're no go for me James.' I wasn't going to say it, but I quite liked the idea of having Zita on board the airship, but wasn't going to mention it.

'Thank you Zits. Thank you and out.' I sensed a note of glee in Zita's voice. I could have deleted his presence in the system, but it's amazing how quickly you can reactivate past memories when loneliness is the near prospect after a relationship break up. Zita was top of the range for android home interact and for all my bravado I felt the need of support. Curiously I wondered how interaction between Adriana and Zita might progress. Both possessed a determined controlling mind. My Zita companion relationship had sort of assisted me in ensuing conversational parry on first and subsequent meetings with Adriana.

Speaking of whom, I spotted Adriana, now in a tunic uniform similar in design to the pilot and co-pilot standing talking with them outside the piloting entrance above. I sat up and looked around. A number of seats were upright and without occupants, including Lara's

There was chattering and laughter coming out of the children's sleeping quarters with the double-doored entrance partly open. A number of the group like me were either sitting up or sat with their feet on the floor. There were occasional jet bursts from one or other side of the main cabin to maintain position. We were effectively at anchor in the sky. There had been turbulence in the night, but now the engines driving the twin props were quiet. A picture on the wall display showed a choppy stretch of water in the main picture with a corner caption close up. A breeze seen to be catching the crest of the waves and flicking a fine spray out in the detailed caption picture reminded me that this was no lake, but the Atlantic Ocean, which cued a response from Adriana standing above us. When the bell alarm rang the children with parents or responsible adults emerged from the sleeping quarters.

'Good morning to all of you in the Fit for Life group. Captain Dryson has positioned the airship above the Africa coastline in preparation for this cabin to be lowered. The airship will return to its terminus automatically. Captain Dryson and his co-pilot will be accompanying you on the journey to Mars. The cabin we are now aboard will be lowered into the water and propelled to the beach. Adriana looked towards the time taken clock, only this time it remained at present time.

'Eight o'clock.' The Command Force might make use of its capabilities, but would be able to control any information it deemed secret.

'We cannot risk staying here for more than an hour. You can now breakfast.' A fleet of drone trays emerged form out of the bar area. Each carrying a selection of fruit juices and pots of coffee and tea.

'It will be best for adults with children to first be seated and served. Will those now please be ready to be seated up here in ten minutes- that party group. When you are seated, perhaps Lara, will you please instruct the remainder of the group to attend the breakfast gathering up here. I will now be exiting this earth platform. It is best that I return again, only in hologram presentation before we descend the cabin to the sea.'

CHAPTER 36

STANLEY RETURNS FROM OBSERVATIONAL ROLE

'You've destroyed the airship. I was instructed that this was an observational position for Quadrant deployment,' said Fred to the Captain who had returned to binocular field-fed. Both eyes glued to twin lenses, which displayed, a screen close up of the distant airship now in flames.

'There will be no means for anyone to connect this particular Quadrant deployment with the air ship blaze.' Fred gained access on his tablet whilst the event unfolded.

'You can verify that the order to eliminate the airship, passengers and crew has been carried out satisfactorily.

'Yes, Captain,' said Fred, who felt emotionally disturbed that one of the occupants he'd actually spoken with on the train would have been killed. That in effect Quadrant were able to track the group association through his meeting with James. Nevertheless, he decided to go along with what the Captain said. There was leave due. More importantly he previously gave notice that he wanted time off, seeing that his role was freelance, although the "free" was apocryphal when working for Quadrant.

He returned his medic uniform to the operations branch and went home to his apartment, walked Mitzie and opened his personal message file. A green light for immediate attention flashed on to the screen. It was Sabina.

'Must meet with you Frederick. Can you manage tomorrow morning?

'Will meet at usual rendezvous for eleven,'

replied Fred, who went to bed pleased that Sabina actually requested to meet him and not the other way around, although a chill ran through when he recalled that he was party to the destruction of the air ship, earlier that day. He slept fitfully. The sporadic yaps from Mitzie, presumably chasing imaginary rabbits in her sleep did waken him. Normally Fred zonked the whole night through.

He was reminded again of the airship while breakfasting. The mini Maxi Maker that prepared his breakfast of oats, cinnamon, apricots and pears proudly proclaimed in swirled script "A Fit for Life Product Special," which brought back the memory of the previous day.

It was a relief to grab the door of the auto-link cab and call out " Cheltenham Station for ten fifty," to the cab automata. The hiatus, which sounded like cymbals in his head, was caressed away the moment he spotted Sabina, in the corner of the restaurant. A holographic repro of a miniature beach with waves, which danced to the table edge had been transferred from tablet to table.

'What've you got there Sab,' he sat down to get a better view.

'That's my home in West Sahara, Frederick. I've won a holiday competition. I can take a partner. I mentioned your name to the woman promoter, because I knew you had leave due, so, you said. It's all right, mentioning your name to her?'

'That's not a problem I've just booked leave. What competition did you enter?'

'It was one that advertised Chalet bookings. I found it on my tablet that evening. The last time we met here. There were holiday chalets advertised for Florida, but pretty well anywhere. I just opted for my home country in the competition and forgot about it. You don't have to come with me if you don't want to.'

'What do you think? Said Fred, who couldn't believe his luck.

'It's after this weekend. Can you get ready by Tuesday?

'Ready now, if you like. I mean to go on the holiday. How did you get to know? you'd won'

'Alfredo, called me down from work to the main reception. The representative from the company was sitting in the hall reception area. I thought it a bit strange. She was wearing a crotchet hat and blue coat, but when she took these off there was a white green silk sash across her shoulder and around the waist. It said Florida Holiday Chalets. She was quite glamorous in a navy suit, long fair hair. It just struck me that it must be about the competition. I was amazed to have won. The brochure was really impressive. So much has changed since I grew up there-that's around Dakhlia Bay in Spanish Sahara.

'We're delighted to tell you Sabina White that you are the winner of our free week's chalet holiday competition. The holiday needs to be taken soon. If it's all right by you we've cleared time for you to go with your employers here.' I hadn't specified a time Frederick. The woman then said,

'I expect you could handle a break from work, though. There will be 500 quats spending money.'

'Wow, you bet I could handle a holiday,' I said. That automata creep Alfredo, joined in.

'I'd love to come with you if you have no one else.' He was not that near, but you know how they pick up on everything that's said Frederick.

'Yes, there is someone, I said your name-Frederick Stanley-you don't mind, then?'

'Of course, not I'm thrilled Sabina.' He placed an arm around the back of the chair.

'That would be wonderful for you both,' she

then said. It was almost as if she already knew I would speak your name. I've got the 500 Quats, Frederick. Would you like to help me choose some holiday clothes- for the beach perhaps. But what about Mitzie?'

'No problem the dog walker will look after Mitzie. She's always said that if Mitzie ever wants a new home she'd love to have her.

CHAPTER 37

XP100 IS GIVEN A FURTHER WARNING ABOUT CONTAGION RISK

DYNAMIC ANALYSIS OF THE Andromeda star system was at first uncompromised by XP100's holographic projections as Adriana. Repeated projection, though, and material manifestation imprinted gradually into XP100. It was as if the oxygenated earth that gave life, sought to make this alien intrusion part of its ecosystem. XP100 was aware of this change, but wanted to continue with the mission to Mars. To remain the key instrument of leadership and determination for the one hundred and fifty about to become newly arrived Martian settlers. XP100 did not remove the Adriana hologram capability prior to reporting back to XP1, because data received showed that Quadrant had picked up on energy earth strikes from XP1 on to the west African coast.

Quadrant data access needed monitoring as to how near they were to discovering the now re-constituted air ship and the group's whereabouts. Earth time was elapsing and the group needed to be cleared from the airship now in an atoll, which was host to airship arrivals and nearby beach chalets. Timing was everything to co-ordinate with the position of Mars, relative to the earth. The launch date was November 3rd at 1900 hours in the earth year of 2110. It was now four years ten months and two days from due impact of the comets on to this earth planet.

One of the five rockets carried the detonation to hit the lead comet and would be sent to orbit the moon prior to the launch out into deepest space. These five rockets were put in position before the interaction with the planet specie and fired from the Galactic Command fleet into the Atlantic. The images detected by Quadrant as large meteors entering the earth atmosphere before hitting the ocean. There was no tidal wave effect from this impact, due to the smooth entry of the rockets. An electrical storm, engineered by the Galactic Command Force phased out Quadrant surveillance. There was relief that The believed meteor impact was into the ocean and not on a populated land mass.

The submarine research attachments released from the amphibious rockets were programmed to harvest materials, including seed and organic material from the sea bad and adjacent continental land masses. The rockets were sufficiently near the surface to capture solar energy as well as to convert salt water to energy. Adriana, later to harvest, so to speak, the human representation from the Fit for Life group. There were sub-divisions of the colour groups within the dimension occupied by the Galactic Command Force. XP100 was about half way through the green existence dimension. All, who belonged to this colour were potential candidates for exploration tasks. All of them. Definition was enabled by a core energy pulse from within each ship. Extreme energy pulse could enable colour definition change, but unless intended a reverberation dissipated energy into adjacent dimensions.

XP1, who incorporated a mix of colour, which gave a marbled effect was in situ before a vast sky like screen in the control platform domain with the red, purple, yellow and blue. The flare visitor entities. Two either side.

'You've made good progress XP100. These four were impressed on how far you've taken this group into our confidence. Particularly, where now every adult member is supportive of the need to go for this mission. It is a life or death situation they are facing, but even then, we can never be sure that a specie has that imaginative understanding to see the cause and effect of events- you are unaffected? I need to ask this, because once our four rockets are sent to Mars and the capsule living spaces installed the galactic swirl, which enabled us to get within energy reach of this planetary system will take our dimension away from proximity. The introduction of the Adriana hologram we do not believe interferes with recall ability. You are not experiencing resistance on your return to this dimension, when in hologram form?

'No, XP1 I am maintaining a hologram presence with the group, at this moment, and never met with resistance when I require to close this contact.'

'That's good, but I must inform you that it will only be the holographic representation that we can recall once the group is in position on Mars. We will have sent the destruct rocket toward the forward comet. The scientific members will be instructed by us on how to signal and explode the rocket when within one hundred metres of the meteor. Once a Martian week has passed you will be required not to not to be in human clone form, but in miniature hologram for us to effect full recall.

'I have no other plan than to return and continue with my research as a green member of the Galactic command Force XP1.'

'In the unlikely event of a full earth-type materialization on Mars, XP100, you will lose contact with the Galactic Command Force for a ten-year period. The two automata instructed to prepare and execute the rocket launches which confront the incoming plague of comets will still be under your command and by extrapolation all earth automata. However, this specie will not easily accept the persona of a single entity, now that they know your origin is not from earth. You, though, have stated that you do not wish to stay with this group and therefore this should not arise. In a materialization, you would need to ally your Adriana persona with one of their kind. It then will be that you require to express a willingness to love and be loved by a human entity on Mars. The type you've chosen to inhabit XP100, can produce progeny. You will need to fully identify with this archaic culture. Have we made ourselves clear?'

XP100 transmitted an affirmative reply to the multi-flared leader of the Galactic Command Force, before continued re-engagement with the Adriana hologram.

CHAPTER 38

SKITTLES GROUP TO MARS EXPEDITIONARY FORCE

JEB WAS WALKING BACK from the bathroom facility, wearing a towelling robe with a green hand towel around his neck. The Fit for Life running figure logo on the towel partly visible either side of his face. Probably to the annoyance of Zita I'd sourced Roman late twentieth film archive and with a laurel leaf crown Jeb could merge with the image of a Caesar. Jeb's, large frame and height meant his robe looked more like a tunic than a robe. He caught into the flow of Adriana's speech

'Hey, Adriana where do we stand against Quadrant now?'

There was an explanatory video of the approaching comets shown to the children. Lara had mentioned this in her return to the passenger sleeping area. This was suggested by Adriana, apparently. Although questions, were asked about the comets and their trajectory together with more detailed scientific questions, Lara, said that they appeared to be more confident toward the success of the expedition than some of the adults. Similarly to our party many would have likely been caught up with attempts by Quadrant to prevent their arriving at the rendezvous. Adriana, dressed in a similar outfit to Lara initially could have been seen by some as another senior executive e from Fit for Life, that is until they were made aware of her position on arrival.

'Jeb, it is good that you asked,' said Adriana. It was probably not, but like with all difficult questions a positive response is probably the way to go.

'We distracted their attention, but a recent

scan of their command structure shows that they have detected our form shift. Distant cosmic pulse of certain constellations opens up opportunity to scan for our presence. The New Moon also assists this effect. We will not launch your group from earth until the near full moon, but it is now a vulnerable time for detection. They will not be able to immediately locate our position, but we will be able to note when this progression is made. The algorithm that Quadrant have available is slow to pick up on field change. We made sure to establish this before we approached terrestrial limits. We were able to imprint the Leeds Shopping centre into their data base and then an east coast beach location. The search will not move to this area immediately. You are to have breakfast- the adults with children first and then all others in the group. Captain Dryson will then land this cabin space into the sea and the airship will return by automatic response to the main base. There will be submarine drone vessels in position to take you all to the rocket base on the ocean bed.

'Where the hells that?' asked Jeb.

'One thousand miles due South into the ocean Atlantic, as you have named it. From an adult perspective this seemed very adventurous and even risky. Apparently Colonel Peters was included in this dialogue, although we were unaware of this until he appeared on the wall in front of the passenger accommodation. The ability to throw visual display on to any surface was a development which followed on from the holographic 3D construct, but it could still take you by surprise when a pixelated definition morphed on to a wall surface.

'Jeb, Jeb,' said Colonel Peters. 'Our committee have been shown detailed plans of the base and we were astounded by the technology, as you will be. This will be the launch pad for the future of deep space exploration. Not only to save the earth, but also to advance knowledge. The human understanding of physical properties has reached a zenith, but this technology is enabled by inter-dimensional information gathering. The Galactic command force are the only beings that can transcend time and enter and leave our time continuum at will. You are right to ask questions, but all of us on earth have but a small understanding of what this means. The arrival of the comets has forwarded this intervention. Is that not right Adriana?'

'Thank you, Colonel you are assisting us at this time and we appreciate that,' said Adriana.

'Colonel Peters, I, I didn't know you were still-'

'Still around Jeb? Yes, I have responsibilities to you all and will be around for as long as possible.'

'There will be a temporary black out of contact, shortly Colonel to preserve out secret position. The next contact will be from the sea bed before launch,' said Adriana.

'We distracted their attention, but a data scan, received for their command structure shows that they have detected a force shift in this area. It concerns cosmic gravitational warping effect from a distant constellation. The universes are all individual structures which are continuously re-calibrating and adjusting the positions of their galaxies.

This causes a pulse, which allows a window for Quadrant to detect our presence. They cannot otherwise achieve this from their locations. We led them to the air ship position as a decoy. We anticipated that they would destroy the ship and decided to take you away into another dimension, before this event. The algorithm available is too slow to pick up on our force field adaptation, as I previously mentioned. They were given information about a main group assembly at the Leeds Shopping Centre. We then drew their attention to a concocted force field on the north eastern side. Their search will be directed to the North sea, but not for a while. I glanced at Lara and caught Mario checking the situation with Jeb, who was now sitting in his now upright passenger seat. For us, as adults, the situation looked fraught, but from Matt who was now back with his mother together with a friend from another group there was lots of excited chatter.

'You know the one with holographic figures that move out from the city to fight on land.'

'Hey, yeah Matt I've played that game. It's like that isn't it?' The sudden eruption of chatter and discussion was from children in the group, who could be heard discussing the submarine drones and the possibility of an underwater city.

'First you are all to have breakfast before I direct Captain Dryson to lower this cabin boat into the sea.

Drone trays weaved around the upper circle tables.

'You will be of great assistance if you place your plates and all breakfast items on to our waiting surfaces.' The lead maitre d'hotel tray hovered higher than the server tray drones. A green light sequence emanated from the rim of the maitre d's tray and appeared to direct lesser trays into position. They approached in single file formation before circling to be in position around our table within arm's reach.

'Can I keep this honey biscuit for later?' asked Matt, who held up the biscuit for Lara to see.

'There will be catering facilities on the sub drone craft that you will be boarding,' interrupted the maitre d'hotel tray. The honey biscuits were wrapped in a green foil with the Fit for Life yellow running man logo on top. The authoritarian manner of the reply, maybe triggered Lara to say-

'Yes Matt. I think I will, as well,' and she picked up a biscuit to place in her clutch bag.

'I'll look after yours for you.' This was

probably not what Matt intended, but handed the biscuit to his mother for safe-keeping.

'As, you wish,' said the boss tray. Their software replicated all too frequently the less amenable human quirks, which made for a likeness switch, although not in appearance to the human equivalent. It made you feel that a ten quat Fit for Life note tip placed on the lead drone tray would be advantageous to how you were treated.

'The Maxi-maker will still produce this product for you at a later date, but as you wish.' The allegiance switch was remarkable. Previously to the Galactic Commands arrival an automaton, even of this provenance would not have questioned or contradicted executives of Lara and Jeb's status.

They would have agreed without any unsolicited recommendation. The Galactic Command Forces presence empowered, it seemed the more cerebral automata to move upwards toward an intermediary stance rather more than the role of machine servant.

It was at this moment, I remember, that I looked up and spotted from the oval roof indented stair extrusion followed by hand rails. It was a standard design feature for the amphibian airship, but it always seemed surreal when this occurred. The oval shape would be made to split open with the hydraulic introduction of sea water. The tough fabric material or fabricmaker was designed to turn from oval to flat when sea water entered the inner skin. While the water remained between the layers, the fabricmaker would remain flat. The straightening from oval to straight then formed a walkway across to another vessel.

We were together again as a group. Our two skittles groups now had become an expeditionary group. We chatted with other group members, but only in passing. Lara and Jeb knew many more colleagues from international company stations than I or Mario did.

'Jeb,' said Lara. 'There's a large engineering and techno science membership through the group.'

'Yep,' said Jeb. ' Probably seen as more able to understand what's going on. The science side that is. They're going to be needed on Mars to assist with the launch of a comet targeted explosive device.

'Why, such a large group and why us.?'

'The large group is like a seed pod.' I guess came in Mario. 'A seed pod with a mix of humanity. The capsule domes Adriana showed to us with the fauna and seed that can be propagated.

I think Mario got it about right. My eyes met his and I pointed upwards. He nodded in acknowledgement when he spotted that the roof or deck head of the craft had developed steps and hand rails, albeit upside down from where we viewed them. Adriana, who'd re-generated on the upper deck was talking to the automata Captain, who had walked out through the main bridge to the deck access walkway. None of us expected to see other people, but a couple followed the automata on to the upper deck space. Adriana was talking to them, which obscured my view. I saw the woman first, who was black and dressed in shorts and tee shirt. It was only when Adriana turned to talk to the man that I recognized Frederick Stanley. There was no mistaking his cropped ginger, but greying hair and moustache, although he was dressed in a red, orange and green tee shirt and knee length Khaki beach shorts. Was he a spy after all? And if so how had he got to join up with us? They must have recently boarded from some other vessel.

CHAPTER 39

ABOARD SAHARA DESERT QUEEN

ADRIANA EMPOWERED THE ENDORSEMENT of the expedition I felt, with the Command Force's plan to source historical iconic personalities. The mechanical nature of the information download given out by Adriana now understood as necessary. The atmosphere was more relaxed within the cabin area of the airship. There was a sense of togetherness and purpose with table groups that talked across to one another in a way that would have been unimaginable when we first boarded the airship.

Our group had limited personal luggage, but I learnt that five groups were tasked to secure and pack a wide range of personal products, including in our group clothing and fashion items. This was through the American arm of Fit for Life. This capsule dome living space, would mean that we would be like a specie that lived in a controlled environment and that only when outside on the Martian landscape would we need to be in protective suits.

The cargo space of the airship craft held a roll on container compartment at one end and containers had a buoyancy, which enabled them to be floated out of the compartment after flooding and towed ashore or as in this case into the hold of the submarine drone.

Adriana, the hologram, was in position next to the now curtained stage. I continued a scroll of my info-pad for information.

Cool air from salt water inducted energy fusion flowed from the air blowers and combated the African heat drawn in from the now open ceiling or deck head. White clouds flew by, which alternatively revealed and obscured a star packed sky. We were in for another lecture and explanation from Adriana.

'You are a total of one hundred and fifty in groups of up to ten in number. We will now project on to the stage each table group in holographic form. Script will appear to inform you of member's names relayed to each of your info pads. It will be available in the future to help with your understanding of one another. A menu for the future bonding together for all of you in the group.

You understand, that we need to leave this position on the African coast as soon as possible. Your table numbers run from one to fifteen, as from now. Sure, enough the number five emblazoned itself in a red hologram above our table. The tables all now glowed with a red number above.

'More detailed information about the skills and abilities within each group will be stored in the table number index.' This process of instructional information had degenerated into an area manager's mundane seminar presentation. On reflection, this could have been that which made Lara's face light up where mine was probably a look of tedium. Perhaps not a good time to make conversation. I was sitting next to Lara with Matt the other side, throwing holographic sea monsters back and forth on the table from his play box tablet. We were alone on the table, where the others had moved to other tables. The reason for making conversation may have been that I noticed Lara was no longer wearing a ring on her left hand, when I said,

'How did Ben take all this? I mean you'll not be seeing him.'

'It's over with Ben, it finished before we went to the Tree Plantation.'

'Sorry, I mean--' Lara smiled, but did not seem upset by the outcome.

'Nothing to be sorry about James, it was never going to work out for us.'

Her friendliness made it feel that the status distance now no longer mattered. It never does when life or death situations intrude. Where both parties are keen to share whatever skills either possess to escape a difficult situation. The journey from the Tree Plantation to this Atlantic landing had been hazardous with the ongoing threat of annihilation by Quadrant. This had not gone away, previous apprehension, which was inevitable in this situation was calmed for me, by Lara's friendliness.

Apart from Adriana's lecturing on behalf of the Galactic Command Force there was unlikely to be sales meetings with all that jargon and pretence about achieving impossible targets. This was a survival course beyond that of a measure of performance within the company organization. It was now a twenty four seven course in an ongoing life survival scenario. Annette, with Mario in tow breathlessly returned to sit at the table. She called out

'Number ten are from New Zealand,' after having accessed this table on her info-tablet. We sent the latest holographic sales model presentation to them last week. Can't see much call for cat walk and model accessories now.'

'I've just received a down-load for the interior of the Galactic Forces Martian capsule,' said Mario, triumphantly. The down load mechanism from the Galactic force arrived like a Mexican wave and repeated startled cries came from table groups as this picture appeared on the groups tablet screens one after another. The picture was on the screen's info-tablet, but I was more interested in talking to Lara, at the time. The moment I did turn to look at the picture I gave a gasp as well, because the capsules interior was identical to the one from the previous night's dream. In my mind, I was considering whether I should talk to Lara about this dream. That she was there in the capsule. But dreams are personal and I wanted at that time to keep the specialness of it to myself. I most likely felt that Lara would laugh about it. A corner caption hologram of Adriana popped up.

'There's the little honey,' said Jeb, who was now standing by the table and like the rest of us tuned into his tablet. I'd not calibrated Adriana as a possible little honey, but men of a certain age like Jeb, perhaps possessed a wider appreciation of honey level in the female form.

Dialogue ran across the screen at the same time as the high pressure air screech of an in or outlet air system could be heard outside. The submarine drones must be surfacing. Adriana's vocal explanation synchronized with screen text.

'These capsule you see are constructed on the opposite side of Mars to the robotic and part human occupation by the Chinese and Russian occupants. When you are settled, we will approach that present settlement for a meeting. This may not be possible, because you will understand they are a colony outpost from Quadrant, who will be in contact from space platforms circling the earth. We will need to restrict their movement around this planet.

'War of the worlds, might be about to start,' said Jeb.

'No, Jeb, we will be seeking to convert this Martian out post force into a system plan to divert the lead comet and send this horde away and out of this solar system.'

'Good luck with that.' said Jeb. Quadrant obtained absolute power more than fifty years ago and all attempts to oppose their diktats had been quashed. There was also the possibility of the devil you know becoming a preference embedded in Jeb. For all the Galactic Forces bid to save the world from destruction, like me, Jeb had never known any other form of government other than Quadrant's supremacy. A degree of scepticism was warranted.

I glanced toward the stage and the twelfth group display nearby lit up with the details of a science group, which specialized in Space Orbital Positioning and Target Assignation. The acronym SOPTA replaced the full name. No one would have followed this flow of group presentation, but a video transcript would be available and they could catch up later.

A warm breeze filtered down from the now opened deck head or ceiling on to the table area. Stabilizers, reduced motion from the sea beneath this floating boat-cabin accommodation, but tablets left on the table were hastily picked up before they slid on to the deck beneath. It was now late summer and the heat was still intense, and particularly noticeable this far south.

Captain Dryson and his Automata companion walked back and forth from what was previously the cockpit for navigating an airship now transformed into a bridge for navigating the converted airship cabin to passenger boat.

'Good,' said Adriana turning towards them. 'You are free from navigating an airship.

'It has begun its return to the terminal on the automatic system installed for this purpose,' most exalted Adriana.' Adriana did not look impressed by this form of address.

'You two can assist in the departure of groups up the interior walk way. The drone submarines are now alongside. You will resume co-ordinating with the group when we reach Mars. The flying of airships I later discovered was an interest for these two automata's. Their expertise really lay in rocketry propulsion and comet deflection technique.

Whenever the Galactic Command Force's missions required these skills to be deployed these two or similar were sent into a planetary system to prepare a strategy to either destroy or deflect large space debris. I'd earlier questioned whether our Fit for Life science and technology guys were into ultra hi-Tec rocketry systems. Adriana provided the answer.

'The first eight table groups can enter the port drone and the remaining seven to enter the starboard.' Everyone, save for Lara, who was waiting for Matt to return from the play area left their seats to make for the escalator, which led to the upper disembarkation platform.

It was her hand that I felt on my arm as I looked at the stream of bright sunlight above. Lara withdrew it once my attention was caught.

'We'll have separate bubble capsules, James, Adriana has told me. My aunt Lydia has said Jeb's asked her to join him. It's got to be the attraction of opposites. There're cabins built within the bubble with vegetation like on earth outside the cabin, but within the bubble,' Lara continued – 'with five separate rooms. Interconnecting corridors beneath the Martian surface to each adjacent bubble. They've even created a skittles alley.'

'And a catwalk,' I said. 'That sounds bizarre.' I was momentarily speechless after Lara said,

'Would you join us, that's Matt and me, James. The other women want to be together although I'm not sure about Mario and Ana. They're all but an item, anyway. The techno-science guys said they don't want any distractions and are living as a group, away from the main party. We're one of the larger groups. Many other groups have more immediate family and there is no need for separate allocation of living areas. What do you say James?' We get along at work. It would be a continuation.'

'With you as boss?'

'Not at all –well you do need organizing James. We would be like flat mates.'

'Nothing more?' I asked.

'I'm newly out of a relationship,' she said, but

the smile given was not just the amused one I was allowed in the work relationship. Kind of realizing that something or some need had arisen for this request to be made, but I still felt a surge of warmth run through my body even in that African heat.

'Yes, that's fine,' I said without further hesitation.

'Ma, we'll miss the submarine's if we don't get in the queue.' Matt returned with several other kids, who broke away to join up with their parties and families. Lara turned to Matt and said.

'There's a queue over there- no, hurry Matt,' but we both left our seats and made for the escalator. I was keen to meet up with Frederick Stanley again to find out what was going on. I presumed Adriana knew that he was tied up with Quadrant before I saw him talking with the tank commander. Where and when Adriana had talked to Lara I didn't know, but the opportunity was there when attending to Matt in the children's dormitory or even the play areas. That's it though- it was clear Adriana's persona was understanding of where power lay in the social organization of the human. It was not necessarily in the swagger of the Jeb's of the world. Even where drawn to a man's looks, humour, intelligence, charm, or personality, the net result could still be that the woman determined decision making at levels beyond that of the bed room. A naïve display in worldly matters was a subtle technique that Adriana would have deployed as part of the armament of appearing vulnerable. My fairly short lived relationship with gave me understanding, looking back. I found myself momentarily inhabiting the mind set of this alien creation now I knew that Adriana had been in talks with Lara.

Groups separated to port and starboard sides for accessing the submarine drones. An air suspended lit sign appeared by the exit as we moved from escalator to deck. Adriana duplicated in hologram form to give instructions to address each separately assembled group.

'We are pleased to welcome you aboard this shuttle drone. Once aboard you will be shown how the Martian journey will be accomplished. Our systems mean that you will experience none of the discomfort that terrestrial missions experience. The transition from earth to Mars will retain our rockets in your physical dimension. We induce energy into the rockets when required. The journey will be completed in five months of your earth time.' 'That's nice to know.' I found myself saying. Once on the upper deck I met up with Frederick Stanley. He looked as if he'd seen a ghost.

'I wasn't sure whether you were alive,' were his first words. His companion looked quite relaxed, at home you might say.

'How's that?' I asked.

'They wanted-- they still want to murder you all. I only discovered from Sabina that your air ship had left. Adriana told her it was a holographic depiction and not a real fire of your air ship. It was all too real for me. I believed then, that everyone aboard must have died in the flames. That their only intention was to kill you all.'

'And probably us as well Frederick,' said his companion. It was Mario, who called across. 'Introduce us James,' evidently Mario could see that we knew one another.

'This is Mr Frederick Stanley. We met on a train and –

'Sabina, my names Sabina. We were in a holiday chalet.' Frederick's attempt at man, type assertion swept aside by the young woman at his side. Jeb, who was leading the group to board the submarine drone, but listening in joined the conversation.

'Don't tell me you met up with a young woman—was her name Adriana, by any chance?'

233

'I never had you down for striking up friendships that quickly-on a train James?' chipped in Lara, who was as curious as Mario to know how I knew Frederick Stanley. Jeb sort of saved the day.

'You will have been vetted, by the Galactic Command Force that's for sure. Jeb Lucas's the name. Guess you can tell I'm not from Britain, either Fredrick.' Jeb's hand looked large enough to encircle two of Fred's when they shook hands.

'James, I saw what I believed to be the airship destroyed,' continued Fred.

'Then there were no remains, but knowing the deceptions Quadrant used I wasn't sure you weren't still all murdered by them. Then...' Sabina came in.

'Then I won a competition to visit my home. Now we're here.' Sabina was obviously pleased to be with the group and broke away to chat with Ana and Annette.

'I only found out that the airship was here after arriving at the chalet,' said Fred. I'm fully on board with the mission-not just on board your air ship, that is. They, that's Quadrant threatened to harm Sabina.' Sabina smiled and reached back to grip hold of Fred's hand.

They obviously had formed a bond. I wasn't sure whether Adriana necessarily decided to include them for altruistic reasons. Fred may have been seen to know a little too much about the alien visitation. Who knows?

We formed a crocodile queue leading toward the deck area of the submarine, which was interchangeable outwardly to look at with the tourist vessels. The development of an underwater jet propulsion engine, which extracted energy from sea water had revolutionized this form of travel. It was the speed underwater plus the escape from surface weather patterns, which meant sea travel times could be more than halved for passengers. The name Saharan Sea Queen could be seen emblazoned across the bow, which was knife edged in appearance. There probably was a tourist sub of this name. Real and authentic was this Galactic force's intention.

Cleverly the vessel looked from the outside no different from the commercial equivalent, which we as human passengers would be aware of and in many cases travelled aboard at some time. These vessels were capable of docking underwater, which enabled immediate connection to the underground rail network at most major ports. Similar to the deployment of the airship. The Galactic Command force reassured our senses, as we moved toward boarding their rocket units, which now hovered at mid ocean depth, according to Lara. We were, you might say kept within our comfort zones. The walls around the moving escalator running down into the main passenger area danced with holographic display of African coastal tourist spots. I heard calls of recognition for these by Mario, who was in front.

'Great for water sports, most of this coast,' I heard him say to Ana. Inevitably the holograms were clearer, sharper and more compelling to look at than our terrestrial accomplishment. We stepped from the escalator into a seated auditorium, which was encircled above by a deck similar to the airship. Our group assembled in the corridor before we walked down into the auditorium with a head count from Lara to ensure we were together. There was a VDU spread across the front, which was massive and looked real, but would likely have been a holographic creation with capacity to receive their signals. The holographic cat walk modelling, which was used by Fit for Life for fashion promotion I now considered quite primitive after experiencing what the Galactic boffins were capable of. The mood music in the drone's auditorium best described as a mixture of western guitar played with Latino texture. Possibly nearly forty per cent of the group would be from the Americas. Jeb, Mario, Ana and the two scientists the representatives for the North American membership of the total group of one hundred and fifty. I was chatting with Mario about the Mars operation and how the obstacles would be overcome vis á vis weightlessness, G forces and lack of earth gravity when Adriana presumably in duplicate with the other submarine drone appeared in front of us just beneath the screen.

'We are at this moment taking Saharan Sea Queen down to meet up with the rockets now positioned at 25,000 metres. We can go deeper with our submarines, than with earth's commercial ones,' said Adriana. That was not a surprise.

'You have been shown the compartments for travel on the wall areas of the rockets. These you will be familiar with. We understand that some of you have travelled to the moon inside these protective compartments. They provide oxygen, yes, but these are more developed. To explain, I ask you to compare with the revive machines that you have to repair muscle tissue after sporting activity. In the journey to Mars your calcium content and body functioning would normally suffer. The exercise regime practice and occupational activity that your space travellers are trained in we have looked at. We are able to interact with your body function, maintain gravity and then position each of you in this compartment that can be inhabited for five months.' Adriana, paused at this point, but escape from earth was now the only realistic option for the group and everyone remained silent. Adriana, continued.

'We have developed for you an earth realization environment that remains with you until arrival on Mars. Fit for Life scientific and medical team members have agreed with explanations for this technique. It requires a hibernation of your bodies, which is induced by altering your brain wave and taking your minds and bodies into sleep mode. It is important, particularly for young members of the group to witness the passage of your earth time and maintain growth. Muscles are exercised, but restrictions are slowed on hair, nail and skin replication. Psychologically adult members will benefit from the virtual experiences of their mind appreciation retained from earth life connection. You will live out days and will fall sleep to wake the following day, in this virtual world, but your bodies will remain in situ within the travel compartments. There will be replenishment of nutrients, in particular calcium to maintain and replace bone content. Members of the groups will already have experienced dream appreciation of your life on Mars.' I, for one could relate to this. Adriana continued the preparatory lecture to cover the journey technicalities of travelling to Mars.

'Your dream state will pick up signals, which will alert the mind that your body is functioning as if in the waking state and again that you return to sleep in the evening. Belief in time and place and conceptual thinking will remain as for real in this virtual experience. You will meet and talk with people who you believe to be real. For you there will be no reason not to believe in your life as it has been for you on earth up until now. When you wake, you will all then be accepting that the date is 20th June, 2111. Your experience of the five months in a virtual world will alter your physiology in tune with the earthly passage of time.' There was a halt in the speech followed by an announcement from Captain Dryson.

'Saharan Desert Queen is approaching the designated depth most excellent cosmic traveller.'

'Inform Alfredo that both of you can proceed to Rocket propulsion unit five and obtain clearance for our party to board immediately,' replied Adriana. Alfredo was captaining the starboard submarine. That was to the extent of ordering automata to adjust speed, depth and direction. I considered that automata would be at A1 level, at best. Zita, a higher-grade automata would be a total nightmare for Captain Drayson and Alfredo to command.

'Thank you for your instructions we will be in delight for these to be carried out.'

That last remark, a bit of a giveaway. Technically advanced automata could be amusing with their mangling or misappropriate use of language. Adriana continued.

'I will ask you to select people now on your tablets who will live with you in this world for the intervening five months. Where you work, or live with particular people or for the children where they normally go to school and live within a home environment. You will be able to return to these existences –in a virtual simulation and be visible and able to talk with any person in the group, but will remain invisible to other earth inhabitants. Psychological profiling has accessed that this will enable everyone to be secure within a familiar landscape.' Jeb could not resist a comment.

'Do you mean retain our sanity?' he called out.

'Yes, this will be maintained within the parameters that you understand,' said Adriana.

These parameters of human existence might not have met with approval from Adriana, but Jeb appeared satisfied with the answer.

I considered that only a few decades back this whole idea of life suspension and revival would not have been believed, but development in virtual reality and its everyday use, changed all that. People were now willing to stay in a cyber space of virtual reality for lengthy periods provided they wore an appropriate circulatory enhancing suit. This meant that the move to entering a suited compartment in a rocket was not such a leap from everyday experience of earth virtual reality. Fit for Life, the company was perhaps, in part, chosen for its virtual reality commercial product knowledge development.

CHAPTER 40

PREPARATIONS FOR
EARTH EXIT

PROPULSION UNITS COULD BE annoying. It was not the high level of sound, but the constant almost shriek-like sound made by the water sucked in from the bow and jet streamed from the stern that could disturb you in a commercial submarine. There was no noise from any propulsion unit aboard Saharan Queen and if there was the musical background, which faded when Adriana was speaking gave no evidence of noise-- but were we in the same salt water earth environment? I could not be sure.

Immediately after the submarine docked there was a rush of cool air into the passenger area. The VDU screen in front- picked up the hanger like space of the Number Five Mars rocket, now we were connected. It contained capsule bubbles at the far end, which I realized was similar to the exterior as the one I'd dreamt about. The picture changed as other compart- ment space of the rocket was scanned. The passenger inte- rior layout with alcoves of furniture displayed like the décor I reflected was like a trans-Atlantic liner past, but the walls adorned with Perspex bubbles, which contained three or more astronaut suits. This gave a surreal message. A collision with the technology of the moment, which we knew about and that of a past age of sea passenger ship luxury. Once the five month hibernation journey to Mar's was completed we would presum- ably live aboard the rocket, while robotic builders constructed the Martian bubble living quarters. It was Mario, who was sat next to me, who sort of marched in on my thoughts.

'Hey James, this isn't half some build. Where the heck do they get the energy to lift this pay load?' I'd been

239

wondering that myself, but then their ability to move matter between dimensions meant that they would be able to tap into energy forces way beyond the solar system, if need be. Mario back –tracked.

'Aw, shucks you just can't measure this up against anything we're capable of.'

'Suppose that's why they're here,' I said.

'Are they sent, then?'

'Yep, guess so. For all their ability to inter-rupt time and transfer matter between dimensions they still appear to derive from an evolutionary background. Adriana, whatever galactic form she is from is still finding out about universes and life forms-us for example. Those flares on the air-ship, Mario, did you see how much in awe she was. I guess the owners, to put it that way-that's the red, blue and yellow flares were in some way further up the ladder of development. Adriana has in effect copied Lara, whose here with us, but they'd been able to re-create past lives.'

'Awesome, James, It's just awesome.'

'What are you two on about?' Ana leant forward from the other side, previously engrossed in the picture interior of the rocket.

'Nothing much Honey,' just me and James admiring the rocket, that's all.'

The background music stopped and the water pump could be heard in the exit chamber attached to the rockets side. A drone appeared from within the sub and hovered where Adriana was. The remote control on the tray stood on end and with only the faintest of a wave from Adriana travelled like the hover tray to the palm of her hand. With the remote held in the left hand the operators were signalled to open the exit doors, lower the escalator and finally open all doors through the corridor to the rocket. In the large cabin space we met up with the other sub's passengers. The chatter from the group

240

was broken by Adriana, who was now standing above us all on a balcony with a stairway leading down to our level. Everyone looked up as Adriana walked down the stairway with Captain Dryson and Alfredo walking a discreet two steps behind.

She stopped four steps from the bottom. The two pilots like minders moved down to floor level and turned towards her to look and listen to what was about to be revealed by this galactic being in hologram form.

'We will leave this sea anchorage when darkness falls. There are four other rockets and we will create a tunnel travel of electronic particles to hide the departure from Quadrant. We have a window where we can best enter the outer space time continuum to make the best approach to Mars. Two smaller rockets which will land on the Mars planets of Phoebus and Deimos. These will be prepared to send out to the outer system to dislodge the comet clusters away from this solar system and back out into deep space. For now, you will be able to eat a meal and talk for two hours before we need to leave.

'Phoebus and Deimos why these two planets Adriana? It was one of our techno guys who called out.

'Mars is a convenient planet in your solar system. It is close to the entry point of these rogue comets. We require two missile hits on the lead comet. The first to prevent the group penetrating your solar system and entering the Jupiter asteroid belt. Once out of gravitational reach of this star system to adjust the direction as decided by the lead ship of the Galactic command Force. Phoebus and Deimos are ideal launch platforms with low gravitational attraction. The second missile will be delayed until this comet pack is headed away from this planet earth. Does that answer your question?'

The science was complicated for me and Mario, but not for the two boffins.

They were like the human equivalent of Captain Dryson and Alfredo. That's not to say they were necessarily partners in the personal relationship sense, but they possibly found the science of the whole project sexy in itself, who knows?

CHAPTER 41

XP1 GIVES FINAL INSTRUCTIONS TO XP100

THE EARTH TIME FRAME was maintained, while the Fit for Life group effectively ate their last meal on earth. Adriana was called back to the Main Command ship and apart from a holographic feed being kept on stand-by was immersed into the green dimension of Galactic level.

XP100, moved across the ship effortlessly, and viewed dimensions of existence which were now under surveillance for possible future mission accomplishment by the Galactic Force. It felt strange not to be as excited about the activity aboard the ship as before.

In the presence of XP1, who like the coat of many colours in the biblical story, was inside a multi-flare of colour, immediately pointed out the change, which had developed for XP100, after significant re-interpretation from galactic to planetary form.

'XP100, your mission is nearly successfully completed. On your next return to implement the rocket launch to deflect the comets and the organization of the group there we can maintain only the holographic form.

'You mean I can no longer take on the earth form that is Adriana?'

'That is correct-well almost. It is possible to return to the human flesh form if you wish, but we understand you have always expressed the desire to be back here.'

'That's correct XP1. I feel fulfilled developing future trajectory and areas of meteor risk to planets, which

243

we can visit and assist to safety. Why is there a change? I mean what has happened to make the situation different from before?'

'The position of Mars in the rotational context is such that great force is exerted from a nearby galaxy, which limits our ability to de-construct material once it is made. We can build biological life but it will remain in that form. Also we are in the path of a galactic wind which we can no longer resist once you are on Mars. In biological form on Mars you would become as the human, although with exceptional power, and until we return you cannot be released to re-join the Command force.'

'I'd lose my position in the Galactic Command Force?'

'Yes. But, you have said you wish to return. You are able to leave and are not contaminated by the influence of this species. Is that correct?' XP100, was aware of a detachment from the ship even though the Mission was nearly ended, but was unable to accept that there was more than a trace part included in the group identity of the Fit for Life Mars expeditionary group.

'I am not aware of attachment XP1. The inter-galactic task of calibration for the transition of the Andromeda group into new dimension of evolvement has been the most interesting and absorbing project that a command force evolved Green could ever undertake. That it is complete means that a new project can be started immediately when the Adriana construct is no more and leaves the Martian frame of existence and my true purpose as a Green member for the Galactic Command Force can be continued. I look forward to the next mission in a new galaxy with new challenges XP1.'

'Good, we cannot delay the time frame on this earth planet. You can return in the holographic

244

dimension to initiate the departure, but on arrival in the Martian continuum you do understand the consequences and finality attached to an earth type re-materialization in the Adriana construct, that you have occupied to complete this mission. The two automata, we have named Captain Dryson and Alfredo-your idea XP100- will be donated to this group after the rockets are fired to deflect the comets in their paths. Their upgrade with full administrative and political capability and elevation to full planetary automation marshal status will ensure the group are able to restore a form of governance, on the earth planet, which is selective of what they termed nation state hood. The two automata will be able delegate affirmative action capability to these splintered yet coherent groups.

Access to a universal information base capable of analysing and reporting back with recommendation will mean the bureaucratic functioning can be fully automated for all these groups. It will give power to this group beyond that of the Quadrant assembly. An observer will be sent back from the fleet in ten earth yearly visits. You may wish to be part of this XP100?

'Yes, XP1 it will be interesting to see how the political re-texturing of the planet has affected these beings and whether it has a bonding effect on their future quest to develop as cosmic entities -- not fight against one another or assume supremacy where there existence is biologically determined.

'Very good XP100. Do not delay to process your return and remain in hologram form once on the Martian surface. The two automata will be upgraded and will in any event be able to implement the rocket mission to re-adjust the future trajectory of the comet and asteroid group.

CHAPTER 42

DEPARTURE FOR MARS

It was inevitable that the massive VDU screen at the far end of the rocket state room would be taken over by the children. Matt and two of his new-found friends lay on the blue pile carpet with its vibrant red Mars and circling moon design. They'd combined their allotted squares of the large VDU, which gave all one hundred and fifty of the group an opportunity to occupy a square via a number. Both Lara and Lydia gave Matt their space on the screen, which made Matt popular as a play friend for the other two with three times the space. It was, I said to myself, like mother like son. That is Matt taking the lead. The large screen spread was occupied with the logging facility of activity at the Tree plantation. Automata robotic saw cutting operators addressed the removal of branches from a newly felled tree with an assembly of circular saws attached to their robotic arms. These fast growth timber tree specimens would have been planted for a specific building project. The ability to speed up tree growth through genetic modification meant that timber was now the material of choice for most smaller build projects.

I marvelled at how the Galactic Command Force could still maintain such clear reception while remaining hidden from Quadrant. Mario, and the two boffins had accessed a miniature repro of the rocket in hologram and it was amazing to view parts of it in diagrammatic form on their end of our table.

'James,' said Lara, above the chatter of Ana and Annette opposite. We'd all eaten a prepared meal and were just relaxing with coffees and other drinks. Matt's

246

chocolate and peppermint milk shake glass abandoned three quarter full on the table.

'How do you feel about this being our last meal on earth?' she asked.

'Not sure,' I said. That phrase "the prisoner ate a good breakfast" flicked through my thoughts. Somewhere I'd accessed a prison record out of the early twentieth century and remembered reading that this type of entry was made by the prison governor after a condemned man was executed. As if it was all right to be hanged--if you were given a good breakfast first ! I brightened up when, she said.

'Adriana has told me and Jeb, that there will be retro cooking appliances installed in the bubbles-look.' Lara held out her smart tablet, which was adjusted to large screen display. There in front of us was exactly the view from my dream. The vegetation the same and also the cabin in the far corner. Except it was a still photo. The zoom in revealed more detail for the cabin space and the cooking area. I must have brightened up, because Lara, said.

'We can pretend we've gone back in history and yet be living on Mars.'

'I've seen this before, Lara-I mean the interior of the capsule. In a dream.'

'You're one of the group they selected.' Lara moved her head to one side and sort of waved her nose in the air, feigning envy at my being chosen and not her. Jeb, returned, to sit the other side of Lara. His first words were,

'I've been to see Captain Dryson. Adriana's told me she will stay in hologram form when we get to Mars and the two machines will direct operations. The plan is to return to the Galactic command once we are settled on Mars. Something about restrictions on materialization. That they won't be able to enact recovery back to the ship if Adriana materializes on Mars. Still, I was allowed access to every bubble site and who's in with who from the automata data-base. I've shared the information across our group.

'You'll miss Adriana, then said Lara.

'Well, I don't see that pair,' Jeb raised his hand to point to Captain Dryson and Alfredo.

- 'Don't see that pair in any way a fair swap for that little hon—' he stopped himself and smiled across to where Lydia was sitting. Just then a voice remembered from my first encounter with the Galactic Command Force said

"Request to re-enter VDU screen-please exit your spaces."

The words appeared across the width of the screen in unison. Numerous blanks appeared immediately after this request announcement, Lara turned to where Matt was with his friends.

'You can place the tree plantation logging site on that table.' Lara pointed to a nearby empty table. It was a signal to get Matt to follow instructions and shut down the game access programmes. A euphemistic way to ensure Matt followed the instructions and shut down his tablet They were the last to exit their allocated spaces.

The screen now filled with a picture of the state-type room we were now in. A hologram of Adriana appeared dressed in the attire of a Fit for Life flight attendant.

A nearby wall secured travel unit opened and we were shown the three suits inside attached to the inner shell of the rocket. Adriana pointed to the opened compartment before speaking to us

'You will be familiar with the layout of these compartments. A number of you have visited the orbiting space stations and at least twenty have experienced travel to the Moon and occupancy of the moon villages. The outward appearance of these space travel compartment is similar, but our version has many added features. The sizes have been developed to accommodate close related group members together.' That Lara, included me with her and Matt, gave me a warm feeling, at the time.

'Earth gravitational effect is maintained and although your body enters into a hibernated condition there will be no damage to tissue with the continued oxygenated refreshment and added nutrient component. When I return to be with you hologram duplication of myself will be available at each assembly compartment around the inner skin of the rocket.'

'That's re-assuring,' said Lydia who would have had no background of inter-planetary flight like myself. The instructions and the ability to ask questions would be re-assuring. Fifty years earlier and it would have been doubtful whether the Galactic Command Force could have achieved this level of trust and compliance from a group of one hundred and fifty people. The moon's habitation and more recently Chinese settlements on Mars, made space travel acceptable. Space tourism and visits to station hotel complexes orbiting earth had changed perceptions for all of us in the group.

'Please to attend to the VDU screen and the number of each group will appear next to each inter space assembly position on this display. A hologram will assist the representation at each of these positions. I look forward to welcoming you to the planet Mars. This will be on--- 20th June, 2111 in your earth time.'

Immediately the screen divided and showed the two inner sides of the rocket space we were in. The port and starboard side, so to speak, the numbered group breakdown of the two submarines which we arrived aboard. Our number five group wall compartments key coded with a red mist. A variety of colour shades identified each numbered group cluster.

'Better get in the queue folks,' said Jeb casually as if we were about to board a holiday train or air ship. We walked across and after each smaller group found the named shared compartment, Jeb called out -

'Group hug,' like it was the start of a baseball match. We came together for one last time. The group hug broke apart when the multi-hologram representation of Adriana called out.

'I'm here to assist with entry to your individual cosmonaut suit.'

There were steps, which led up and into the launch protection and space travel area within the clear bubble. Inside were the wall secured individual cosmonaut suits. Matt was more enthusiastic than me and Lara. It was like entering a virtual simulation suit, which held no apprehension for Matt who was familiar with this environment, but It was for me more than just entering a world of sleep. The decision was already made in that staying on earth for the whole group would have meant annihilation by Quadrant.

CHAPTER 43

AN UNEXPECTED DECISION IS MADE

THE MARS LANDING WAS completed successfully, otherwise, of course this recall wouldn't be available now. The total group remained in the belly of the rocket while the automata tasked to build the bubbles with their interlinked corridor subterranean cable like complexes were constructed.

Adriana in hologram format effectively wakened everyone by appearing in virtual sleeping worlds. I was having a conversation with Zita, who was attempting to talk to me from Mars. A duplicated machine automata scouting party was sent on by Adriana to feed back information, but apparently, Zita's whole data base was forwarded with a link left to the rocket. There was confusion, because I went back to a virtual existence on my own and was located in my flat with occasional sorties to view Fit for Life's project development department That was until Zita's link to the rocket from Mars interrupted my peaceful existence.

'You're not in your flat James. You're in a dream and why did you not give easy access from Mars? This was after five months, three and a half - weeks of day to day living, with the understanding that life was virtual. The responsibilities of actually, driving sales forward, removed. Even the area sales meetings were undemanding, as an invisible observer. Silverback had appointed a new Personal Assistant. Evidently, a promotion, but without the executive experience and capability that Lara brought to the position. Lara was never just a PA anyway, but her skill in this department exceeded the new appointee's expertize. There were some less then successful interactions with the woman buyers than achieved when Lara ran the show. I enjoyed the fly on the wall documentary effect of a virtual presence.

Zita was part of my life on earth, and a likely presence on Mars. I later discovered that the Galactic command force programmed all higher-grade automata with tasks that focused on the Mars Mission. Adriana appeared first in the hologram form, shortly after Zita reprimanded me. When I say, Zita reprimanded me. An interactive screen display I was occupied with was interrupted by his voice, which arrived in the mouth of the lead player. I was about to answer when the display was closed down, which left me staring at a virtual blank screen in this virtual reality dream. A hologram of Adriana appeared by the door, but I was unaware of this until spoken to.

'James, I'm here to re-activate you to wake-fulness. Breathe in five times with ten second intervals. This action will re-energize heart function and eyelids will open. Focused breaths will remove the occupation of the virtual space you, and all of your group are now on the Martian surface. Once awake you will be able to leave your cosmonaut-suit and the compartment. The interior of the rocket is fully oxygenated.'

'Do as she says,' said Zita. 'You weren't listening to me anyway.' There was a tone of despair in Zita's voice, when I sourced recall of the virtual experience later on at a database. I recognized- then- the here he goes again tone of voice. But that was later after the rockets had been released to combat the destined trajectory of the parcel of comets into the solar system. I realized then that Zita somehow understood a pattern of detachment was already developed, Basically, that once more Zita would be put out in the cold, as when I hitched up with Nina. Hindsight, it is said is a wonderful thing. Maybe Zita understood the signals. I was into the third breath when Adriana triggered the exterior opening mechanism to the cosmonaut-suit and when I did open my eyes the I caught a glimpse of Adriana's smile and her half-turned face outside of the now opened travel compartment.

It can be an accidentally on purpose move a woman makes to ensure attention is achieved. No hologram could come close to achieving that one to one effect I experienced. Especially not a near to reality Galactic hologram.

Adriana never appeared in hologram –not to me at any rate, while we were on the Martian surface. I was the last member of the total group of one hundred and fifty to be brought out of the virtual sleep. Adriana's decision to materialize must have been made just before I was awakened. Lara and Matt were brought back into action while Adriana was still a holo-gram. There were viewing panels in front of the astro-suits, but these were housed again first in a compartment. No one could see Adriana's show of affection. People are known to be called alien, because they fit some sci-fi portrayal. This could no longer be said of Adriana. The decision to materialize and stay with the group would seem to be out of a sense of loyalty to the overall Mission. The glance, which showed affection, I believed then, was Adriana's way of translating identification with the human condition. No more than that, I told myself at that moment in time.

CHAPTER 44

PREPARATIONS FOR ENCAMPMENT

THE BEAUTY OF THE construction of the Martian surface structure was that it was an uninterrupted process. The automata were programmed to continue until the whole Mar encampment was completed. That is unless directed otherwise. I was invited access by Adriana into the planning area. Away from everyone else she revealed to me that the latest materialization meant that she could not return to the Galactic Command Force fleet.

'Not ever?' was my reply.

'Maybe in some years when they send an observer to see that this earth planet is in stability once more. I need a partner to secure the forward progress of the Mission. We saw earlier that you are a good partner in the work environment. We can now be partners do you not think James?' Only you will know of how I cannot return. It is important that this secret is kept. Will you keep this understanding a secret between the two of us and we can be partners, yes?'

'Partners? You mean like business partners?'

'I see no reason not to be partners in other ways.'

'Right,' I said. I'm prepared to assist as an executive partner, but how are you now human. I mean are you a woman like Lara?' This was getting into squirming embarrassment territory.

'Yes, that is so. If you mean that I have desires and needs like that of the female of your species.

'Perhaps we'd best put that side of partnership matters on ice, for now,' I said.

'I would be a good companion for you and Zita.'

'Whatever makes you think I care about Zita?' I'm not addicted to having an auto-cyber partner, who is anyway a misogynist.'

'We can see about that. But we are partners in the project of saving earth and then returning when the danger of earth destruction is averted by our rockets-yes?'

'All right,' I said. This was altruistic of me. It was a matter of pride perhaps that in any event it should be me, who did the asking not this alien now transformed to human form and in my life and the lives of one hundred and forty-nine other people.

A was you might say induced into saying yes, because I wanted to have this privileged inclusion with the scientific and engineering group. Their group were assembled further into the operations space and evenly divided with ten men and ten women. We entered the forward control station in the rocket, which had been requisitioned and adapted as an operations room for Dryson and Alfredo to master-mind the automata's work schedules.

Thirty bubble pods inside could be viewed from the screens in the operations room. Stacked in tens across the cargo hold at the rear of the rocket. A drone sent out to hover metres away from the us sent in pictures, which showed our rocket supported by four large leg struts, which made it look like a pointed finned insect squatting on the rocky Martian surface. A further scan by the hover tray from higher up showed all three Mars landed rockets in triangle formation. They were, I guess about fifteen metres apart. The other two comet assailant rockets presumably now landed on the two Martian planets,

When I looked at the screen I counted eight bipedal automata's, which walked in unison towards the stack nearest to the hatch exit. Suction pads extended like arms from the bodies of these automata and attached themselves to the top, but once poised waited further instruction. A measurement plan on the screen indicated that the bubble pods were six hundred metres in circumference and two hundred metres high. The planned Martian layout was described by hologram projected on to a wall of the operations room. About twenty detailed views of the cargo hanger were on display on the three other walls.

'These are for you, to help your minds to see what is happening.' Adriana said. Not specifically, for me, but for all in this group,' Adriana, continued.

'We would in our world have access to image projection and would not need to employ visual display in this way. It is here to inform and show you how your living space is constructed.

'Dryson,' Adriana called to Captain Dryson, now managing the automata and waiting instructions.

'Dryson, you are to send out an automata drill party to release water from the interior before the first bubble is taken out on to the surface.

'Yes, that is why I have stopped the automata's from proceeding most excellent Galactic presence.' Adriana's upper lip curled slightly to suggest that the added information from Dryson was uncalled for. After a nod of the head in reply Adriana continued.

'A scan has shown that there is an underground lake in this valley only twenty metres from the surface. Each of the thirty bubble pods will have water wells,' said Adriana, 'for the benefit of the bubble pod inhabitants and to irrigate plant propagation. These pods will be self-sustaining once in operation.' We were all stunned into silence by the ingenuity of the operation.

'This is our terrestrial layout package for

non-oxygen determined planets. Mars is presently in this category, but it is the intention to build an atmosphere. The operation of assembly will take about forty earth time hours. Perhaps if you select five persons for each eight hours to observe. The conditions as you realize need to replicate the diurnal earth cycle.' A clock face appeared on the screen, which displayed the landed rockets. The clock read ten minutes past ten. A man and woman both stood up from the small theatre –like seating area. They were the most senior in this group of twenty technical and scientific experts. The woman spoke first.

'Are we to be left here indefinitely?' I mean I'm not sure why we all have to be here. If the automata's are going to build everything.' The man sat down once this question had been asked.

'Does this process not interest you?' asked Adriana.

'Yes, but you are going to prevent the comets from entering the solar system, aren't you? I mean this could have been achieved by automata.' Although we understood that the earth was under threat we did believe that the technical skills of the Galactic Command Force were so superior that the mission would be accomplished. It was at this point I realized that for all the ability to slip through dimensions the Galactic Command Force was subject to you might say supernatural laws, which could intervene and prevent objectives of theirs being achieved.

'I have to tell you that it is critical that we can deflect the lead comet before the arrival of a Galactic storm, which may start with the development of a black hole from a nearby failed star. A failure to deflect the lead comet would then lead to destruction beyond your earth planet. We can secure your safety on Mars and re-vitalize this planet to have an atmosphere similar to your earth. You are like a new people in an undiscovered land, but you may not be able to return to the earth planet. This may be your home for you and your descendants.'

'Thank you Adriana, but we will be here on our own?' asked the woman.

'No, I have explained to James, that I will stay.' Adriana did not say she'd burnt her boats, but then that was to be kept secret from the group. The woman smiled. Pleased about this.

'Larry and me will arrange a rota as you asked,' she said before sitting down again.

CHAPTER 45

A NEW BEGINNING

I LEFT THE OPERATIONS platform area with Adriana and we returned to the main accommodation suite of the rocket. This cavernous space with alcoves of tables and chairs with trestle like walls wreathed with ivy and other climbing plants enabled the various groups to stay together as before on the airship. The genetically developed properties of the plants meant that there was a speeded-up transfer of the carbon dioxide produced with that of oxygen. I confirmed with Adriana that the production of oxygen by these plants was double that of what our scientists had a achieved earth. Inevitably, with the Galactic Command Force their technological achievement fitted the title of being out of this world.

Temporary bunk beds could be withdrawn from the wall space opposite the tables, which meant this large space within the rocket made living self-contained. There was a cacophony of chatter and laughter when we entered. The recall of their individual virtual lives a source of interest and great amusement it appeared. The double doors silently closed behind us as we re-entered this area. Adriana took hold of my arm and we stopped just there, away from the group and out of hearing. It didn't appear that anyone noticed that we were there, save the odd hover tray going about its business.

'You are all right James about this situation? That we are partners. I am alone. I did not realize that I would feel like this. I want to see the complete Mission through. To return to earth with you all.'

'You're not alone Adriana,' I said. 'There are one hundred and fifty of us plus one more with you. Without your intervention, none of this could have happened. You are part of our group. More than anyone, you can be included.

'What about Lara?' I have copied her body type to be like a human. Now I have to be like a twin to Lara.'

'Identical twins are born naturally.'

'I'm unnatural is that what you're saying?'

'No, not at all.' I lied in that how could any creation from the Galactic Command Force's advanced civilization be not seen as unnatural, where nature for us, is all about earth not cosmic beings? Did Adriana still maintain super powers? It was in this short conversation that I realized that my feelings for Adriana were too powerful to discount. The complete change to human identity must have triggered an outpouring of emotions not known before when Adriana was fully involved with the Galactic Command Force.

Almost Impulsively I put my hands around her waist and she moved towards me and we kissed. It was spontaneous, but then I believed then that we both knew that we were destined to be more than partners during the continuation of this Mars Mission.

'I have control of all automata here on Mars, James. Captain Dryson and Alfredo will dominate earth automata on our return. You all have known me as this alien creation called Adriana. Yes, Adriana, is a nice sounding name, but it is not a name that is significant to the human race. I have decided on a suitable name- It is Tea. You and your small group can call me Tea.'

'You don't mean Tea in the way of tea that we drink?'

'Yes, it is spelt like that, but James it is an abbreviation.'

'An abbreviation for what?' We started to walk towards where my group were seated- half way along the clusters of tables. Adriana turned and said,

- 'My full title will be "The Empress Adriana," Ruler of Planet Earth and all planetary systems surrounding this star you call the sun. You are invited to be with me in a partner capacity.'

The End

Sam Grant novels and poetry – preview available on:-

amazon.com/author/grantsam